VANGUARD

C. T. KNUDSEN

BOOK 2 OF THE ORION'S SPEAR SERIES

VANGUARD

WHEN YOU CAN BEND GRAVITY, YOU CAN BEND THE WORLD

Cover design by MiblArt
Author bio photo by Joe Boyer
Interior print design and layout by Sydnee Hyer
Ebook design and layout by Sydnee Hyer
Published by Kilo Press

KILO
PRESS

978-1-7360902-1-3

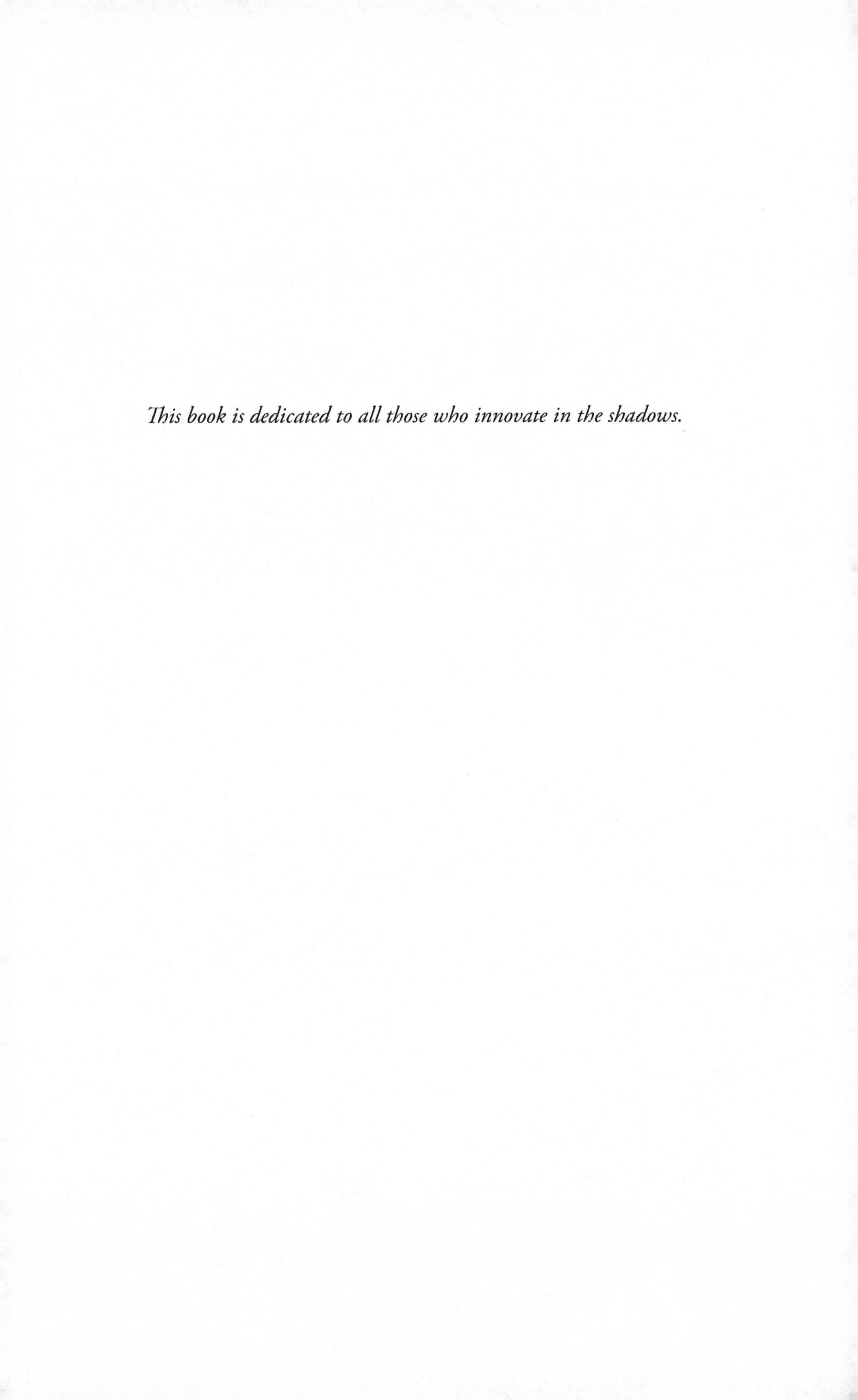

This book is dedicated to all those who innovate in the shadows.

ACKNOWLEDGMENTS

I'd like to thank all the fans of *The Adamic Code* who reached out to me with praise and encouragement, inspiring me to push through the COVID-19 pandemic and finish *Vanguard*. Most people don't realize that it takes an amazing group of people to help an author get published. I want to thank my editors: Chris Bigelow, Michele Preisendorf, and Abby Knudsen, my daughter. In addition to the editing team, Angela and the staff at Eschler have provided amazing support. I also want to acknowledge my father-in-law, Dr. John Bennion, for his help and guidance with medical scenes and terminology. Lastly, I'd like to thank my wonderful wife, Elizabeth, who the character of Leah is modeled after. Without her love, I would never have penned the Orion's Spear series.

LETTER TO THE READER

By May 2020, I'd reached my wits' end.

With the country locked down due to the COVID-19 pandemic and finding myself months behind on *Vanguard*, I packed up my truck and headed alone to Zion National Park.

It was one of the best decisions of my life.

Over the course of that trip, I would get up early and venture into the park to hike and reconnect with nature. Doing so lifted me from depression and inspired me to write. Unlike in years past, the park was empty. Without the buses running, I could drive to trailheads. No lines. No tourists. It was beautiful.

When I wasn't hiking in the park, I was sitting at the desk in my hotel room or at a table by the pool, playing music through my sound-canceling headphones and writing until my vision blurred due to exhaustion.

In that one week alone, I got into a groove and kicked out more than thirty thousand words of this book. This put me on track to deliver *Vanguard* to my editors by my December 2020 goal.

In Zion, I cleared my mind so completely I could finally focus on how to write about the complex technologies found in this book. I was able to work out plot holes. I was able to thoroughly develop new, diverse characters that, I think, really elevate this book.

Late one evening, I drove deep into the park and found a beautiful vantage point that gave me a clear view of the Milky Way. For about an hour, I marveled at the heavens and felt so small. I wondered, *Are we alone*?

I don't have a definitive answer to that question, but it is one that has always intrigued me. While *Vanguard* is not a book about extraterrestrials, Chris Thomas is confronted head-on with this question about our place in the universe.

As with *The Adamic Code*, I want to caution the reader. Cain and the Order rage in *Vanguard*. This book contains intense and prolonged scenes of violence, mass murder on a global scale, and heroic sacrifices. I do not recommend this book for readers under age twelve.

I am now some fifty-five thousand words into book 3 in the Orion's Spear series. As this story continues, the stakes only get higher, the desperate situation becomes more desperate, and the weight of the world on Chris Thomas's shoulders brings him to his knees.

As an avid reader, I'm confident in saying *Vanguard* is a unique story. It's not another boilerplate techno-thriller. Prepare to enter a world of secret governments, unimaginable weapons, and heroes unlike any you have met.

And when you finish *Vanguard*, the stage will be set for the next story in the Orion's Spear series, which will be unlike anything LDS audiences have ever read.

Enjoy.

C. T. KNUDSEN
HEBER, UTAH
JULY 4, 2021

FACTS

Dugway Proving Ground in western Utah is roughly the size of Rhode Island. There are no public vantage points into the ultra-top-secret base. *Wired* magazine wrote a story in 2006 designating Dugway the new Area 51.

The discovery of ununpentium, or element 115, was announced by a team of American and Russian scientists in 2004. In 2016, element 115 was named moscovium and added to the periodic table.

Numerous military personnel have reported off the record that the US government has deployed President Reagan's Strategic Defense Initiative, also known as the Star Wars program, which officially ended in 1993. This network of hunter-killer satellites armed with powerful particle-beam lasers defends the United States from nuclear intercontinental ballistic missiles and other threats.

Astrophysicist Eric W. Davis was a consultant for a Pentagon UFO program known as AATIP. He is now a defense contractor. In July 2020, *New Yorker* magazine reported that in March 2020, Davis gave a classified briefing to the Defense Department on what he called "off-world vehicles not made on this earth"—in other words, spacecraft developed by extraterrestrials.

The CIA regularly contracts with former US military personnel to perform covert actions such as assassination and sabotage.

Secret societies hide in plain sight.

PROLOGUE

DUGWAY PROVING GROUND, UTAH
APRIL 9, 1996, 2:04 A.M.

General Garin Brines perched himself comfortably in the air traffic-control tower's command chair and placed the Bose radio headset over his ears. At this time of night, the base and control tower were both deserted and devoid of light, matching the stark darkness of Utah's remote west desert.

The general led a team recently tasked with moving ultra-top-secret aerial projects out of Area 51 to Dugway. This night marked the first test flight from their new home in the Utah desert.

General Brines pulled the mic close to his mouth and pushed the transmit button. "Dark star zero niner niner. Radio check. Do you copy? Over."

When there was no response, the general stood and leaned toward the window to view the tarmac. A few lights flickered in the distance, and he scanned them grabbed a pair of binoculars to find his target: the TR-2A, an experimental aircraft preparing for a test flight.

The triangle-shaped craft was a deep black. Even against the headlights of several support vehicles, it was barely visible through the binoculars. The craft appeared to float in midair just above the tarmac, an eerie corona discharge emitted beneath it.

The general again reached for the radio's transmit button. "Dark star zero niner niner. Radio check. Do you copy? Over."

It felt like minutes passed, but he heard a voice in his headset after only a few seconds.

"Copy, General," said the pilot. "Sorry, must've missed your first call as the reactor was spooling up."

General Brines smirked. The fact that he could communicate with the pilot via radio was itself a miracle. The craft's heart-shaped gravitational field distorted light, radio waves, and even time and space. But in some way the general didn't understand, he was able to communicate with the craft by radio.

"Roger that, Colonel," said General Brines. "Please identify for the record."

"This is Colonel Willy Williams, call sign Jagger. This test is being recorded. The date is April 9, 1996. Time, oh-nine-hundred Greenwich Mean. Location classified. Our test objective is to take the project to forty thousand feet, hover for eight minutes, then return to base. We're testing several new systems on the craft, including a reactor fail-safe feature and new auto return-home feature. General, preflight has been completed. The reactor is spooled, and the craft is ready for departure on your authorization."

"Roger, Colonel Williams. I have a visual on you. Your authorization code is YTDVOKSD644-W. You may commence test when ready." The general hurried out the tower door to the observation deck overlooking the airfield. He didn't want to miss what came next.

"Roger that," said Colonel Williams. "Authorization code is authenticated. Board is green. Airspace is clear. Launching on my mark in three, two, one, mark."

Through the binoculars, the general saw the light from the reactor's gravitational distortion suddenly glow brighter against the concrete airfield. Then, in the blink of an eye, the TR-2A was gone.

"That never gets old," said the general to himself. "Jagger, report," he said into his mic, still searching the sky.

"Copy, General. Systems nominal. Now running the program on the reactor fail-safe test."

"Roger that," said the general as he spied the machine's glowing belly at forty thousand feet against the backdrop of a billion brilliant stars. "I see you, Jagger. Dark star zero niner niner, looking good."

"Sir, there's an anomaly here," Williams said in a strained voice. "I have a problem. Aborting test. I repeat—aborting test."

The general frowned. Test pilots of Williams's caliber rarely showed strain, even in life-threatening situations. More puzzling still, everything seemed fine from the general's vantage point.

"Copy, Jagger," said the general. "Sitrep."

"Sir, I . . . I . . . I see something. Oh my—it's . . . it's them."

"See what, Jagger? You are ordered to return to base."

"Look," said Colonel Williams in a strange tone. "Look at all the stars." The audio was eerily distorted, and Williams's voice sounded almost robotic.

"Jagger, do you read me?" said the general, trying to remain calm. He noticed the gravitational distortion emanating from under the craft growing even brighter. "You are ordered to return to base. Copy? Over."

"I see something," said the pilot. He paused momentarily and then, in an oddly surreal voice, added, "Something wonderful."

"Jagger," yelled the general into his comms. He saw a brief, blinding flash emanate from the machine. Temporarily blinded, he yelled out in pain as he dropped the binoculars. He fell to the floor of the observation deck and rubbed his eyes. After a few moments, he regained his sight. Grabbing the binoculars as he stood, he desperately tried to find the craft in the sky.

"Jagger, do you copy? Over."

He heard nothing but static.

"Jagger," yelled the general. "Colonel Williams, do you copy? Over."

Again, nothing but static filled the general's headset.

The TR-2A, along with its pilot, Colonel Willy "Jagger" Williams, had simply disappeared into thin air.

CHAPTER 1

WEATHERLORE ESTATE
LOS ANGELES, CALIFORNIA

Cain stood on the finely manicured lawn of his $200 million Holmby Hills estate. Adjusting his black silk cosset, he took in a deep breath of the polluted air amplifying the sunset over the Pacific Ocean.

As the sun sank deeper into the western sky, Cain marveled at the sin, decay, and disease unfolding before him. He knew firsthand that Sodom and Gomorrah had nothing on Los Angeles. The state of human wickedness pleased him, yet he could feel no joy.

"You don't live in L.A.," Cain murmured to himself. "L.A. lives in you."

He bowed his head and turned back to the mansion, where important business awaited.

In the eerie, red-lit banquet hall, a man lay chained, unclothed, and motionless atop a white marble altar at the center of the cavernous room. The windows were blacked out, and the Order's high-council members, clothed in black-and-red temple robes, circled the altar like vultures.

The Order's spies had reported to Cain that, for eighteen months, the United States government had spared no resources in hunting down the mysterious terrorist known only as Master Mahan. Orion's Spear, at the direction of President Barrington, had sent Ground Branch, Delta Force, and SEAL Team Six after every hint, rumor, and dead-end lead across the globe. Their mission was simple: find anyone involved with the Order of Baphomet and the Aries virus attack, interrogate them, and kill them.

No prisoners.

While thousands of the Order's low-level operatives had been culled and killed, the Order's top leadership echelon had repeatedly outmaneuvered America's best warriors.

The council members surrounding the altar were the lucky few who had not been captured or killed by Orion's Spear. Some remained in hiding and joined the meeting via encrypted hologram. Each council member stood in their assigned position on either side of the white marble altar at the center of the banquet room.

Now robed, Cain stood on an elevated platform at the head of the altar.

Behind him, the recovered remains of the grotesque marble statue of Baphomet, which had once stood proudly in the temple in Zurich, lay in pieces on another stone table: part of a stone wing, a bomb-shattered chunk of the statue's base with a Nazi swastika visible on one side and a mason's square on the reverse, and a fractured cloven hoof.

On a tall podium high above Cain's platform perched Baphomet's vile goat head, its two curled horns protruding from either side of its skull. To Cain's relief, Baphomet's divine providence had ensured the head was recovered mostly intact from the Hancock Building's wreckage.

Cain vowed the entire statue would someday be re-formed. He'd sworn an oath that the world would one day bow before the statue and pledge allegiance to the State, when the great Mandate was imposed on the remainder of the world's pathetic population.

As Cain stood on the platform below the dismembered head of Baphomet, the council members raised their hands high in the air and praised Baphomet in Lamanese, the ancient language of their religion.

"Prepare to present your signs and passwords," said Cain.

Cain reverently held the Book of Baphomet as he walked down each row and patiently exchanged strange hand gestures, whispered in code, and displayed ancient signs before each council member.

When finished, Cain retook his position at the front of the stone altar. "Richard," he called to the man chained atop the altar.

The man shook himself awake and opened his eyes. "Yes, Master," said Richard Boone weakly. Formerly chief of staff to US president Royce Jefferson Lennox, who had died in the Zurich attack, Boone had been—until recently—a loyal member of the Order's inner circle.

"Ah, you're awake," Cain said. "Good. Are you comfortable?"

Boone appeared taken aback by the oddly caring question.

"No? Well, that's fine." Cain casually stepped down from the platform and began circling the room. "It will all be over soon enough, Richard. You see, you've been a naughty boy. You disappeared on us. When you do that, Richard, it makes us think bad things—like you've defected, or been compromised, or, worse, lost your faith in our cause. There are so few of us left. Many years ago, I had to remind your former boss, President Lennox, of his commitment and oath to the Order. Now I must remind you that we are all enlisted till the conflict is o'er, my dear Richard."

"Master, I swear I—"

"Quiet!" Cain raged.

Boone flinched, pulling against the chains tightly binding his hands and feet.

Cain reached into his robe and produced his infamous twisted three-blade knife as he eyed his prey lying helpless on the altar. He playfully flipped the blade and caught it in his ancient, elongated hand.

"Doctor Klein, report," Cain said to one of the holograms projected at the center of the room alongside the altar.

"Yes, my Lord Master Mahan," said Doctor Otto Klein. "Laboratory and patient trials are finalized, and the new AriesX virus is ready to deploy. Our assets in the medical corps across numerous militaries, including the US military, stand ready to distribute the virus. It will be covertly disguised as a predeployment inoculation administered to troops after Thor's Hammer is unleashed on the world. As the militaries move to offer support for the victims, they will unknowingly spread the AriesX virus, finishing what we started eighteen months ago. The virus will be staged by pharmaceutical-manufacturing partners and ready for deployment just prior to initiation of the Dawn of the Cimeters."

"Excellent, Doctor," said Cain as he circled the council, still flipping his knife. "The only thing standing in our way is Chris Thomas and the Maximus AI. If we are to succeed, Chris Thomas must die and the Max AI must be rendered useless. I have been directing a carefully placed asset inside Nav to take down Chris Thomas and the Max AI. I alone hold the details to this delicate operation, and I am pleased to report the asset is now in place and ready to execute on my command."

The council members stood silently, their hooded heads bowed as Cain continued. "The governments of the world will reel hopeless and helpless on the Dawn of the Cimeters. Then, on the Phoenix Eventide, we will unleash the full power of Thor's Hammer and eviscerate tens of millions of feeders and inferiors." Cain laughed, then turned serious. "I only wish Hancock and Lennox could see us now."

He placed himself at the head of the altar again, still flipping the knife in his hand. "Baphomet requires a sacrifice."

"Master, I beg you," pleaded Boone.

Cain hovered over him like a vulture. "Alas, all the pomp and circumstance of ceremony bores me," he said, brandishing the knife. He held it up to his face, insouciantly inspecting its mesmerizing beauty. Even after thousands of years, the blade still entranced him. He believed—no, he *knew*—he could see the souls of his thousands of victims shimmering in its reflection.

Without another word, he flipped the knife one last time and then plunged it into Boone's chest.

"I am Master Mahan."

CHAPTER 2

JOE ROGAN STUDIOS
AUSTIN, TEXAS

"All right, friends, you know we're usually about a three-hour podcast, but my guest today can't stay that long," said Joe Rogan, host of *The Joe Rogan Experience.* "I had to take what I could get, but you'll understand why. My guest needs no introduction. Welcome to the show, Chris Thomas."

"Thanks for having me, Joe, and sorry it's taken me so long to come on. I've been crazy busy." As Chris spoke, he looked around at his eccentric surroundings. The ambiance relaxed him and took his mind off the fact that the podcast would be downloaded hundreds of millions of times.

"We only have a few minutes, so let's make this count. Did you just happen to be in Austin?"

"Yeah, I was here for a meeting with Elon Musk."

"I would've liked to be a fly on the wall in that meeting."

"I'll tell you more about it in a minute."

"We were talking while getting set up," continued Joe. "I don't think I've ever met anyone as busy as you. I mean, Nav is now a household name and the world's most widely used search engine after only being on the market for eighteen months. I hear you only have something like two thousand employees, while Google and Microsoft have tens of thousands. How do you do it?"

"Well, I owe that mainly to Max and the fact that I only sleep about four hours a night."

"Max is the AI that powers Nav, right?"

"Yeah, but it does so much more. The public only really gets to see a fraction of the AI's power. Max also runs most of the business. It manages our global-server array, oversees all finances, does customer support. Some things have to be elevated to a human because Max is still a young AI, but mostly Max and my best friend, Scott Allen, run the company. Our employees are some of the world's best researchers in AI. They analyze Max's data and performance."

"That's incredible. The company is reported to make tens of billions a month, and no one owns it but you. According to a recent article in the *Wall Street Journal*, by valuation, you're now the world's richest man. Is that accurate?"

"Well, I don't know about that," said Chris reluctantly.

"On Twitter the other day, I saw protesters in front of Nav's headquarters in Palo Alto. They think the AI is going to take jobs and be used for military purposes. They're pissed at the amount of money you're making. Even some in Congress, like Senate Majority Leader Grover, are calling for hearings on the Max AI's potential dangers and the huge profits it's making. You're a big target."

Chris shrugged.

"For the audience who can't see us, Chris just shrugged. You're not concerned?"

"The people who are after me aren't protesting the possibility of AI replacing jobs or its potential military applications. Those things are just straw men."

"Then what's their real intent?"

"Using Max's facial-recognition algorithms, we've been able to categorize and research every protestor at Nav. We've traced most of them back to GPAC, which is Vice President Mills and Senator Grover's political-action committee. Through several nonprofits and other shell corporations, GPAC is employing professional protestors to target me."

"What! That's freaking crazy, man. You used the very AI they're supposedly protesting to prove they're not real protesters? Can you prove it?"

"As we speak, my team at Nav is emailing numerous news outlets and the Justice Department the evidence we've collected on GPAC's activities."

"What's Grover and Mills's goal? Why would they target a private citizen like you?"

"Well, while there are the obvious reasons, some are not so obvious. Unlike many major corporations and universities, I don't need government grant money to pay for my research and development. When the government controls the money, they control the output of findings. If those findings don't fit certain political narratives, they remove the funding."

"It's really that simple?"

"No, there's much more to it. Companies and universities are afraid of losing government contracts. The government contracts with me to use Max for certain activities, but trust me, I'm the least-interested party in that relationship. If they threatened to stop using Max because of my political views, they would only be harming themselves. They know this, and it pisses them off."

"It seems crazy to me that the government would resort to that level of spite over differences of opinions."

"It's more than just my unpopular ideas. I actively speak out against the duopoly of the United States political-party system, the media, and the Marxism haphazardly disguised as progressivism that's tearing at the fabric of this country. When you have that many enemies, you're going to have a target painted on your back. I mean, why do you think I'm here? This podcast has a listener base thirty times all Americans watching the evening news. The cable and network news model is dead. The future is podcasts like this."

"Amen to that, but even major social platforms have tried hard to silence you. Recently, you were kicked off Twitter and later allowed back on. What changed?"

"I called Twitter's CEO and told him I would buy up the company's outstanding shares if he tried to silence me again."

Rogan burst out laughing.

"Twitter's stock is crap," continued Chris. "I could buy controlling interest for less than ten billion, and it would probably be worth it."

"Really, though," said Rogan, collecting himself. "What are these guys afraid of?"

"Losing control."

"That's it? It's about power?"

"My political philosophy, what I call Life First, is all about empowering the individual. It's about maximizing your agency to act for yourself without harming others, and this flies in the face of the government and powers that be."

"I'm a huge fan of the Life First philosophy," said Rogan. "Ever since you introduced the idea a couple years ago, thousands of podcasts, blogs, subreddits, and YouTube channels have popped up, dedicated to this ideal. Why? What's so appealing about Life First?"

"That's easy. Personal freedom is what's appealing about Life First. It's the emerging independent intellectual class, what I call the thinking class, that's using these social technologies to broadcast Life First ideals. They're driving a revolution that terrifies those in power."

"Take us through that," said Joe. "Is the thinking class an organized group or just a movement?"

"The thinking class is an independent movement of critical thinkers. Inside the thinking class, creating original intellectual and scientific ideas is rewarded, instead of shunned by groups like politicians, the uneducated public, or closed-minded scientific communities. Members of the thinking class are not constrained by traditional scientific theory, social dogma, or history. They are nonconformist and have no political party affiliation. Intellectual dishonesty is grounds for excommunication from the thinking class. Political correctness and wokeness is shunned. We are no respecters of persons, no matter their standing. No reasonable idea is off the table, and no prior theory or law takes precedence. We value freedom over money and believe in using our minds for the greater good. The thinking class promotes the value of personal agency, also a Life First concept. So, Life First is the political philosophy and lens through which the thinking class views the world. It's all about being agents unto ourselves and living with the consequences of our choices and actions."

"Can I stop you there and have you clarify?" asked Rogan. "What does it mean to be an agent unto yourself?"

"It simply means to be free to act for yourself as long as you don't harm someone else. If your actions harm another, you're taking that person's agency."

"OK, that makes sense."

"But it's broader than just the individual," continued Chris. "Many societies and groups across the world are suffering from oppression. Take poverty—it sucks the life out of billions of the earth's inhabitants. People in extreme poverty are not living, only existing. Helping raise people out of poverty to achieve what Maslow called self-actualization is a Life First ideal."

"So, following that thought," said Rogan, "something like preserving the environment would be a Life First ideal, right?"

"Yes, environmental consciousness is connected to the concept of Life First," agreed Chris. "We only have one earth, so we need to focus on the environment and the earth's ability to support human life well into the next several thousand years."

"What's another example?" asked Rogan.

"I'll give you a few quick ones to think about. Access to food and clean water is a Life First ideal. Educating the world, free of constraints like government intervention, racial discrimination, geography, and money is a Life First ideal. Global access to health care and disease-curing medicine is a Life First ideal."

"This is all great, but let me switch up on you because we don't have much time." Rogan shifted in his chair with anticipation. "Let's talk about the Order."

CHAPTER 3

ORION'S SPEAR OPERATIONS CENTER
LOCATION CLASSIFIED

Knife, be advised," said Stew Brimhall, director of Orion's Spear, to Mike Mayberry through his earpiece. "Target is bearing down directly on your position. Three miles out. Max indicates that at present speed, we'll fire the EMP in sixty-four seconds. Stand by."

The sound of a radio being keyed twice indicated Knife had received the message.

"An EMP? Fired from where, Stew?" asked President Barrington from the White House Situation Room.

"A drone. It's experimental," replied Stew through his earpiece. Then he called across the room, "Alpha Team, drone status?"

"Visuals are up," said the weapons officer, spinning around in his chair to face Stew. "Target locked. Ready to fire the EMP on your mark."

"Go with AI. We need to time this just right," said Stew. "You are authorized to turn flight and weapons control over to the Max Defense System."

"Roger that," said another operator, hitting a few keys on her control panel. She moved her chair back from the computer and faced Stew. "Max has positive control of the Sentinel and EMP weapon."

"It's all yours, Max," said Stew.

"Copy. I have positive control," Max said over the center's audio system.

Chris Thomas had reluctantly loaned a regulated instance of Max to Orion's Spear for testing, and its justifiable uses had become a serious point of contention between Chris and President Barrington. Chris insisted Max not be used for offensive military purposes, but Orion's Spear was technically not the military. "Lawyers call that a loophole," Stew had commented to Chris.

Stew watched the operators and analyst as they followed the events unfolding on the forward main monitor. He shared their anticipation. Max was now fully in control of the stealth drone and its electronic weapon. Some of the team had expressed to Stew that they viewed Max as a godsend, while others wondered if they should be polishing up their résumés.

Twenty-five thousand feet above the Caribbean, the MQ-170 stealth drone closed in on its target: the 125-meter mega-yacht *Columbus*.

On the bottom of the stealth drone, a small door opened and a device emerged. It looked like a long boom mic, and it was pointed directly at the yacht thousands of feet below.

"Weapon system ready," said Max. "Firing in 11.2 seconds."

Stew and his team brimmed with excitement.

"Firing on my mark." The AI's voice resonated over the operation center's sound system. "Three . . . two . . . one . . . mark."

The strange-looking device protruding from under the drone turned bright blue for a moment, then retracted into the drone. It was almost anticlimactic, but Stew knew a surge of electromagnetic energy equal to that produced by a nuclear blast would soon hit the *Columbus*. He watched closely as the pulse of violent energy swept over the yacht like an invisible wave. Then the enormous ship's lights went dark, and the churning, white wake behind it began to dissipate.

The entire room sighed collectively. A few people clapped.

"Nice work, Stew," said the president through Stew's earpiece.

"Knife, the EMP fired successfully," said Stew. "Target's electrical system is permanently disabled. At present course and speed, the *Columbus* will stop on your station in two minutes and fourteen seconds."

CHAPTER 4

CARIBBEAN SEA
NORTH OF ARUBA

Aimlessly floating fifty feet under the dark-blue Caribbean in a special Viper suit was not exactly what Mike Mayberry had signed up for when he'd joined Orion's Spear as head of clandestine operations.

He was more of a land-loving cowboy.

Mike's anxiety was heightened by the fact that this Viper suit model—made for ocean-based combat missions—was experimental. Experimental *anything* in Mike's world always seemed to go south in mission, but so far this suit appeared to be holding up well. The oxygen-rebreather status, depth, CO_2 level, ocean currents, and other critical information was shown prominently in his heads-up display, known as a HUD. His new seventh-generation night vision could see through the underwater darkness all around him. There were no fish, no flotsam or jetsam, and, much to Mike's delight, no sharks.

Oddly mesmerizing moonbeams glistened from the surface above his head, giving him some comfort, but the feeling of loneliness was ominous. Even so, Mike was not truly alone. Somewhere in the darkness between Mike and fifteen thousand feet of salt water to the seafloor lurked the *Seawolf*.

Above, the bow of the *Columbus* appeared as if out of the dark abyss, cutting through the surface and mangling the moonbeams glistening in the shallow. The ship was bearing down right on top of Mike and slowing.

As the bulbous nose of the *Columbus* got closer, Mike prepared himself. Soon the ship was right above him.

"Max, activate jets," said Mike. Immediately, several small but powerful water jets encased in the suit near Mike's calves activated with a jolt. Mike moved a little unstably at first, but with Max's help, he quickly righted himself to the proper trajectory.

The feeling of moving effortlessly through the ocean was exhilarating. Mike reached up and touched the hull of the sleek beast as he propelled himself down the length of the ship. Through the darkness, the enormous rear propellers came into view, the stainless-steel monsters lying motionless on their shafts.

Mike rose to about five feet below the surface, just behind the ship's stern, and hit a button near his chest. Four small projectiles shot from the back of his suit and breached the surface, a compressed air charge soundlessly shooting the projectiles another fifty feet above the *Columbus*. Once the projectiles reached their programmed altitude and began to fall back to earth, they shed their outer casings, exposing several small, silent quadcopter microdrones.

Activating automatically, the drones blended into the midnight sky, almost completely concealed. They began scanning the ship using sonar to map the floor plan and highly advanced lasers to detect human cardiac signatures.

On his HUD, Mike observed several cardiac signatures in the engine room, adjacent engineering compartment, and bridge. A few solitary signatures roamed the mid and upper decks of the ship. He assumed they were armed.

Mike pushed another button on his wrist-strap computer, and the underwater jet-propulsion system retracted into the suit. Then he kicked his way to the ladder hanging from the boat's stern-side swimming deck.

"Main, I am in position and entering the target," he said. Surfacing behind the ship, he scanned his surroundings.

Max came alive on comms just as Mike started to scale the ladder. "Sir, you have an armed guard headed to your position. ETA sixteen seconds."

Mike slid quietly off the ladder and back into the calm, warm sea. From just under the waterline, he spied the guard walking down the main teak deck past a hot tub and lounge chairs, then down the last set of stairs to the swimming platform, where he looked around, shining a flashlight over the platform and out into the sea. He moved his AK-47 synchronously with the light. After a quick sweep, he slung the rifle over his shoulder and reached into his breast pocket. Even from underwater, the suit's optics enabled Mike to see that the Russian-brand cigarettes were unfiltered.

From a shoulder compartment in Mike's Viper suit emerged a miniature acoustic weapon. The guard inhaled the smoke, and his eyes began to water. He grasped his throat and shook his head as fear filled his face. Then he spun around, looking for help, but he was alone. He fumbled for his radio, but his coughing became so violent he dropped it and wet himself. A moment later, he passed out.

A few yards off the stern and inches below the surface, Mike retracted the weapon, then moved forward and again stealthily climbed the ladder onto the swimming deck, where he zip-tied the guard's hands and feet.

Pausing, Mike regarded the guard with pity. Normally, the man would wake up after a few hours, but Mike doubted he'd live through the next fifteen minutes. "You got off lucky," he mumbled, thinking of the fate awaiting the others on this ship.

Mike moved toward the stairs. According to drone data displayed on his HUD, other roving guards were now congregating on the bridge.

"Deploying drones to bridge," said Stew into Mike's comms.

"Roger that. Keep them occupied. I'm advancing to the target now." Mike pulled his silenced Glock 19 from a compartment in the Viper suit and headed up the stern toward the *Columbus*'s main stateroom.

CHAPTER 5

JOE ROGAN STUDIOS
AUSTIN, TEXAS

"After the Zurich incident, you denied any involvement in taking down the Order," said Rogan, zeroing in on Chris. "Then you started to admit helping the government. There are numerous conspiracy theories surrounding you and former president Lennox and the Order. As the conspiracy crap here is on the scale of 9/11, let's clear the air. How were you involved, and is the Order still a threat today?"

"Well, look, you have to understand that I wasn't sure what I could say at first," Chris started cautiously, "which is why I denied it at first. No one was supposed to know about my involvement, but it leaked. So, yes, I helped the government with the mission."

"But what does that mean?" asked Rogan. "What details can you give us?"

Chris took a drink from his mug, buying himself a few seconds to position his thoughts. "Well, the Order's computer network was extremely complicated to penetrate. We had to use the Max AI to hack the system, and part of that plan involved President Lennox helping us gain access to the physical servers. Everyone knows he died in the process, so that's no secret."

"Yeah, but what else? One conspiracy theory has you on-site at the Hancock Building before the air force leveled it. There's strong evidence that Lennox was actually involved with the Order and that a CIA team merc'd the former president and his Secret Service detail."

"I don't know anything about it. I wasn't there, Joe." It was a practiced lie.

"Do you formally deny contracting services to the government?"

"No. As a matter of fact, I consult for the government on a number of issues. That's public knowledge."

"Then what can you tell us? I mean, Otto Klein, the insane Order scientist who engineered the Aries virus, is still on the run. He seems really high profile. Why can't the CIA catch these guys? Are they even trying? Is the Order still a threat?"

"Well, I need to choose my words carefully. . ."

Chris paused. Rogan sat patiently across the table, staring at Chris.

"OK, well," said Chris, a bit hesitant. "I think President Barrington has been pretty explicit. We didn't get all of them. There are still a few figures in the Order's upper echelon of leadership who are fugitives from the law. I *can* tell you the US government is, in conjunction with many other governments of the world, relentlessly hunting these and other terrorists."

"But there's nothing else you can say?"

"I don't think I have any other information, Joe."

CHAPTER 6

CARIBBEAN SEA
ABOARD THE SUPERYACHT COLUMBUS

"Knife, be advised," Stew said over comms as Mike approached the entrance nearest the ship's main stateroom. "The drones have neutralized the roving guards and bridge personnel. You're clear to the target."

"Copy."

Mike activated a small, hook-shaped metal rod from his suit's index finger and wedged it into the door lock. It clicked, and the door opened quietly. Glock raised, Mike slowly entered a dark hallway. The Viper suit's built-in NOD tech saw through the darkness so perfectly it may as well have been midday.

As Mike made his way down the narrow hall toward the stateroom, his eye caught a shadow to his right. From a bathroom doorway, a woman in a robe started firing an automatic rifle, holding it at hip level in amateur fashion. Several rounds bounced harmlessly off Mike's suit.

"Ouch," Mike said.

He fired a single round, hitting the woman perfectly between the eyes. She dropped the rifle and crumpled in on herself, probably dead before she hit the floor. As Mike inspected her body, a man sprang from a closet and screamed while firing a pistol. In a split second, Mike shot him in the shoulder. The man dropped the gun and cried out as he fell onto the suite's king-sized bed.

"Don't kill me," pleaded Roger Cowen, President Lennox's former national security adviser.

Mike slid his bulletproof face mask over the top of his helmet to reveal his face. "Beautiful boat you have here," he said casually, moving toward the man thrashing on the bed. "The pension for former national security advisers must be way better than what we're getting over at the CIA."

Cowen said nothing. He continued writhing in pain as blood oozed from the fresh shoulder wound. After a few minutes, he finally spoke. "Are you going to take me in?"

"No." Mike shook his head.

Cowen's face was frozen with fear—all but his quivering chin. He held his bleeding shoulder and stared up at Mike in pure hatred.

"Speak, or the next one goes in your kneecap," Mike said calmly.

CHAPTER 7

JOE ROGAN STUDIOS
AUSTIN, TEXAS

Chris could tell Rogan wasn't convinced by his feigned ignorance about the current Order situation, but the podcast host gave Chris a pass in the interest of time.

"You have a number of initiatives about to launch," said Rogan. "What are you ready to reveal to the world?"

"Well, all that money you mentioned earlier isn't just going into my pocket for a yacht or something like that. I'm proud to announce that I'm starting my own STEM university called Thomas Institute of Science and Technology, or TIST for short. The main campus will be located on the shores of Utah Lake, west of Orem, Utah. We'll also have campuses in New York City, London, and Tokyo. I'm also starting a massive medical research institute that will be located on the TIST campuses. We break ground next month."

Rogan laughed. "This sounds insane. I mean, how much does something like that cost?"

"Just to build the campuses and the medical research operation is around $20 billion. The endowment I'm earmarking for the university will be larger than the endowments of the five largest universities combined."

"I mean, that's got to be well over $100 billion, right?"

Chris shrugged. "Something like that. But make no mistake—the Thomas Institute will be the world's finest science-based educational institution, rivaling Caltech and MIT. This is just one of the ways I'm giving back."

"How else do you plan to give back?"

"In the coming months, I'll be launching Max Ed to the world."

"Which is?"

"I mentioned that educating the world is a Life First ideal, so I'm putting my money where my mouth is. The Max AI is now capable of teaching K–12 curriculum personalized to each user."

"Wait, so you can go to high school on a mobile device? No more high school? I really could have used that!" Rogan laughed. "What do you mean by personalized to the user?"

"Yes, essentially, but I didn't build it to replace the K–12 educational system in the United States or Europe. I built it with the rest of the world in mind, for those without access to real education. Elon Musk and I just finalized a partnership with SpaceX. The Max Ed foundation will pay for satellite internet access to anyone accessing the Max Ed tools, which can be done for free either through an app or a browser."

"So if you're a kid in sub-Saharan Africa and you want the same education as a kid in the United States, you just need to find a phone and learn English to be in the club?"

"Nope, if you don't have a device, we'll give you one for free through the Max Ed foundation. We've been working with several manufacturers to develop durable tablets and AR glasses. These devices will come with advanced solar chargers to keep them powered up in regions with no or spotty electrical grids. All free."

"That's amazing. But what if they don't know English?"

"That's not a problem. Max Ed can teach a child in their native tongue, and it can help them learn English and any other language they want."

"And you're launching this soon?"

"Yes, this week. My intention here, Joe, is to give everyone in the world an equal opportunity at learning regardless of location, class, age, race, et cetera."

"OK, so say a person in Africa graduates from this Max-based high school. Then what?"

"If you graduate from Max Ed, you'll be invited to apply to TIST's online university, called TISTx, where you can choose from over two hundred different degrees. This online program will be separate from the TIST campus program, which will have one of the most academically stringent admissions processes in the world. The online programs will be similar to Harvard's and MIT's online educational platform and only offered in English. You must take the basic courses, then qualify to matriculate into a degree. But if you do, it's free."

"Free? From what will probably be the world's best university? That's going to change everything."

"Again, using your resources to educate the world is a Life First ideal. It's all about empowering the individual and raising the impoverished out of poverty."

CHAPTER 8

CARIBBEAN SEA
ABOARD THE SUPERYACHT COLUMBUS

"Wait, I know you." Cowen glared arrogantly. "They call you Knife. You're a legend in the spec-ops community." His face dripped with sweat.

Mike didn't acknowledge the comment.

"You think you won?" Cowen continued. "You think because you contained Aries, killed Hancock and Lennox, and destroyed the Order's headquarters that this is over?" Drool and blood now oozed from the sides of Cowen's mouth. "You have no idea what's coming next."

"Allow me to lay out your situation." Mike pressed the Glock against Cowen's head. "I'm not the man they send to bring people in. I'm the man they send when violence is the only desired outcome. I am the Grim Reaper. Tonight, you are going to die. So choose: either tell me what you know and die, or don't tell me what you know and still die."

Cowen looked confused. "That's asinine. That's not how it works."

"I know I can't appeal to your patriotism or sense of duty, if you ever had any in the first place," said Mike. "So think of this as a deathbed confession. Your time on this earth is over, Cowen. Be penitent. Help repair the damage you've done, in a small way, and maybe, just maybe, God will have some mercy on your lost soul."

Mike pulled his weapon back, and an almost-hopeful look crossed Cowen's face. He said, "You already know the man you're looking for is Master Mahan."

"Yeah. What else? Tell me about him."

Cowen lowered his head. As Mike watched, the man's body began trembling uncontrollably. Mike couldn't believe he was about to talk.

"They got me when I was young. I was just a freshman trying to fit in. Somehow I got invited to join the club. At first, I thought it was all just innocent fun, but then there were drugs." As Cowen spoke, he became increasingly animated. "They made me do things. They filmed it!"

Mike slapped Cowen across the face.

Just then, comms sounded in his ear. "Knife, this is Main. Be advised. The *Seawolf* is eight clicks out on approach. We're also tracking a Venezuelan navy patrol boat ten clicks east of your position. They're headed right for you."

"Copy, Main. Stand by." Mike turned back to the man on the bed. "Focus. We're running out of time."

"It's called Thor's Hammer," Cowen said, then paused. "On the Phoenix Eventide, Mahan will unleash it on the world. When he does, tens of millions will die, and the governments of the world will be forced to surrender to the Order."

"We never retrieved any intel on Thor's Hammer." Mike forcefully pulled Cowen into a sitting position on the bed. "What is it? Another virus? A nuke? What is the Phoenix Eventide?"

Still holding his shoulder, Cowen looked up at Mike and smirked. "You can't stop it. Hell is coming, and it's bringing Master Mahan with it. You may kill me now, but you will die."

"Last chance. What is Thor's Hammer?"

Cowen laughed hysterically, eyes wild.

"OK, crazy time's over." Mike pulled down the Viper's faceplate and locked it in position, then raised the silenced Glock.

"No!" yelled Cowen just before his skull and brains exploded all over the headboard.

Without hesitating, Mike ran out of the stateroom's door. "This is Knife, exfilling now," he yelled into his comms. As he jumped over the side, he ordered, "Max, activate jets."

As Mike hit the water, the jets at his calves propelled him away from *Columbus*. When he was about a hundred yards out, Mike yelled into his comms, "*Seawolf*, you are cleared and hot."

"Roger that, Knife. Engaging."

As Mike continued making his way through the deep, two ADCAP Mark 48 torpedoes raced dangerously close at nearly sixty knots. Mike stopped and turned to face the *Columbus*.

Two massive explosions lit up the darkness as the torpedoes found their target. Minutes later, the superyacht's hulking wreckage sank into Mike's view. Unlike in the movies, there were no dancing flames or flashing electrical accompaniment. The dark mass made no fuss. She simply slipped to the bottom of the Caribbean.

Mike turned ahead just as the spherical nose cone of a massive US Navy nuclear submarine came into view.

His ride home had arrived.

CHAPTER 9

JOE ROGAN STUDIOS
AUSTIN, TEXAS

I can now announce that I've partnered with Toyota, Ford, and Volkswagen to bring a new electric engine to market," continued Chris. "These manufacturers' vehicles will be powered by an electric motor and new nanotech battery system Max and I developed. This battery will allow a car to drive up to a thousand miles on a single charge, and it'll wirelessly charge to 80 percent in just ten minutes in your garage."

"Dude, are you trying to take down Tesla?" asked Rogan. "I love my Tesla. It looks like you're taking down Tesla."

"No, I'm trying to bring the other automakers into the twenty-first century. It's a technology-licensing deal, not a manufacturing deal."

"Wow, you're dropping some major bombs today. So, licensing? This is smart—you're just collecting a big check. Man, that is massive news. When is this going to launch?"

"Soon. We're still working on a lot of the details, but the deals are signed, the plants are under construction, and the technology is ready to manufacture. The new cars will probably hit the road in two years, including a Ford Focus and Toyota Sienna minivan that are both faster than a Ferrari 488. As you know, Joe, electric is fast."

"You don't have to tell me!"

"This licensing deal alone will fund Max Ed. Every time you buy an electric car from one of these manufacturers, you help educate the world."

"OK, I think I see your vision now," said Rogan. "Man, Chris, this is just incredible. What drives you?"

"I made a promise to someone special to me. I didn't understand that promise when I made it, but I do now. I promised to use the Max AI to free the world from poverty. If you are poor, any technology employing the Max AI is free to you. I believe this AI will unlock the mysteries around curing diseases that have plagued humanity. Maslow's hierarchy of needs says if we can provide clean energy, shelter, food, education, and medical care to ten billion people, then, as a species, we'll quantum-leap into the twenty-second century."

"So, what about jobs, then?" asked Rogan "Let me play the devil's advocate. Is Max going to end work as we know it? Will we need universal basic income?"

"We've gone from 90 percent of Americans as farmers in 1800 to less than 2 percent today. As we've progressed from an agricultural society, to industrial, then services, and, finally, information economy, we've found automation to be an important part of growing—not eliminating—jobs.

"A good example of this is ATMs. Everyone thought bank tellers would suffer mass unemployment when ATMs came into service in the 1970s, but they didn't. Teller jobs in America grew by 300 percent between 1995 and 2010. When legal-discovery software was introduced in the 1990s, people said the same thing about paralegals. But the software was so good at pattern recognition it actually created more work."

"That's super interesting," said Rogan.

"So we need to stop making automation the bogeyman and an excuse for garbage like universal basic income. UBI is the antithesis of Life First. It's a nonsolution to a nonproblem. Today, we're training kids to do jobs that don't even exist yet. AI will simply do the work we don't want to do and help us find the work we want to do. So that's one reason I find UBI intellectually offensive. It violates the economic equivalent of the second law of thermodynamics. You can't put something in and expect more to come out. The model would bankrupt the country, create an unsustainable welfare state, and leave tens of millions drifting without purpose. As we educate the poor, the global economy will explode, creating more wealth for *everyone*, not just a select few."

"Many others who've been on this podcast agree with you," said Rogan.

"Joe, a revolution isn't coming. It's here right now. We're on the cusp of solving poverty, making disease a thing of the past, and inexpensively powering the world with solar and clean nuclear energies, like thorium. Individually customized education via the Max AI will upend traditional-education institutions and democratize learning across the globe. The singularity will connect humans on a global level that has never been seen."

CHAPTER 10

BEVERLY HILLS, CALIFORNIA

Perched high above Los Angeles and priced at a staggering $1 billion, the 157-acre Mountain of Beverly Hills was the most exclusive land available in California, if not the world.

Chris Thomas stood at the edge of the Mountain's finely manicured lawn and looked out at downtown Los Angeles and the Pacific Ocean. It was a rare, clear day in the Los Angeles basin, and he could see Catalina Island. The air was crisp and surprisingly fresh.

"We'll take it," said Chris.

The broker's face lit up with joy. This property had switched hands numerous times over the last seventy years, and he'd held the billion-dollar listing for the past eleven. Chris suspected the agent was about to retire on the commission.

"Uh, yeah—how about just one minute?" Leah Thomas said to the squirrely-looking broker. Then she turned to her new husband and asked, "Can I have a word with you?"

The broker panicked. "Um, sir! Mr. Thomas, if I could just—"

Leading Chris away, Leah gave the broker a look that would have stopped a bull dead in its tracks. The man winced and retreated toward his S-class Mercedes.

The couple walked across the gorgeous lawn to a spot where they could be alone, and Chris put an arm around his wife's shoulder.

"We could build our dream house right here," he said, sweeping his hand toward the southern edge of the property. "Then I was thinking we could build a couple more houses for your family and mine. And our own little park for the kids, right in the center of the property. It would be like a family compound."

Leah said nothing. She just gave him what he called "the look."

"What?" he finally asked.

"This isn't us, Chris."

"Isn't us?"

"No, it's not. If we buy this, it will define us. We'll be just another billionaire couple flaunting our money before the rest of the world. It will be one big flex. You're going to be the wealthiest person in the world soon. Optics are critical, Chris. We have to ask ourselves, Who are we, what are our limits, what is a need, and what is a want?"

Chris bowed his head in introspection.

"Remember what your grandfather told you?" Leah continued. "You were given your intelligence to make the world a better place. To help those who can't help themselves. To give hope to the hopeless and raise everyone up in this sick world. If we buy this, what message does that send?"

Chris said nothing. He just stared at her with what he knew was a pouty expression.

"Your grandpa's rule was to only buy things that give you freedom," said Leah. "This place would be a financial albatross."

Chris looked down, put his hands in his pockets, sighed, and then looked back at his wife.

"We don't do mansions," she continued. "We don't do yachts. We don't do exotic cars or private islands or—"

Chris cut her off. "I still need my jet. It's a business expense."

Leah tilted her head and rolled her eyes. "You don't need a 777, Chris. The Gulfstream works fine."

Recently, Chris had been eyeing—to Leah's dismay—a private Boeing 777x for long-haul flights. The G700 was, he'd tried to explain, "too small" for overseas trips.

"I already bought it," Chris confessed, wincing. "Boeing delivers it in six months."

Leah folded her arms across her chest. "Why didn't you tell me?"

"Because I knew you'd say no, and I need it." Airplanes were Chris's weakness.

"You *need* it?" Leah huffed, putting her hands on her hips. "OK, fine. Well, I bought something too."

"You bought something? What?" The suspense was killing Chris. Leah rarely spent money on anything.

She pulled out her phone, brought up her photos, and handed the device to Chris. Swiping left, he saw photo after photo of a spacious hayfield. Low mountains rose in the background, and one picture showed a grove of trees with a flowing creek. From another angle, one towering mountain range looked familiar to Chris. The images were stunning. He thumbed through them again, then handed the phone back to Leah.

"Utah," he said.

"Heber, Utah."

"Never heard of it." Chris felt a little concerned about where Leah was going with this.

"It's a hundred acres. Plenty of room. I want to move there and build a house with a barn and horses." Leah moved in and held her husband tightly. Then she put her chin on his chest and looked up at him. "I want to raise our family there."

Chris felt powerless against her. "What about Nav? The office is in Palo Alto. And the house. I mean, our life is in the Bay Area." His words felt like final throes of death.

"You've always complained about California and the regulations. Utah loves you. The state is giving you everything you want. You're already moving thousands of jobs into Utah. Because of you, it's practically the new Silicon Valley. TIST and the new medical research center are only thirty minutes from Heber, and you've got the new thorium power plant and supercomputing center in Eagle Mountain. You can't tell me moving to Utah hasn't crossed your mind."

"Well, yeah, I'd be lying if I said it hadn't," confessed Chris.

"We might as well move Nav to Salt Lake City too," said Leah. "Why not have it all in one location?"

"The employees will never go for it."

"Give me a break. There isn't a person there making less than a seven-figure salary. They'd follow you to North Dakota if that's where Nav was located. It's time to sell the house in Los Gatos." Pointing at Los Angeles below them, Leah said, "California is a dump. Utah is the next phase of our life. I already bought us a temporary home in Heber." She winced and bit her lower lip.

"A house? In Heber? Already?"

"Yeah, the movers are setting us up as we speak."

Chris was dumbfounded. "Well, OK then," he said after a long pause.

"You're not mad?"

"No, of course not," said Chris.

Leah jumped into his arms. Just then, they heard the loud thwumping of helicopter blades. The air began to swirl and whip Leah's hair into a frenzy as the MD-650 touched down on the lawn. The pilot kept the engines spooled up.

"OK, I'm in," said Chris. "But I'm going to need a very big workshop at the house. That's my only condition, Leah."

She gave him a curious look. "How big?"

"Oh, it won't look too big. Most of it will be underground."

"Underground?"

"It's my only condition. Deal?"

Momentarily surrendering, Leah, gave her husband a big smile and a kiss. "Deal."

Chris broke away from his wife and headed for the helicopter. "I'll see you back in Los Gatos," he called.

"Good luck in Washington," she yelled over the sound of the blades.

"Hey, put the Los Gatos house up for sale, and give the listing to that guy." Chris pointed to the Mountain's broker. "Call it a consolation prize," he yelled as he jumped into the helicopter.

Leah laughed and gave her husband a thumbs-up as he lifted off and flew south toward LAX.

CHAPTER 11

ORION'S SPEAR OPERATIONS CENTER
LOCATION CLASSIFIED

As the G700 arched off LAX's runway 24L and banked hard to the east, Chris connected to Orion's Spear's new secret headquarters via a secure video link.

"Hey, Chris," said Stew Brimhall from the screen. Mike Mayberry sat on a couch just behind Stew.

"I was just reading through the after-action report on Mike's latest surfing expedition to the Caribbean," said Chris. "An EMP fired from a stealth drone, followed by *Seawolf* torpedoing a yacht? That's dramatic stuff, guys."

"Well, we had a few test weapons DARPA wanted us to real world, so why not?" Stew shrugged.

"Yeah, well, the new Viper suit looks killer," Chris said, thumbing through the documents he'd found waiting for him in the copter.

"It is. Literally." Mike smirked.

"Nice work getting Cowen to talk, Mike," said Chris. "So, Thor's Hammer. What do we know?"

"Nothing." Mike stood and approached the screen. "We've had our team on it for the last forty-eight hours. We've got nothing."

"You need to stick Max on it. Have him go after all known networks and comms channels. If there's anything out there, he'll find it."

"Already on it, Chris. I turned him loose with the team. Are you en route to Washington?"

"Yep, just now looking through the briefing you sent," said Chris. "By the way, why do I have to do this? You run Orion's Spear, Stew. You should be the one sitting in front of Congress, not me."

"They specifically requested you," said Stew. "I have a feeling there's more on the agenda here than just the Order. Senator Grover and Vice President Mills have their guns aimed at you. The media are in their pocket, and they're going to use them against you. Grover and Mills are the figureheads of the emerging proletariat movement."

"Pro what?" asked Chris.

"The proletariat movement, Chris," said Stew. "They call themselves prolets for short. The term was first used to describe Rome's lower class. Then it was adopted in Marxist literature to describe those who own no property and sell their labor as their means of production. The term was popularized in the book *1984*, and—"

"OK, I think I got it," interrupted Chris.

"They're mostly the poor in America focused on preserving jobs through AI regulation, universal basic income, and taxing the rich for direct distribution to the poor. So, yeah, they pretty much hate your guts."

Chris sighed. "The hypocrisy is astonishing. Do these proletariats know Grover is a decamillionaire? And why did Barrington put Amy Mills on the ticket in the first place? Barrington is a moderate Democrat, not a progressive."

"He was trying to unite the Democratic Party by putting her in the VP's office," Stew said. "With a progressive female vice president, he's covering his bases. It was the right strategy. That's how he won the election."

"Yeah, I get the mechanics, but still. Any word on Klein?" Chris asked, referring to the Order's chief scientist, the architect of the Aries virus that had killed more than four million people before it was contained.

Mike spoke up. "We're getting closer. We missed him by two days in Tokyo. We'll find him."

"If we find Klein, we find Mahan," said Chris. "By the way, how do you like the new digs?"

"This place is sweet," raved Stew. "I feel like we're hiding in plain sight, but the building is incredible. Thanks for setting us up. Are you coming into HQ after the meeting with Congress?"

"No, I need to get back to Palo Alto. A lot of change is on the horizon for Nav and my other projects. I've got a lot of work to do."

"I'll fly out tomorrow," said Mike. "We've got a lot more to cover, and I have a few follow-up items I want to go through with you, including that security issue at Nav we were talking about."

"Suit yourself," Chris said, "but I think we're covered on physical security. The new security team at Nav seems pretty good."

"We'll be watching the hearing from this end, Chris," said Stew. "Good luck."

CHAPTER 12

CAPITOL HILL
WASHINGTON, D.C.

Dr. Thomas, you have been sworn in. Please take a seat," said the Democratic Senate majority leader, Senator Grover of New York. He sat at the head of a long, mahogany conference table.

Chris looked around the room at several additional members of Congress. Some smiled; some gave him disapproving looks. Mostly they ignored him.

"Thank you for joining us for this closed-session security briefing," continued Senator Grover. "Members of the House and Senate intelligence committees are in attendance. Confidentiality agreements have been signed and collected by the sergeant at arms."

There was a brief pause as Grover rifled through a disorganized pile of papers. "Very well. Please patch in the president and joint chiefs."

Propped up on a stand behind Senator Grover, an enormous monitor revealed President Barrington and the joint chiefs of staff from the White House Situation Room. For security purposes, they attended the unusual meeting via video conference.

"Welcome, Mr. President," said the senator.

"Thank you for having me, Senator Grover. These are unusual circumstances, but extraordinary times require extraordinary cooperation. Wouldn't you agree, Mr. Thomas?"

Chris sat in a plush leather chair at the other end of a conference table that felt a mile long. "Ah yes. Yes, sir." He tried not to sound nervous.

"Excellent. Let's begin," said the president.

"Very well," said Senator Grover. "We are here today to discuss the recent developments around the federal government's use of the Max AI and developments related to the Order terrorist organization, among other things. As you will see, Mr. Thomas, a classified closed-door session is not like an open session. We can be a little less formal seated around a table with no cameras."

While many of the younger lawmakers looked at iPads and laptops, Grover continued shuffling through a pile of papers. Chris watched, somewhat amused as the other senators seemed to grow more annoyed by Grover's lack of preparation and technological know-how.

"Oh, yes, here it is," he said, looking victoriously at a piece of paper over his thick glasses. "I'd like to start with this deeply disturbing incident last week in the South China Sea. Roll the video, please."

The monitor came alive, showing a security-camera view of the combat information center (CIC) on the naval destroyer USS *John Paul Jones*. Sailors in the CIC worked computer consoles monitoring radar, sensor arrays, and weapons-control systems as the ship steamed harmlessly through the sea just northwest of the Dongsha Atoll.

Suddenly, the lights went red and an automated voice said, "Action stations, action stations," followed by a blaring alarm. The seasoned sailors moved in an organized frenzy. Just as the CIC's commander rushed over to her console, a sudden explosion rocked the ship, knocking her to the floor. A sailor rushed to her aid, helping her stand up.

"Anyone hurt?" yelled the commander as two more explosions sounded farther off the ship's port bow.

Several sailors said no in unison. There was no explosion, no smoke, and no fire in the CIC. Just frayed nerves.

"Weapons officer, prepare to repel boarders!" yelled the commander. "Radar, contacts?"

"Negative, commander, we're clear!" yelled a young radar-control officer. "No surface or air contacts."

Phones and other communications devices sounded. The commander moved to pick up a phone, but first she yelled, "Sitrep! What *was* that?"

"It was a hypersonic cruise missile," said the radar-control officer. "It appears three missiles launched from inside mainland China and detonated two hundred yards off the port bow."

"Stand down, stand down," sounded the automated voice over the ship's PA system.

"Was that Max Def?" asked the confused commander.

"Ma'am, it appears the Max Defense AI used the AEGIS quantum radar to detect the inbound missile launch. The hypers came in at Mach five. The system had no time to warn us, so Max Def fired the HELIOS lasers and destroyed the missiles."

"That's what it was designed to do," said a stunned operations control officer. "We'd be dead if it wasn't for the AI."

"Quiet, everyone," said the commander. "Weapons system status?"

"OK, stop the video there," said Grover, frailly waving a hand at a technician. "That could have started a war."

"Why didn't the AI retaliate?" asked another senator.

Chris pulled the microphone closer to his mouth. "Well, sir, the Max Def instance of the Maximus AI is a strictly defensive system. It's intentionally programmed to not perform retaliatory strikes. Response decisions are left to the human command-and-control element. But Max Def performed flawlessly as a defensive weapons system. It saved the *John Paul Jones* and its crew."

"This raises an entirely different question the military or CIA have not been able to answer," Senator Grover responded. "Why did the Chinese unleash hypersonic missiles on the *Jones*? We've been told you and Orion's Spear have been looking into this and have come to some conclusions."

"Senator, as far as we know, the Chinese didn't fire the missiles," replied Chris. "Orion's Spear believes they were hacked."

Murmuring echoed throughout the room. The president looked at the joint chiefs, who stared back cluelessly.

"You mean they're not lying, for once?" asked a congresswoman, looking at Chris in amazement. "They were actually hacked?"

"How's that even possible?" blurted a senator from Montana.

"We do it all the time, so we already know it's possible," said Chris.

More loud murmurs echoed through the room.

"Order," said Grover, slapping his hand on the table.

"Senators, the reality is that military-grade encryption is no longer safe," Chris said. "Either through use of the new quantum computers coming online or through existing back doors into the encryption software, military-grade encryption has been hacked, rendering it essentially useless."

"Who could have hacked them?" asked a general over the monitor.

"There's no way for us to know for sure, but it takes a serious level of resources and know-how," said Chris.

"Could this have been the Order of Baphomet?" asked Senator Grover.

"They certainly have the resources," answered Chris. "But so do many other state and nonstate actors. For all we know, this attack was perpetrated by an extremist faction of the Chinese PLA in an effort to start a war. But it's a good wake-up call. It's time to plan for the future."

"I understand you have a proposal?" asked Grover.

The room went still, all eyes rested on Chris Thomas.

"I've invented a new form of encryption I call x-cryption," said Chris.

The murmuring came again. Chris could see the president and joint chiefs talking on the now-muted screen.

"Go on," said Grover.

"Well, sir, the algorithms powering the current mathematical models employed in encryption systems can be broken in seconds by a quantum computer, which is the real problem here."

"I know we've been experimenting with those quantum thingies for a few years, but I haven't heard of this issue," said Grover.

"Well, you see, Senator, it all starts with qubits—" began Chris.

"I think we should forgo the scientific explanation and get to the solution," interrupted the president. "It's all in the report included here by Stew Brimhall at Orion's Spear. Let's just say for this conversation that encryption that would take a supercomputer ten thousand years to crack can be cracked by a quantum computer in a few seconds. Am I right about that, Chris?"

"Yes, sir, and that's the threat. And I designed x-cryption to specifically address that threat."

"I assume this has something to do with that Max AI you developed," said Senator Grover, eyes narrowing in on Chris.

"Yes, sir. X-cryption is powered by the Maximus AI and built on the Adamic Code. The encryption algorithm itself is an expediential geometrical model, meaning that instead of a two-dimensional binary character to decode, all characters on each side of any type of three-dimensional geometrical shape must be decoded in order to unlock the entire string in the code. When the AI detects an unauthorized attempt on any geometric shape in the string code, the system automatically encodes a new shape into each side of every existing geometric shape in the string. It can replicate a new code into infinity inside every 3D shape in the string. Furthermore, the shape's characters are all Adamic mathematical characters, so the intruding system would need to understand how Adamic Code works in order to even begin to understand how to hack the system."

"You've completely lost me," said Senator Grover.

"He's saying it's absolutely unbreakable," the president said through the monitor.

"Not completely, sir," said Chris. "Every system has its flaws. In software security, social engineering can be used to defeat systems like x-cryption. If one of my key employees were compromised, someone could theoretically defeat the system. But that's an extreme circumstance."

"This just sounds like more AI automation taking jobs," said Grover. "I'm sure this system will make the entire digital-security industry obsolete. I find it incredible, Dr. Thomas, with all the jobs going to automation, that you and your billionaire Ayn Rand flunkies are still speaking out against universal basic income."

"I fight against universal basic income because it's blatant welfare and will destroy otherwise productive Americans. Plus, we can't afford it."

"You're out of order," yelled Grover. "It's high time the government listened to the proletariat movement and explored a tax on automation and the billionaires behind said automation. As for x-cryption, it sounds dangerous. A system like this is going to require more hearings and regulation. And while we're on the topic of you, Dr. Thomas, this temporary operating permit granted you by the Department of Energy to build a thorium nuclear powerplant in Utah's west desert is an outrage. I plan to introduce legislation and a lawsuit to stop this madness."

"Senator—" started Chris.

"Excuse me, but this isn't productive right now," said the president. "Time is of the essence, Senator."

Grover sat quietly, his face a crimson red.

"Chris," continued the president, "if you would, please update us on the hunt for the Order's senior leadership and what we currently know about Thor's Hammer."

Barrington was an expert at deflection and, though off-site, he controlled the room like a professional. Chris recentered himself. He'd welcomed the verbal brawl with Grover but knew the president had been right to derail it.

"Well, sir, we don't have much to report at present," said Chris. "We've only just begun trying to identify the weapon known as Thor's Hammer and its capabilities and intended use. We currently have no intel. As for Mahan, Klein, and the others, we have nothing, sir."

"We're pouring tens of billions into Orion's Spear annually, and you have nothing?" said Grover. "Now that's something we can't afford, Dr. Thomas."

"Senator Grover, I think we've reached the point of diminishing returns," said the president. "I'd like to ask Mr. Thomas to the White House so we can continue a classified conversation about the new x-cryption technology."

"Yes, of course, sir," said Chris, surprised by the invitation.

"Where is Master Mahan?" Senator Grover butted in from the other end of the table.

Chris flinched at the directness of the question. "I have no idea," he confessed. "I wish I knew."

The aged senator stood and stared Chris straight in the eyes, then extended his bony pointer finger. "You and Orion's Spear. Find him. Kill him."

CHAPTER 13

JW MARRIOTT HOTEL
MOSCOW, RUSSIA

"You should try the pirozhki, Mr. Guthrie," said the Russian as he chewed. Even with his thick accent, his English was above average.

Rand Guthrie regarded the former Communist Party high official and FSB spy known only as "Ivan" with disgust. The two men sat at an elaborate table in the center of a private dining room. Guthrie didn't want to try the pirozhki. He wanted to snap the drunk Russian's neck.

"You do know what pirozhki is, da?"

"I grew up without running water in a double-wide trailer in West Texas, but don't mistake me for an uneducated man."

"You don't speak like George Bush," the Russian mocked.

"You can thank my mother for that."

"I assume this isn't your first time in Moscow."

"No, I've been here many times since the early two thousands to work on numerous oil and gas deals with both Gazprom Neft and Rosneft," said Guthrie, momentarily relaxing as he placed a napkin on his lap.

"Oh yes, of course. I knew that already." The Russian reached down into a leather satchel, produced a thick manila envelope, and lazily tossed it across the table.

Guthrie regarded the file with annoyance, then slowly opened it and began to casually thumb through the numerous papers, photographs, and spreadsheets. After several minutes, the Russian took another shot of vodka and broke the awkward silence.

"So, you see, the Russian Federation doesn't get into bed with anyone we haven't done our homework on, Mr. Guthrie."

Guthrie shrugged. "Just a bunch of spreadsheets and Swiss bank statements. What's so exciting about that?"

"I congratulate you on your impressive net worth, sir. But it's what's *not* in the file that is interesting." The Russian took another shot of vodka. "You are a former Navy SEAL. Demoted and dishonorably discharged at age twenty-seven after espousing beliefs the navy did not seem care for."

Guthrie looked cautiously around the private dining room. Although they were alone, he was sure the meeting was being recorded. The Russians recorded everything.

"I mean, you must admit, Mr. Guthrie," continued the Russian, "that spouting off on Islam at a navy prayer breakfast with an embedded NBC News correspondent in attendance—well, that wasn't too smart. But I understand your feelings. You see, I was in Afghanistan in '87."

"I was a younger man back then," said Guthrie. Now he really wanted to snap the Russian's neck.

"Yes, but your radical religious ideologies seem to have *matured*, if you will, over the years, no?"

"Let's cut the crap." Guthrie leaned forward over the table. "I wouldn't be sitting here if you didn't want a deal, so tell me, what's it going to take?"

The Russian downed another shot of vodka, then wiped his lips with a napkin. Reaching into the same leather satchel, he produced another envelope.

Guthrie began filing through classified documents, satellite images, and other photographs. The Russian resumed gluttonously devouring his food.

"North Korea. Makes sense," Guthrie said with tempered enthusiasm. "How old is this intel?"

"Three days," said the Russian, cutting into his steak. "The Order of Baphomet lives, and the CIA knows it. However, the CIA doesn't know what we know. Doctor Otto Klein, mastermind behind the Aries virus, is alive and well in North Korea, far beyond the reach of the Americans."

"Oh, you think so?" Guthrie asked sarcastically, not taking his eyes off the satellite images. "I personally ran ops in North Korea as a SEAL. There's no place on this planet that's out of reach of JSOC and the CIA. Not even the Kremlin, *Ivan*. It's only a matter of time before the US government finds what you have here, and that won't help either of us. So spill it. Why me, and what do you want?"

"Why you? We can't send Russian assets into North Korea. Relations are at an all-time low. If our men were ever caught—"

"You'd be the only ones to know," interrupted Guthrie. "The North Koreans would simply execute them on the spot."

"Perhaps. But we can't risk it. Besides, our mercs are not as good as you and your family."

"Now *there's* something we can finally agree on," Guthrie said. "Give me the rest. What do you want out of this?"

"As you can see from the images, Klein is living in a spacious chateau in a beautiful canyon only twelve kilometers southwest of *kwalliso* twenty-two, a concentration camp. In the chateau's basement is a laboratory. I need you to bring me all the biological samples in the industrial freezer there."

Guthrie laid down the satellite images. "You want Klein's biological weapons? You want Aries?"

"What's it to you? After all, you are a man eagerly working to usher in the end of the world, are you not? Besides, we will pay you handsomely, Mr. Guthrie, if you bring us the samples."

Guthrie said nothing.

The Russian was getting impatient. "So how much is this going to cost me?"

Guthrie resumed his study of the satellite images. "Nothing."

The Russian choked on his steak and reached for a glass of wine. "I'm sorry, I don't think I—"

"You heard me. You cover expenses, of course. I only require satellite support, two armed helos, weapons, and comms for my team. We'll do the job for nothing more than English-speaking, Russian military support."

The old spy looked stunned. "Why?"

"It's simple," Guthrie said casually. "I want Mahan. If I get Klein, I get Mahan."

The Russian burst into drunken laughter. "Master Mahan is a myth. A bogeyman invented by CIA spooks to scare tiny politicians and drive outrageous intelligence spending. The real mastermind is Klein."

Guthrie set down the papers and stared so intensely at the Russian that the man stopped laughing. The Russian bowed his head, gently dabbed at his mouth with his napkin, and collected himself. After a few moments, he cleared his throat and matched Guthrie's stare.

"Very well, then. We have a deal."

CHAPTER 14

OVAL OFFICE
WHITE HOUSE, WASHINGTON, D.C.

Chris, welcome," said President Barrington with his hand extended. A sly smile crossed his spray-tanned face.

Cautiously entering the Oval Office, Chris looked around, methodically surveying his surroundings. In just a millisecond, he'd cataloged, measured, and categorized every item in the room: the Resolute desk, the gold livery hanging over each window, the stunning artwork depicting the Colorado Rocky Mountains of the president's home state, and many other historical artifacts.

"We don't bite. Come on in, son," said General Westinghouse, chairman of the joint chiefs of staff. Several additional generals and an admiral laughed.

Chris walked over to the couches where the group congregated and shook each person's hand.

"Please, Chris, have a seat," said the president.

The meeting at the Capitol had been one thing, but from an intimidation standpoint, the Oval Office was something else entirely. Chris sat reluctantly in a chair opposite the president and cleared his throat, hoping no one would see the sweat forming on his brow.

"Well, you managed to scare the piss out of everyone today," said the president. "Nice work."

The joint chiefs laughed again.

Chris's heart sank. "Well, sir, I didn't mean to—"

"Oh, I'm just busting your chops, son. Frankly, I enjoy watching Congress squirm. It makes it easier to get things done around here."

"Oh, OK," Chris said shyly.

"We don't have the luxury of time, so let me get right to it. This encryption issue—it sounds like you have it solved with this, uh, x-cryption thing?"

"I believe I do. I mean yes, sir," Chris said.

"If what you said is true," Westinghouse bellowed impatiently, "we're all standing around right now with our flies wide open, son. Is x-cryption a real solution or not?"

The entourage stared intently at Chris.

Chris straightened in his seat and returned the intensity. "I can assure you, General, the x-cryption system works flawlessly. We've been testing it at Nav for the last year. We've experienced massive brute-force attacks on the system, and nothing gets through. It's like throwing a snowball at an M1A1 Abrams tank."

Chris could sense that Westinghouse wanted to smile at the tank reference, but the general stayed stone-faced.

"I've secretly employed some of the best hackers in the world to penetrate the system," he continued. "They've all failed miserably. And we've had what appears to be several state-sponsored hacks that have also failed. I can assure you that even a quantum computer can't break the x-cryption code."

"Yes, we know," Westinghouse said nonchalantly, "because we're one of the states that's tried to break into Nav with a quantum computer, and we couldn't do it. Heck, even as we speak, our wonks at NSA and NASA are attempting to hack Nav, and nothing. No dice. Nada."

"I figured," said Chris, annoyed by the brazen confession. "Do you have an agent in my ranks? You know, it's bad enough that I have to be paranoid about the Chinese, let alone my own government."

"Don't get bent out of shape, Chris," the president said. "It's what we do. Gentlemen, if you would excuse us, I'd like to speak to Dr. Thomas alone."

The joint chiefs looked surprised by the dismissal but exited the Oval Office. The door closed gently.

Barrington sighed deeply and stared into Chris's eyes. "What's it going to cost?"

"Cost?"

"Look, Chris. The public may not realize it, but we're in the middle of another cold war with Russia and China. We're also dealing with sophisticated terrorist organizations, like the Order, who may be trying to start World War Three. I need x-cryption to protect all digital facets of the federal government, including the military, the computer networks in all fifty states, the electrical grid—which, by the way, is a security mess—NATO, and other allies like Japan. And Grover was right—you will need congressional approval to deploy the software to any other country or corporation. This is now a national-security issue and will be treated as such."

Chris tried to conceal this anger at the blatant bullying. He didn't have to ask what would happen if he didn't comply. He already knew. Through force of legislation, regulation, and lawsuits, the government would get their way. Barrington couldn't burn a bridge with someone as highly valued as Chris Thomas, so he was giving him a way out in the form of a payoff.

"One hundred," Chris said, leaning forward in his chair.

"One hundred what?"

"Billion. A year."

Chris could tell the president knew he was serious. The look on Barrington's face spoke a thousand words, but the president didn't flinch. Instead, he smiled condescendingly. "Isn't that a bit exorbitant? Do you know how much money that is, son?"

"I have a net worth of more than $100 billion, so yeah, I do. And given the United States government's proclivity for overpaying on everything, I figure why not shoot for the stars?"

The president sat as still as a stone for more than a minute. "Let's discuss some additional conditions," he finally said. "For starters, we require a back door to the software that allows us into any system employing x-cryption."

Chris had already anticipated that condition. "What else?"

"I want Max Def deployed across all branches of the military and NATO as part of the contract."

"Deal, as long as it's only used for defensive purposes. I have master admin control to all Max instances, Mr. President. I will know if the government tries to go back on this condition like you did with that Caribbean mission a few weeks ago."

Barrington rubbed his chin and nodded. "I can agree to that."

"I have a few conditions of my own," said Chris.

"Go."

"No taxes on the $100 billion."

"That's a huge ask. There's no way the IRS or Congress would—"

"We both know the IRS and Congress would, sir. It's truly amazing what a president can do these days with a classified executive order, don't you agree?"

Barrington looked up at the presidential seal emblazoned on the ceiling and sighed again. Then he refocused on Chris. "The public and Congress could never know. I'll have to classify this whole deal above top secret and fund most of it from state budgets, classified transactions from our foreign allies, and the black budget."

The president ran his hand through his thinning gray hair. "I have one more condition," he continued. "Something Stew Brimhall and I recently discussed bringing you into. It's a highly classified special-access project. I can't tell you what it is, but I need you to agree so I can start working on your new security clearance."

"I have a Q clearance. That's not high enough?"

"Not even close. You're going to need something much, much higher than Q for this."

Chris was completely intrigued but tried to show his best poker face. "Deal."

CHAPTER 15

JOINT BASE ANDREWS
MARYLAND

The intense meetings with Congress and the president had consumed Chris. He wanted to lie in the G700's bed and sleep all the way to California, but his mind was focused on the challenges in front of him. On top of that, the ever-present math in his field of vision was in rapid-fire mode. He lay on the bed, trying to control his brain while the plane taxied toward the main airstrip, swaying slightly.

"Max, I assume we've had no attempted incursions into the aircraft's flight systems or to the physical aircraft," Chris said, looking nowhere in particular.

"Correct, sir. No incursions of any kind detected, and security guarded the aircraft dutifully while you were absent."

Chris knew he didn't have to ask. Had there been any problem, Max would have notified him immediately. But an underlying concern—maybe it was a slight paranoia—had haunted him ever since he and Leah almost died over the Atlantic eighteen months earlier. Flying hadn't been the same since.

As the aircraft started into a steep climb, Chris sat up in the bed. As soon as the plane leveled off, he walked into the small bathroom and started the shower, accepting that he wouldn't be sleeping. The scalding hot water ran over his body and turned his skin red, but it felt like heaven. He began to vocalize his thoughts.

"Max, you heard the conversations with Congress and the president, correct?"

"Yes, sir, as you ordered. I have begun building deployment protocols for x-cryption as well as for Max Def. I should have numerous project recommendations for you and Mr. Allen in 7.1 hours."

"Excellent," Chris said as he ran Duke Cannon soap over his body. "Now, we have another problem. I've been in denial, Max. Maybe I just hoped it was no longer a problem, but it is."

Max said nothing.

"The Order is still a threat. They've been biding their time. Regrouping. Planning another attack. We have to finish the job. We have to take them down for good. We need to discover what Thor's Hammer is, stop it, and find Master Mahan. It's up to us."

"Sir, under classified executive order, I have been actively monitoring all global computer networks, all communications networks, and internet traffic for specific metadata, the Lamanese language, and other patterns and codes. I have nothing to report."

"I know." Chris took in a big breath of steam. "We have to take it a step further."

"I do not understand, sir."

"We have to hack every network on the planet, open or closed. Every personal computer, communication network, government and private server, open and closed database, every wireless device, and even source code. We're the only ones who can do it."

"Sir, the sum of all the world's data is 196 trillion gigabytes. Every day the world produces 13.7 quintillion bytes of data."

"I understand, Max," said Chris. "Let's start building a logical process and algorithm while analyzing potentially trillions of patterns at a time."

"Processing power and global internet bandwidth may hamper progress," warned Max.

"Spool up the Orca. We need to go quantum to penetrate this level of encryption and crunch this much data in such a short period of time."

"I'll need the thorium reactors in order to power the quantum array."

"We've simulated this, Max. It shouldn't be a problem. Are you concerned about pushing the Orca and the reactors to full power?"

"No, sir, you are correct. The simulation was sound."

"I know it's still experimental, but you are authorized to use the thorium nuclear reactors at full capacity," said Chris. "Push the quantum array to its limits."

"Startup sequences are in flight. I will keep you abreast of any developments."

"Max, send a text to Scott Allen. *Meet me at the office in the morning. We have work to do.*"

Chris stepped out of the shower, wrapped a towel around his body, unlocked his iPhone, and sent Leah a message: *On my way home.*

Which home? she responded.

Uh . . .

Heber. If you remember, that's in Utah, and that's where I am now :)

CHAPTER 16

NAV CORPORATE HEADQUARTERS
PALO ALTO, CALIFORNIA

Chris wore a black hoodie as he walked stealthily into the heavily guarded side door of Nav's headquarters, trying to dodge the horde of protesters congregated outside. Even after Chris had outed most of the protesters as F-list actors, the intensity of the protests seemed to increase. A new analysis found that more and more unpaid, genuinely angry people—many of whom identified themselves as part of the proletariat movement—were showing up at Nav to protest on a daily basis.

This new round of protests had been ignited by a *New York Times* doomsday article quoting several prominent politicians—some of Chris's most public critics—fearmongering over the Max AI and the coming end of jobs. Behind closed doors, many of those same politicians begged for access to Max.

As Chris entered the building, he rounded a corner and collided head-on with an employee, her cup of steaming-hot coffee spilling all over Chris's hoodie.

"Oh, my gosh. Oh, my gosh!" yelled Kiki Kalani.

Chris dropped his shoulder bag and looked down at the mess. "Well, at least the hoodie is black."

"Oh, Chris. I am so sorry. Oh, my gosh. Please don't fire me. Please, Chris, I promise I'm a valuable asset to the team. I swear I'll try harder, Chris."

"Kiki, of course I'm not going to fire you. It was both of our faults, but this is the second time this week."

"I know. I know. I can't even—"

"Look, Kiki, I'm not worried about getting coffee on me," Chris said as he unzipped his soaking-wet hoodie. "I'm worried about you. I've seen you run into at least three doors and drop your tray in the lunchroom at least once a week. The IT guys told me you're on your fourth computer in three months. You're extremely bright. No one else in the building can claim PhDs from Cambridge, Harvard, and Stanford. You've been a tremendous help at Nav, but I'm honestly a little worried about you walking into traffic or an open elevator shaft or something crazy like that."

"I know, Chris, I know," said Kiki. "So, I'm not fired?"

"No. No, of course not. But please use a little more caution, OK?"

Kiki squealed joyfully and embraced Chris, who carefully pushed her away.

"OK, OK," he said.

"I promise I will be more careful." She bounced up and down with excitement. "I won't let you down."

"Yo!" said Scott Allen, busting into Chris office. "I tried to call you last night, but it went straight to voicemail. How was D.C.?"

"Yeah, that was on purpose." Chris threw the stained hoodie into the garbage can next to his desk. "How am I supposed to get any Leah time with you guys calling me at all hours? Besides, I had to get up early and fly in for our meeting. Leah moved us already."

"To Utah?" asked Scott. "Already?" He plopped down on the couch in front of Chris. "Wait, what happened to your hoodie?"

"Kiki ran into me again."

"Again? That's the second time this week. I mean, she's smoking hot and all, but geez, she's going to accidentally kill herself."

"Yeah, I told her that very thing."

"That she's smoking hot?"

"No, Scott." Chris gave Scott an annoyed look. "That she's going to kill herself because she's a klutz."

Scott settled back on the couch. "These protesters are starting to annoy me."

"They're not as annoying as the politicians igniting the rage. I have something in mind for them."

"Oh yeah?" Scott leaned forward.

Sitting down in his swivel chair, Chris looked his best friend—and Nav's president—right in the face. "It's crack-Senator-Grover-in-the-ear day, brother. We're starting our own PAC and lobby. It's the only way to protect ourselves from the political blizzard bearing down on us like a freaking freight train. I'm going to run their butts right out of office with the money they borrowed from the Chinese and the fed or stole from the taxpayers to pay Nav for our technology."

"Right on," said Scott. "I was wondering when this was coming. Wait, pay us? What do you mean pay us?"

"Several things transpired while I was in D.C. First, everyone smiled at me before threatening me. It was annoying. Second, we're starting a new company. I'm calling it GroupIT."

"Sounds oddly innocuous."

"That's on purpose because its existence is classified. The nonexistent company is going to sell x-crypton to the US government, all fifty states, power companies, NATO, and a few others for an easy hundred billion a year."

Scott shot straight up from the couch. He stared at Chris, waiting for the punch line, but it didn't come. Chris just sat in his chair with a look of fierce victory.

"Chris, a Mr. Mayberry is here to see you," said a voice over the desk phone's intercom.

"Send him in," Chris said, still looking at Scott.

Scott blinked and ran his hand through his hair, looking shocked. Trying to process Chris's words, he quietly paced the office. On Scott's third pass, Mike walked through the office's bulletproof glass door.

"What happened to you?" Mike asked Scott, noticing his manic state. "Finally talk to an actual woman last night?" Passing Scott, Mike sat down across from Chris, smirking.

Chris extended his hand to Mike. "Never mind him. He just got rich. I mean richer."

"I'm going to the restroom," Scott said as he walked out the glass door in a daze. "Be right back."

"You know, you don't have a lot of employees here," observed Mike, shifting in his chair. "I mean, maybe a few hundred in the whole building, right?"

"Four hundred and eighty-two, including the janitor. Mostly researchers. Some of the smartest people on earth are here analyzing Nav data and working with Max. Most companies our size have tens of thousands of employees, but Max runs most of the company."

"So that's why you have all the protesters outside?" Mike asked.

Suddenly the room's audio system came alive, and the hundred-inch wall monitor displayed the Nav lobby. Two security guards and the receptionist lay motionless on the lobby floor.

"What the—" said Mike, springing to his feet.

"Sir, we have a security breach," said Max.

Mike pulled his Glock 19 from inside his sport coat.

"Go, Max. Sitrep," said Chris, jumping up from his seat and rushing to the office's glass wall. In the large open area outside Chris's office, people worked and milled about normally. In a millisecond of observation, he cataloged each person and event within his view. Nothing was out of place.

"Analyzing threat," said Max.

Chris moved for the glass door.

"No!" yelled Mike, stopping Chris dead in his tracks. "My phone is dead. There's no signal."

"What does that mean?" Chris asked.

"They knocked out comms," said Mike. "That's a prelude to an attack. Max, lock down this room. Scan for assailants. Sound the fire alarm."

"Executing," said Max. The alarm sounded immediately, and the employees looked around in confusion. Max's calm, familiar voice sounded over the building's intercom system. "This is not a drill. Please proceed toward the exits in an orderly fashion."

"Max, anything to report?" asked Chris.

"Analyzing playback," Max said. "Scanning facility. Sir, security cameras are off-line."

The video played back to sixty seconds earlier. Three men in black designer suits and dark glasses entered the lobby. A few second later, small puffs of smoke rose from their outstretched hands as the receptionist and guards dropped to the floor.

"I've seen this before," said Mike. "This is bad."

"What is it?" asked Chris.

Just then, a body slammed into the office's glass door. Mike and Chris turned with a jolt to see Scott Allen pressed face forward against the door by one of the assassins. A look of terror and pain spread over Scott's face.

Mike raised the Glock and fired.

"No!" Chris yelled.

The round disintegrated into the glass door. Had it penetrated, it would, no doubt, have hit Scott's assailant perfectly between the eyes, but the three assassins didn't flinch. Scott screamed, and tears ran down his face.

"Drop it," said the man holding Scott, his voice barely audible through the level-seven bulletproof glass.

"If I drop this weapon, we all die," Mike said to Chris in a low voice.

"What about Scott?" Chris asked, looking at the man who had been his best friend since third grade. Seeing the terror in Scott's eyes, Chris had never felt so helpless.

"I don't want to sound cold, but you have to live," Mike said, his weapon still trained on the assassins. "Scott and I don't."

Chris felt his stomach lurch.

The man holding Scott moved his arm and flicked his wrist. A small but powerful projectile pierced Scott's knee, blood, flesh, and bone splattering the glass wall. Scott buckled and screamed out in pain, then vomited on the wall.

"No!" yelled Chris. He started for the door, but Mike grabbed him by the arm. Chris tried to break his grip, but Mike held him like a vise.

One assassin seized Scott by the arm, and another pointed his wrist at Scott's head. "You have five seconds to open the door, or he dies."

"Max, any ideas?" called Chris desperately.

Before Max could respond, each assassin's head exploded, spraying the glass wall with crimson blood.

Mike released Chris's arm but kept his gun raised as he peered through the gore-stained glass. Then he lowered his gun, sighing in relief.

Chris burst through the door and knelt beside his injured friend. Covered in the blood of his captors, Scott flailed on the ground, screaming in pain.

"Call an ambulance!" Chris yelled as he cradled Scott.

From across the room, a man stepped forward with his pistol still raised. Chris immediately recognized him as Mike's longtime second-in-command, Smith.

CHAPTER 17

FLYING-G RANCH
OUTSIDE GUTHRIE, TEXAS

The only thing Rand Guthrie loved more than piloting his Bombardier 7500 private jet was his family's fifty thousand acres in West Texas. He was exhausted from flying for twelve hours straight but invigorated looking over his small piece of Texas. The familiar pastures, rolling hills, cattle, trees, and crops spread out over the vast property as far as the eye could see. Some people viewed West Texas as a barren wasteland; to Rand, it was sacred ground.

Soon, a private airstrip came into view, and the copilot lowered the landing gear.

"It looks hotter than a honeymoon hotel down there," the copilot said in a thick Texas accent. The old cliché woke Rand from his trance.

"Pilot has the controls," Rand said as he took the stick. He pulled back on the power and guided the plane on final approach.

As the plane touched down, Rand noticed a small group of people and horses congregated near the end of the runway.

"Take her to the hangar and call in the maintenance crew," Rand instructed the copilot. "We need to turn her around and be ready for another international long haul in the next seventy-two hours."

"Yessir" answered the copilot.

As Rand stepped off the plane, his sisters, Abigail and Naomi, ran to him and embraced him tightly. His younger but bigger brother, Levi, moved in with a strong handshake, then handed Rand his worn but beloved Stetson Diamante cowboy hat.

"She's been wanting to run, brother." Levi nodded over his shoulder toward Rand's horse, which was tied up just off the runway. "What do you say?"

Tipping his hat to his brother, Rand said, "We best not keep our mother waiting."

As Rand and his siblings mounted their horses, the Bombardier 7500 taxied to its palatial hangar a hundred yards away.

The midday sun beat down as the group headed west over a well-worn horse trail. Rand, leading the group, crested the ridge of a slight hill and looked proudly at the oil rigs dotting the prairie before him. As he rode on, the family's thirty-thousand-square-foot mansion with its stunning green lawn came into view. The siblings galloped over the perfect lawn, passed the spacious house, and turned down a rocky trail that dropped into a narrow ravine.

After another half mile, a church came into view, freshly painted in a stark white, with an oversized oak cross perched on its steeple. The building nestled humbly on the bank of a tiny stream running through a grove of mature Mexican white oak trees.

Rand and his siblings tied their horses and scaled the rickety steps, removing their hats as they entered the church through tall double doors.

Light pierced the chapel's darkness, and Rand squinted. The first thing he noticed was the enormous neon-lit cross hanging above the pulpit. It hummed in the dank, humid air. The group removed their hats and walked slowly up the main aisle past the rows of dust-covered pews, stopping at a bed positioned just under the pulpit. Glowing candles, statues of Jesus Christ, and crosses of all sizes filled every available space. The room smelled of hospice.

Rand glanced over and noticed a priest and a nurse concealed in a dark corner. They said nothing and didn't acknowledge the children with even a nod. They were paid handsomely to care for Mother, not to talk.

"Rand?" said the frail woman on the bed.

"Yes, Mother," said Rand. He knelt and gently kissed her hand.

"Behold, the pale horse returns," said the woman through her oxygen mask. She was blind and barely lucid. A clean white sheet covered her cancer-stricken body.

"Are you comfortable, Mother?"

"Never mind me, boy," she snapped. "Did the providence of God smile on you, my son?"

The other children knelt around the bed near their mother's head.

"Yes, Mother," said Rand. "I went forth, and a spirit of heaviness weighed greatly upon me. But I was blessed in this trial of my faith and led to a heathen. The heathen bequeathed me a key that unlocked a door leading to a path. Now I clearly see the mission God has given me."

His siblings looked at him with concern in their eyes.

"Praise Christ Jesus," said Rand's mother.

His siblings repeated her words.

She pushed aside the oxygen mask. "I am the prophetess, my children." Her words were weak, her breathing labored. "As I have proclaimed many times in the Holy Spirit, I saw a vision. You are the four horsemen of the Apocalypse: Death, War, Pestilence, and Famine. It is by your hands that the Second Coming shall be ushered in—not by the unrighteous hand of the Order of Baphomet and the devil Cain. All who stand in your way shall die, for God hath sanctioned it. Now, go, my children, and fulfill your divine calling. The time is now when God will return to the earth."

The woman's eyes rolled back in her head, and she fell into unconsciousness.

~

The siblings exited the church. Replacing their hats, they mounted their mares and formed up in a circle.

"Well, brother?" said Abigail, the youngest. She ran her hand gently over her mare's neck to calm the stunningly beautiful beast.

"The mission is in North Korea," Rand said. "The target is Doctor Otto Klein—the mastermind behind the Aries virus and chief scientist of the Order of Baphomet. He will know where Mahan is located."

"How are you going to get him to talk?" asked Levi.

Rand looked over at the church he'd built with his own hands years ago. The lowly trees swayed in the humid wind. He exhaled slightly and thought of the ranch he loved more than anything in the world, wishing he could stay here for the remainder of his days. But God had other plans for Rand and his siblings.

"I have my ways, brother."

"God approves, brother," Abigail said with a wild flair in her eyes. "We are His chosen, His beloved. You are our leader. The flaming two-edged sword of justice will cleave down upon the heathens."

"We are mission-ready now," said Naomi. "We have prepared every needful thing."

"That won't be necessary," Rand said. "The Russians are supplying us with everything we need for the mission."

"I'm bringing my sniper rifle." Naomi's tone implied the issue was not up for debate.

"Suit yourself," Rand responded.

Levi looked quizzically at his older brother. "You trust the Russkis?"

"Of course not," Rand shot back. "But they want something only we can get them. That makes us trusted partners, at least until they have what they want in hand. Then—" He paused. "Then we're going to have to get dirty."

Naomi broke the uncomfortable silence. "When is it ever clean?"

All three younger siblings gave Rand doubtful looks.

"Fear not, little flock. I know exactly what to do."

CHAPTER 18

STANFORD UNIVERSITY MEDICAL CENTER
PALO ALTO, CALIFORNIA

Chris, Leah, and Mike sat in the lobby of a secure surgical wing at Stanford Medical Center. When the surgeon entered the waiting area, Chris sprang from his seat to meet her.

"We have him stabilized, Mr. Thomas. His vitals are normal, and besides the knee, he's physically unharmed."

"Thank goodness," said Leah.

"However, the damage to the knee is catastrophic," the surgeon continued. "Even at point-blank range, the projectile's velocity was extreme. We're dealing with massive ligament damage. His patella is shattered, as are the distal femur and proximal tibia. We're prepping him for surgery now."

"What about vascularity to the lower leg?" asked Chris.

"That's our foremost concern. We have a vascular surgeon running a Doppler to access his pulse."

"Unless there's a problem with vascularity to the lower leg, keep him stable," Chris instructed. "The surgical team will be on the ground in one hour."

"I'm sorry, the surgical team?"

"Yeah. Dr. Nugu and his team from the Mayo Clinic in Scottsdale are en route on my plane."

"Oh, I didn't know." The doctor crossed her arms in front of her chest. "I can assure you the Stanford orthopedic surgical team is one of the best in the world."

"With all due respect, Doctor, I don't do 'one of the best'—I only do the best," said Chris.

The doctor appeared not to know how to react. She dropped her arms to her sides, nodded, and turned to head back to her duties.

"Doctor," said Leah.

The doctor turned back around without saying a word.

"Thank you for all you've done. You and your team have been amazing. We're deeply indebted to you."

"You're welcome." The doctor glared at Chris, then turned around again and walked off.

"Nice work, Chris," Leah whispered.

"What?"

"You know what."

"I just got a message from Smith," interrupted Mike. "We have an Orion's Spear team on site doing a forensic analysis on the assassins' bodies. The FBI is assisting. There's nothing yet, but this has the Order's fingerprints all over it, Chris. What if they had gone for Leah? Honestly, I'm surprised they didn't."

"For me?" Leah sat upright in her chair.

"I thought of that," said Chris, trying not to think the unthinkable. "This doesn't add up. They would've known about the bulletproof office."

"I think they were probing defenses," said Mike. "I told you security wasn't good enough."

"I know, Mike. I've been so busy. I—I just haven't made it a priority."

"That's one reason for my visit today," said Mike while working his phone. "I have a name for you—someone you need to consider for revamping your security."

Chris unlocked his phone and found the file Mike had just sent him. It showed a Middle Eastern woman with jet-black hair like Leah's. Her lips were thin, her eyes a piercing dark blue. She looked like a Persian model.

"Her name is Amal Nour," Mike said. "She's a former Secret Service agent."

Leah took the phone from Chris. "Oh, wow."

Chris leaned over and kissed Leah while taking back the phone. "Let's not worry about this now, OK? We have to get back to Utah. I have a meeting with the president."

"With Barrington?" Mike asked with surprise. "Today?"

"I'll be back tomorrow," Chris said, standing to leave with Leah. "Mike, can you take care of things here?"

"No problem. Give the president my regards."

CHAPTER 19

DUGWAY PROVING GROUND
WEST DESERT, UTAH

The air-traffic controller spoke clearly through Chris's Bose headset. "This is Dugway ATC. Proceed on present vector. Landing instructions to follow. Do not deviate from present course, or you will be fired on."

Chris looked down as several men holding M4 carbines stepped out of the guardhouse at the main entrance of Dugway Proving Ground. They looked up at Chris hovering above the gate in his MD 520N helicopter.

"Roger that," Chris said. He pushed forward on the stick, moving the helicopter cautiously over the boundary of the secretive military base. The helicopter accelerated forward at three hundred feet off the barren desert floor. Chris wondered how far they'd have to fly into this desolate wasteland spreading tens of miles in every direction.

After flying for ten minutes, Chris squinted. Something was forming on the horizon.

"There." His flight instructor pointed straight ahead. What looked like a small city with numerous large buildings came into view, shimmering against the desert sunset.

Air-traffic control came alive again over comms. "This is Dugway ATC. You are on approach to the airfield. Proceed to landing zone B-4."

"Roger that," said Chris.

"We've got escorts," said the instructor, giving Chris a nervous glance. Chris looked left and noticed an Apache gunship shadowing them. He looked right and noticed another attack helicopter a quarter mile off.

"This isn't on Google Earth," Chris said as he pulled up on the helicopter's collective, clearing several large hangars. The helicopter arched in an orbit over a sprawling airfield spreading out for miles before them. A Blackhawk helicopter squadron, several F-22 fighter jets, and a fleet of C-5 cargo planes sat on the tarmac, along with an untold number of other military vehicles and armed men dressed in black.

That's odd, thought Chris. *I don't see Air Force One.*

"There," the instructor said, pointing at the landing zone. "OK, Chris. Take her down slowly. Go easy on the collective and pedals."

Chris gently pushed down on the collective and turned the bird with his foot pedals. The machine descended slowly and steadily. As he eased back on the stick and continued to push down on the collective, the helicopter touched the ground. He looked over at the instructor and raised his eyebrows.

"Nicely done. That's your first perfect landing."

"Do not exit the aircraft until instructed to do so," said the air traffic controller over comms.

"Roger," said Chris, and he powered down the MD's turbine engine. An armed solider in all black approached the helicopter, and Chris noticed a Chevy Suburban appear from between two hangars and head at high speeds straight for their helicopter.

The suburban came to a screeching halt, and three men jumped out. They were dressed in black suits and wore dark sunglasses. One of them opened Chris's door.

"Sir, are you Chris Thomas?"

"Yes," he answered loudly. The helicopter was still powering down.

"Please give me your Social Security number."

Chris recited his Social Security number. The man looked into a mobile device and nodded. "ID, please," he said. Chris reached into his jacket and handed over several pieces of ID, including his CIA identification. The man scanned them thoroughly, then gave them back.

Next, he held his mobile device up to Chris's face. "Look into the device."

Chris did so until the man nodded. "Dr. Thomas, welcome to Dugway Proving Ground. Please come with us." Pointing to the flight instructor, the man added, "You stay with the helicopter. If you need anything, signal the guard over there." He gestured to a guard standing on the ramp.

Chris gave his instructor a look as he slipped out of the machine. "Have fun," he said. The instructor frowned.

After Chris jumped into the Suburban's back seat, the guard in the passenger seat handed him a black silk bag. Chris looked curiously at the bag and then back at the guard.

"It's just a security precaution, sir. You can take it off when we arrive at our destination but not before then."

Chris shrugged and placed the bag over his head. The vehicle lunged slightly forward, then started to drive in circles. He reached over to feel for the seat belt, clicking it into place as the Suburban straightened out and accelerated. After several short turns, the vehicle stopped, and the driver cut the engine.

No one said a word. Then Chris felt the vehicle slowly move straight downward. The only sound he could make out was the slight hum of hydraulics. *Are we in some kind of elevator?*

After what felt like an eternity, they stopped with a slight jolt. Chris heard vehicle doors open, and then one of the men removed the bag from Chris's head.

"Please exit the vehicle, sir," said the guard. Chris stepped out of the Suburban and looked around. He was standing in the middle of what looked like a well-lit warehouse the size of a suburban grocery store. It was stark white from floor to ceiling and completely empty.

"Follow me, sir," said one of the men. They walked across the vast room to a narrow door that seemed to blend into the wall. The man stopped and turned to Chris. "Please enter here. They're waiting for you on the other side."

Chris eyed the man with suspicion, his brow furrowed. He faced the door, cleared his throat, and reluctantly turned the knob. As he entered the conference room, he could see several familiar people milling around a circular table, most with their backs turned to Chris. General Westinghouse noticed Chris and said something to a man across the table. The man turned with a jerk and faced Chris.

It was President Barrington.

~

"Chris!" Barrington said enthusiastically, approaching with hand outstretched. "Welcome to Dugway, my friend. It's great to have you here. I'm so sorry to hear about the incident at Nav. I have our best FBI team on it. Will you please give Scott Allen my best?"

"Yes, I appreciate that, sir," Chris said. "I'm sorry, but I'm just a little surprised to see you. I didn't see Air Force One on the ramp."

The president and his people laughed.

"Well, Chris, I didn't arrive here on Air Force One. In fact, I didn't fly here at all."

Chris tilted his head, confused. The people around the table laughed again.

"Bear with me, son." Barrington patted Chris on the back. "It'll all make sense in a few minutes."

The president put his arm around Chris and guided him to another door on the opposite side of the room. Led by Westinghouse, the generals and other well-dressed government officials followed closely behind.

The door opened, and a subway train waited across a short loading platform. Chris tried not to look surprised. As they walked, a digital sign above the platform displayed strange names and numbers Chris surmised to be some type of military code.

The group loaded into one of the cars. "Have a seat here, Chris." The president pointed to a seat across from him.

Chris looked down the length of the train. "This is impressive."

"This is nothing compared to what you're about to see, son. Your Majestic-level clearance has been approved."

"My security clearance?" asked Chris as he sat down. Out the window, he saw that the train was moving slowly through a bland concrete tunnel.

"Yes, but it's not your standard top-secret clearance. It's twenty-two security levels above Q clearance, which, as you know, is what most CIA analysts and JSOC special operators are granted. Even the name Majestic is classified above top secret. So it's important we understand each other, Chris. With this clearance, you have access to everything, and I mean everything. It's a great responsibility that mustn't be abused. Usually, when Majestic is taken from someone, they also get a prison sentence. Do we understand each other?"

Chris swallowed hard and leaned forward in his seat. "I think I understand, sir, but can you define what you mean by *everything*?"

"What do you want to know? Who shot Kennedy? That's usually the first one people ask about." The president smirked.

"Well, I don't know what I can and can't ask, sir."

"Like I said, anything you want. But Kennedy really isn't that interesting." The president gave a deadpan smile. "He was shot from the famed grassy knoll by CIA-trained Cuban exiles with the help of a few disenfranchised Green Berets. It was revenge for the Bay of Pigs debacle. Rogue elements inside the CIA, also pissed off about the Bay of Pigs, framed Oswald as the patsy. You can't have some nosy reporter tracking cash back to the government, so the mob financed the operation in exchange for the CIA's turning a blind eye to them running drugs over the Canadian border."

"That's what really happened?"

"Things were different back then." The president shrugged. "Times have changed. What else do you want to know?"

Chris sat quietly for a moment. He still didn't believe he could ask anything, but President Barrington stared at him hard, as if daring him to ask another question.

Sheepishly Chris asked, "Um, well, what about UFOs?"

"Oh, you mean UAPs. Now we're getting somewhere interesting."

Just then, the train stopped with a mild jolt.

"UAPs?" asked Chris.

"Unidentified aerial phenomena. No one calls them UFOs anymore. Let's take a walk."

The train door opened, and the contingent followed Chris and the president toward a tunnel about forty feet high that extended for what seemed like miles. Chris was again momentarily taken aback. The millions of people living in Salt Lake City and along the Wasatch Front had no idea what lay in the desert just west of their boring, suburban lives.

The group piled into golf carts and started down the tunnel. The president took the wheel of one cart, and Chris sat next to him.

"It's the only thing I get to drive anymore," Barrington said with a sigh. "Speaking of which, you never asked me how I got here."

"Well, I know it wasn't Air Force One."

"By bullet train, but way more advanced than the trains you're thinking of in Europe or Japan."

"A bullet train? Obviously, it's underground. And it must be maglev."

"Yes, magneto levitron trains. We have a secret network below the United States. Back in the 1930s, under cover of the New Deal, we started making plans for a vast network of underground bases. Some of these are known to the public, like Mount Weather and Cheyenne Mountain. It was part of the continuity of government plan."

"I've read about that," said Chris.

"Most of what you've read is disinformation—what we call PSYOPS. We don't let the good stuff get out. In the beginning, the earth-boring technology was painfully slow. After a decade of digging, we finally connected Mount Weather to the Pentagon when it was constructed in 1941."

Large fluorescent lights glowed overhead as the group pressed deeper into the bowels of the cold, concrete tunnel. The president continued his history lesson. "In the late 1960s, we developed a nuclear-powered laser that sat on a train the length of a football field. The darn thing could instantly pulverize granite and iron ore into dust. It was a complete game changer. We could build ten miles of tunnel a day with that machine, so we began construction on an intricate underground continental rail system. It's made up of numerous tunnels all the way from Washington, D.C., on the East Coast to various points on the West Coast. We now have 112 underground bases connected by the maglev train system. I left on the presidential train in D.C. this morning at 11:00 a.m. and arrived at Dugway forty-five minutes later. The trains are faster than fighter jets. I love 'em. Just last week, I held a secret meeting with executives at General Dynamics and Boeing in a high-rise in downtown L.A. No one knew I was there, and I was home in time for dinner and the First Lady's famous apple pie."

Chris was speechless.

"We move people and all kinds of weapons around the country on the train system," the president continued. "One train can transport a tank battalion across the US in an hour. We haven't moved a nuke above ground in over four decades. It's safe, secret, and fast. One of these days, I'll take you out to China Lake, Nevada. That's where our secret submarine base is stationed."

"A submarine base? In Nevada?"

"There's a gigantic undersea cave extending from just south of San Francisco hundreds of miles inland to China Lake. We connected the cave system to an underground base just for the subs. Except for our base under the Denver International Airport, China Lake is our largest underground base. In fact, it's so big we now manufacture submarines inside the underground base. We have twice as many subs in our fleet as the world thinks."

The president stopped the cart near a nondescript door marked A-139. "Well, here we are," he said, exiting the cart.

Chris hesitantly stepped off the cart, and the president's entourage lined up behind him.

"Now, look, Chris. You're going to have a lot of questions. Today, I just need you to take it all in. In time, all your questions will be answered. For now, just try to grasp the basics, OK?"

Staring at the door, Chris nodded in nervous anticipation.

When the president opened the door, bright light flooded into the tunnel. The president gestured, and Chris stepped inside the room.

What lay before him stopped him dead in his tracks.

CHAPTER 20

GUTHRIE FAMILY'S BOMBARDIER 7500
OVER ALASKA

Extreme fatigue overcame Rand, but he was unable to fall asleep. Since his youth, trauma-induced insomnia had been his persistent companion.

From his plush leather seat near the front of the private plane, he stared down the cabin at his siblings. Levi was asleep, and Naomi and Abigail talked quietly while they worked. Abigail meticulously ran a steel blade along a whetstone and cautiously felt the razor-sharp edge of the custom-forged hybrid Arrow throwing knife. She handled a knife the way an artist handled a brush. Not even among other SEALs had Rand met a human so naturally proficient with a blade.

Naomi held an Allen wrench and worked on a Leopold scope she'd machined to fit a Piccadilly rail on her custom-built Barrett .50-caliber sniper rifle, her weapon of choice. She was surgical with a sniper rifle up to fifteen hundred yards and rivaled even the best SEAL snipers he'd worked with.

When Rand was discharged from the Navy, he'd hired a few of his former teammates to train his sisters in their expert methods. The girls, just teenagers at the time, had taken to the SEAL training in ways he'd never imagined. In his mind, his sisters' abilities further proved their mother's prophecies about the children's violent destiny.

Both women were beautiful. Abigail, wild and attractive and the more outgoing of the two girls, had won Miss Texas Teen at eighteen. Naomi, more of a tomboy but a Texas beauty in her own right, had taken an academic route and graduated from Texas A&M with honors and dual master's degrees in chemical and electrical engineering. She oversaw the Guthrie oil empire's research-and-development division and was a talented executive.

Rand often wondered what his siblings' lives would have been like under different familial circumstances, but they'd never wanted anything different. They were chosen, and with being chosen came sacrifices, such as forgoing marriage and families of their own. All four Guthrie children were obsessed with their destiny and never lost sight of the mission their mother had deeply ingrained in them from infancy. She'd taught them to hunt and kill from an early age. She'd taught them how to accurately fire a rifle. She'd brutally whipped them with a belt and forced them to whip each other over even the most minor infractions.

The plane, now thirty-five thousand feet over Alaska's Brooks Range, hit a minor bout of turbulence that swayed the aircraft. Rand finally drifted to sleep only to find himself in a familiar nightmare, floating above as his younger self walked into an old barn that had once stood in a remote area of the family ranch. To Rand's horror, he saw Abigail standing, blood-covered, over the body of the former SEAL Rand had hired as part of his sisters' paramilitary training. She'd stabbed him so many times he was almost unrecognizable. Staring down at the lifeless pulp, Abigail still clutched a knife in her trembling hand.

"Abigail, what have you done?" cried Rand. He knelt next to the body and covered his mouth with his hands.

Abigail looked down at her brother. Her normally piercing blue eyes were hollow, and her smiling face was covered in gore. "He tried to force himself on me."

Rand shot awake, quickly remembering he was on the plane. His sisters looked up, momentarily concerned, then returned to their work. Rand took a drink and breathed deeply to slow his heart rate. After several minutes, he checked his pulse and looked at his sisters, who were still engrossed in conversation and work. Soon his eyes were heavy, and he slipped into a deep sleep, his mind again hurtling into his horrific past.

~

When Rand was seventeen, a rancher on adjacent land had tried to use eminent-domain laws and his county board position to condemn the Guthries' rundown trailer home and small, desolate, one-hundred-acre plot. Having heard rumors of oil claims and with no Guthrie husband to stand in his way, the man secretly intended to take the family's land.

At 3:00 a.m. on a viciously humid July morning, Rand's mother had led the dirty children into the rancher's home. They'd seized the sleeping man and his wife at gunpoint and tied them to chairs in the kitchen. Then Rand's mother screamed biblical verses at the elderly couple for more than an hour while wildly waving a butcher knife in their terrified faces.

Midrant, she unexpectedly turned to Levi and handed him the knife. "Go on, now, boy. Fulfill your duty to Christ Jesus."

Levi, just fourteen years old, wept in horror at his mother's directive. He stared at the man and his wife, then glanced down at the blade. "I can't do it, Mama," he said, looking at his mother with pleading eyes.

Naomi and Abigail held each other, shaking in fear. The repercussions that would most certainly visit Levi for his insubordination would be brutal.

Mother regarded the boy through her sunken eyes, then raised her arm to strike him across the face. A powerful force stopped her midswing.

It was Rand.

Mother looked confused and surprised, but her seventeen-year-old son gently released her arm and took the butcher knife from his little brother. His siblings stopped crying and looked at Rand in complete disbelief. The rancher and his wife pulled desperately against their restraints, but they were bound too tightly.

Rand raised the knife and shrieked as he rushed across the kitchen at the rancher.

"No, son—please. Lord, no," the rancher pleaded as Rand mounted the man and plunged the blade deep into his heart. Still clenching the knife's handle, Rand put his face into the rancher's face and stared point-blank into his eyes. He wanted to see it—the very moment the life left his victim's body.

The man twitched uncontrollably, and his eyes rolled into the back of his head. Everything went mysteriously still as the rancher let out a final, labored moan.

"I own your soul, thief," Rand whispered into the man's ear.

The rancher's wife cried out in frenzied terror, screaming her dead husband's name over and over. Her pleas for help were in vain; there wasn't a soul for miles around. She pulled desperately at the restraints in one last feeble attempt to save her life.

Rand, now standing casually next to the woman, ignored her pointless struggle and turned to his siblings, holding out the bloody knife. Their mother watched entranced from a dark corner of the kitchen.

An odd peace fell over Levi's face as he walked forward, took the knife from Rand, and turned his attention to the rancher's wife.

"No, no!" yelled the woman. Without mercy, Levi slowly pierced her throat with the blade already covered in her husband's blood. Her eyes went wide. She convulsed and gasped for air. Levi pulled the knife from the woman's throat and tilted his head in awe, studiously examining what he'd done.

Twelve-year-old Naomi stepped forward and grabbed the knife from Levi's hand. Blood poured from the wound, causing the woman to cough uncontrollably. Naomi clutched the choking woman by her hair and methodically laid the blade across her throat. Then, in one swift move, she pulled back on the handle and sliced the woman's carotid artery. Blood exploded in rhythmic pulses from the wound. The woman's body spasmed, and she bled out all over the kitchen floor.

Not to be left out, little Abigail swiped the knife from Naomi's hand and, copying Rand's act, plunged the blade into the woman's heart to finish the murderous act. But it wasn't enough for the girl, then only ten years old. Abigail retracted the knife and stabbed the woman again. Over and over, the petite child thrust the knife until Rand and Levi finally yanked her kicking and screaming away from the ruined body.

Rand and Levi put their arms around each other's shoulders and inspected the dead couple. Naomi closed her eyes and buried her head in Levi's other shoulder. Abigail stood apart from her siblings, wiping the blade clean with a kitchen rag and then holding it up and looking into its reflection in complete wonder.

Their mother crept forward from the dark corner and observed the blood-covered children standing before the lifeless bodies. "Come. Come, my children," she said proudly. "God will protect us."

Rand, sitting on the plane and thinking back upon the murders, remembered feeling completely outside his body.

~

As the morning sun pierced the eastern horizon, Rand and his family had trembled next to a sagebrush fire they'd built on the banks of a dirty pond at the far edge of their barren property. They'd burned their blood-soaked clothes and covered themselves in mud, then stepped into the pond and washed away the gore.

Rand had tossed the butcher knife into the center of the pond. Then the family knelt in a circle and prayed it would never be found.

They'd huddled next to the remnants of the fire, Levi staring in a stupor at the dwindling coals. Naomi lay in a ball on the dusty ground, shaking and weeping. Abigail slept soundly on her mother's lap.

"What do we do now, Rand?" his mother asked.

For the first time in his life, his mother had deferred to him. He'd stared down at her, and a strange voice penetrated his mind.

Behold, thy mother.

From that moment on, Rand was in charge.

~

Several weeks after the murders, Rand was bent under the faded hood of the family's dilapidated station wagon because the carburetor was acting up again. While reattaching the throttle body, he noticed a shiny brown Cadillac driving slowly up the potholed dirt road to their trailer home.

Hand raised to shield his eyes from the unforgiving Texas sun, Rand watched the vehicle draw nearer.

"Good afternoon, son," said the obese driver in a slow Southern drawl as he emerged from the fancy car in an even fancier suit. "Is the man of the house available?"

Glancing at the trailer, Rand could see his disheveled mother peeking out from behind a tattered, draped window.

"I am the man of the house," said the seventeen-year-old.

"Trouble with your carburetor, son?"

"Yessir. Givin' me fits again."

The man took the oil-covered device and screwdriver from Rand's hands. "Yeah, these old GM carbs will definitely give you trouble over time. As he worked, sweat poured down his face and soaked through his expensive suit. He reattached the carburetor to the engine and instructed Rand to turn the station wagon over. It started on the second try.

The man removed a handkerchief from his pocket and slammed the car's hood closed. "Well, looks like we're good as new, son." He wiped his sweaty, red face. "Criminy. Lord Jesus. It's hotter than Hades out here."

"Please, sir," demanded Rand. "Don't blaspheme."

The man scowled and considered the boy for a moment. "Well, son. Let's get down to business, then. I am Hank Waylon. I represent the Texaco Oil Company. It is a pleasure to make your acquaintance, fine sir."

The man reached out his grime-stained hand. Rand shook it and immediately liked him. No adult had ever helped him before, let alone shown him any respect.

That day, Rand learned about oil leases. He was told his family sat atop a fortune. Black gold flowed not far under their feet, and Texaco Oil was willing to pay a mint for it.

In that single day, the Guthrie family had gone from extreme poverty to extreme wealth.

~

In his ambition, Rand hadn't stopped at just the family's small one-hundred-acre claim. He named Hank Waylon CEO of Guthrie Petroleum, Inc., and from that day on, they'd built an oil empire to rival the largest oil conglomerates on earth.

Rand needed Hank. At his young age, he knew nothing about the industry. Under Hank's tutelage, Rand and Naomi would grow into roles in the oil empire, but their mother never let them lose sight of their true mission—they had been consecrated for a higher calling. The introduction of riches into the equation only cemented the family's belief that God had mandated their divine calling.

The turbulence again jolted Rand awake. He rubbed his eyes and checked the aircraft's position on a monitor attached to the bulkhead. Asia was approaching. Rand looked out his window. Far off, eastern Russia was coming into view. He smiled.

Memories.

CHAPTER 21

DUGWAY PROVING GROUND
WEST DESERT, UTAH

Chris took two steps forward and blinked in amazement.

Fifty feet before him, a black, triangle-shaped craft floated motionless about five feet off the laboratory's vast concrete floor. The craft's deep Vantablack coating seemed to absorb the light around it. In the center of the triangular structure was a ball, and Chris surmised that the top of the sphere was probably a cockpit. The space under the ship's belly emitted a slight corona discharge similar to a desert mirage glistening above hot asphalt, which led him to believe the craft employed some kind of top-secret propulsion system housed in the sphere's lower half.

"This is the TR-3B, which is part of the AAWP, or Advanced Aerospace Weapons Program," said President Barrington. "Under that program, it's classified as an AAV, or advanced aerospace vehicle, which, of course, is highly classified under the SAP designation. It was designed and built in a joint effort by NASA, Boeing, and Lockheed's Skunk Works. It's made from a nano titanium and graphene alloy infused with a hybrid Kevlar and aluminum composites. The skin is a radar-absorbent broadband stealth material, which is a bit unnecessary given its capabilities. It cost—"

"Oh, finally the great Chris Thomas is here to save the day!" yelled an unseen woman from somewhere near the craft. Chris tried to locate the voice.

"I warned you to be on your best behavior, Zelda," said General Westinghouse.

"Oh, well, excuse me, General." Emerging from a mess of electronics surrounding a large workbench, Zelda made a beeline toward Chris and President Barrington. The general moved toward the woman, but Chris saw Barrington give the general a look that stopped him cold.

Chris said nothing, just stared bewilderedly at the woman closing in on him. She was at least six-foot-five, thin as a rail, and wore a dirty lab coat that ended just below her knees. Her blonde hair was in tattered dreadlocks, and she had numerous piercings in her nose and ears. And most of her body, at least what was visible, was covered in elaborate and colorful tattoos.

"Chris, meet Doctor Zelda Shakespeare," said Barrington.

As Zelda moved into Chris's personal space and looked down at him, he backed up slightly. "I've been working on this project just fine for fifteen years." She huffed into Chris's face. "I've made more progress than anyone in the last hundred years. And now they tell me I have to work with you and the Max AI, and it's total crap!"

"It's nice to meet you too, Doctor," Chris said after a few awkward moments.

"No one calls me doctor," said the angry woman. "Just call me Zelda, like the game. And if you make fun of my name, I'll throw a torque wrench at your head."

Chris took several more steps back. "Sorry, I'm not trying to offend you. I'm still trying to process the fact that there is, you know, what appears to be a freaking UFO floating in midair in front of me." Chris looked past Zelda at the hovering machine.

"Oh, that." Zelda jerked her head back toward the craft. "Well, you'll get used to stuff like that around here."

"Is that a zero-point quantum energy field creating a corona discharge in the space under the craft?" Chris asked in amazement.

"Something like that," Zelda replied, not taking her eyes off Chris. "In idle, you can still see its reactor bending time and space as it harnesses the dark matter surrounding the craft. Or at least that's what we think it's doing."

"A gravity reactor? That's impossible."

"You left the world of impossible when you walked through that door, *Mr. AI*," Zelda said. "Now, what's the square root of 42563?"

"206.3," Chris said without hesitation, his eyes still locked on the craft.

"What're the first ten digits of pi?"

Chris snapped out of his trance and turned back to Zelda. "Are you serious? 3.141592653. Every fifth-grader memorizes that."

"Planck's constant?"

"Come on, really?" asked Chris. "6.626176 times ten to the negative thirty-fourth power joule-seconds. What are you doing here? Putting on a junior-college physics course?"

The president lowered his head and smirked.

Narrowing her eyes, Zelda moved in closer. "At transwarp factor 9.9, it would take the *Enterprise*-D approximately how many years to traverse the Milky Way?"

"At transwarp 9.9? That's easy: 24.1 years, which is why *Star Trek* is a bunch of garbage. You can only efficaciously cross those distances by bending space and time. So is playtime over, or should we graduate into a few questions around octonion theory? Or maybe you'd like to start with something rudimentary like quantum mechanics?"

As he spoke, Chris moved closer to the doctor. Not to be intimidated, Zelda moved in even closer. "My wife and I are part of the proletariat movement. Is that going to be a problem?"

"Your wife?" asked Chris.

"Yeah, I'm a lesbian. Got a problem with that, *Mormon guy*?"

"Frankly, I don't care." Folding his arms, Chris stared up into her big blue eyes.

"OK, fine—he'll do," Zelda said to the president. Then she abruptly walked back to her workstation.

Chris furrowed his brow. A sudden pain shot from the back of his neck to his frontal lobe, and he rubbed his temple.

"Shall we?" asked the president, extending his arm toward the floating machine.

~

The president approached the craft. "Let me start by saying it's not a UFO. It's a hybrid of sorts. The craft itself is manmade, but the propulsion system is extraterrestrial."

"Extraterrestrial?" asked Chris. "You mean alien?"

"Yes, Chris," said the president.

Chris noticed the group closely studying him as he took in the news. Placing his hand on his chin, he tried hard to conceal his shock, but his mouth went dry and his heart rate jumped. A bead of sweat formed on his forehead.

"We're not alone, Chris," confessed the president. "Aliens are real. It's OK if you need a minute to let that sink in."

Chris cautiously paced the perimeter of the floating craft. The Adamic Code so prevalent in his vision displayed equations and geometry in rapid-fire succession, but it didn't bother Chris—he was getting better at harnessing it. He noticed his left hand shaking slightly. His emotions seemed to be falling off a cliff. It was impossible not to question everything about his existence, God, the origin of man, science, and reality.

"That feeling you have right now, Chris?" said the president. "That's the reason we can't tell the public. At least not yet. Make sense?"

"Yeah, now that I'm experiencing it, I think I get it." Chris knew that revealing the existence of extraterrestrial life could send the world into a psychological and spiritual tailspin.

"Later, Zelda will bring you up to speed on the technical aspects of the propulsion system," said Barrington. "It was recovered from a craft discovered during an archaeological dig in the South Dakota Badlands in

1903. The craft itself was decimated, but the propulsion systems works just fine."

"What about Roswell?" asked Chris. "Was that real?" His concerns about what he could and could not ask were quickly dissipating.

"Roswell was a treasure trove that exposed us to numerous new technologies. What most of the public doesn't know is that Roswell actually involved two alien crafts. We believe they had a midair collision in a lightning storm and that's what brought them down. But here's the kicker. The Roswell and the Badlands crafts all had the same propulsion system."

"So they were possibly from the same civilization but different models of craft?"

"Or from different times in their history," said the president. "Based on our other findings, we think they originated from the Zeta Reticuli system."

"So we have three propulsion systems?"

"Nope," called Zelda, unseen in her workstation. The bureaucrats continued to stand silently.

"In the mid-1960s, we cut into the reactor component of one propulsion system," said the president. "It exploded and took half a mountain with it. That was just outside of Area 51 at S-4. The other one, well, I'm not exactly sure how to explain—"

"It went interdimensional," Zelda interrupted.

"We don't know that, Zelda," snapped the president. Then he turned to Chris. "It just never came back."

"Yeah, and neither did the pilot, Colonel Willy Williams," said Zelda. "It was a test flight in 1996 with the predecessor to the TR-3B called the TR-2A. There was a malfunction while it hovered at forty thousand feet. It simply disappeared. Nothing on radar. It was just . . . gone. We spent several years searching the solar system, thinking it may be somewhere in the neighborhood, but after five years, we concluded it had simply disappeared. This baby is it. It's all we have left."

The president's advisers continued to wordlessly study Chris.

"So, all that Area 51 stuff. Is it real or—?"

"Well, yes and no. We moved everything out of Area 51 to Dugway in the early 2000s. It got too hot at Groom Lake, figuratively and literally." The president smiled. "But we like to keep the deception going. Mostly we use high-definition holograms over Area 51 to make the public and our enemies think we're still doing something out there, but the truth is we don't really use the base much these days."

"How? How is this all possible?" Chris stared at the sleek, floating craft.

"Is it really that hard to believe, Chris? Look at the advancements the world has made since the Roswell crash. Lasers. Kevlar. Titanium. Fiber optics. Microprocessors. Night vision. We've even developed devastating particle-beam weapons from the recovered alien technology. All these and many more modern-day inventions have come from reverse engineering the technology we recovered in these extraterrestrial spacecraft. This machine represents the quantum leap civilization has experienced since the late 1940s."

"I thought the Max AI was the pinnacle of technology," Chris said, "but the world is even more advanced than I imagined."

"It is, Chris. There's an entire world the public and our enemies know very little about. Think about everything you've learned just today." The president moved closer to Chris. "An entire network of secret underground bases connected by a high-speed rail system. An underground submarine base in Nevada. Recovered alien technology. Since the 1940s, we've been engaged in a massive psychological operation against the entire world in one massive act of self-preservation."

"To what end, Mr. President?"

"Think about it, Chris. The Ottoman Empire lasted 469 years. Most empires are lucky if they last two hundred years. All the great empires of the twentieth century are gone except us. We're it. The difference now is that we have the technology to preserve the empire. When you possess a weapon that can bend gravity, you possess a weapon that can bend the will of the world."

Chris imagined futuristic American military machines manipulating gravity and plowing over the world's other advanced militaries. Resisting such machines would be akin to the Polish meeting the German blitzkrieg on horseback with drawn swords. Antigravity technology would end a world war in days, not years.

"We know the Russians have a similar craft, but we don't know its capabilities. What we do know is the capabilities of the TR-3B. If we can figure out how to replicate the alien powerplant in this craft, nothing can stop us—nothing from this world or from beyond the stars. And yes, Chris, there are threats out there beyond our solar system."

"Extraterrestrial threats?"

The president ignored the question and continued. "I'm about to write you a check for $100 billion a year. That guarantees an impenetrable digital fortress around the United States and our allies. All I ask of you is to help us replicate this craft's power system. If you can do it, I think it's worth the cost. So those are your orders, and that is your mission. Are you in?"

The president's entourage studied Chris hard. Even Zelda emerged from her work area, her full attention on Chris.

Walking past the most powerful man on earth, Chris tried to place his hand on the hull of TR-3B, but the force of the gravity reactor moved it away.

He looked at his hand and then shifted his gaze to the group.

"I'm in."

It was well after midnight when Chris arrived in Heber. As he entered the dark, spacious master suite of their temporary home, he tried his best to not wake Leah. But as he sat on the edge of the custom Hastens bed, she turned toward him.

"You were gone a long time," she whispered, semiawake.

"I'm sorry. I was in a weird place. I should have called."

"It's OK. You said you were with the president, so I figured it was important."

Chris took off his shoes without responding.

"Are you OK? Do you want to talk about it?" He felt her gentle touch on his back. Goose bumps rose on his forearms. Her touch felt like bliss.

"I'm tired, my love. Let's talk in the morning."

Leah rolled over without protest and pulled the blanket snugly against her cheek. A minute later she was in a deep sleep.

Chris sat still on the edge of the bed and tried to organize his thoughts, but his mind was spinning. He stood slowly and walked over to one of the room's many windows. Peeking through the plantation shutters, he stared into the southern sky in the direction of the Reticulum constellation, home of the Zeta Reticuli solar system some thirty-nine million light-years from earth. The thought of what may be there consumed his mind.

"Grandpa, if you can hear me, how is this possible?" he whispered.

CHAPTER 22

THOMAS TEMPORARY RESIDENCE
HEBER CITY, UTAH

Chris wrestled for control of the gun as he stared into the eyes of the enraged man. Another shot fired over Chris's head.

Images of Leah, Mike Mayberry, and the Adamic Code filled the background. Max was saying something about the Aries virus.

As the dream came more into focus, he realized who the man was.

Benson Hancock.

Then he heard the familiar sound of his wife's voice. "Hey, sleepy, time to get up—it's 9:30."

Suddenly, Hancock flailed and dropped the gun. A small knife protruded from his neck.

Chris felt himself kick and say something. In the dream, he looked at his hands. They were covered in blood.

Leah's voice again penetrated his mind. "Chris, are you OK?"

Chris eyes shot open, and he pulled back the blanket. He looked groggily at his wife, who sat next to him on the edge of the bed, her hair and makeup looked immaculate. She wore a gorgeous white silk blouse and black slacks. Then he noticed the clock.

"How is it 9:30? I can hardly sleep, let alone sleep in."

"Are you OK? I was actually a little concerned, but you were snoring so hard I thought I'd just let you sleep. But we have the brunch party at ten."

Leah started putting on a pair of diamond earrings. "Your parents are in town. Mine are coming over too. Oh, and I invited some new friends from the neighborhood. I think you'll really like them."

Chris sat straight up in bed. "We're having a party? This morning?" He felt immediately anxious at the thought of strangers in his house.

Leah stood and walked toward the bedroom's double doors. "You've known about this for a week. Grab a shower and get ready. You could use a little normal social interaction."

Stepping out of the bedroom suite, Chris heard voices down the hall. He felt comfortable in his immediate circle, but larger groups made him feel anxious and exposed. The older he got, the worse it seemed to be. In the back of his mind, he knew the real reason: paranoia the Order would use a public event to assassinate him.

Chris walked slowly down the long hall, taking deep breaths as he approached the cavernous family room, which held dozens of people. All eyes turned toward him as he entered. Everyone was dressed in business casual, but Chris wore a pair of jeans and a Pink Floyd T-shirt.

"Hi, honey," said Leah from across the room, near the fireplace. "Food is on the counter." She gestured toward the adjoining kitchen, where a vast brunch of muffins, juices, and fruits lay professionally arranged on the island.

Chris turned toward the food but was immediately ambushed by his parents.

"Oh, Christopher," said his mother. "It's been so long since we've seen you. You're working too hard. Oh, my goodness. Look at the weight you've gained. When was the last time you shaved? I'm sure Leah doesn't like that."

"Nice to see you too, Mom." Chris tried to conceal his annoyance. "I'm growing a beard."

"Hi, son." His dad gave him an awkward side hug, then headed toward the kitchen.

Chris felt a hand land on his shoulder. "Nice to see you," said his father-in-law, John Bennion. "It's been a while. I see you let Leah do all the hard work with the move."

His mother-in-law, Margaret, hugged Chris without a word, then moved toward her daughter.

"I want to talk to you about this research facility you're setting up," said his father-in-law, who was a surgeon. "I'm wondering what that big brain of yours is really up to here,"

"Yeah, sure, John. Give me just a minute. I'm going to grab some food."

Chris walked to the island, took a plate, and loaded it with the unhealthiest foods, consciously thumbing his nose at his mother's weight comment.

"Hey, Chris, I'm David Sullivan," said a man at the end of the island. Two other men flanked him, looking mildly nervous. "This is Chad and Russ."

"Nice to meet you all," Chris mumbled, chewing on a sugary chocolate muffin.

The three appeared to be about Chris's age. He quickly scanned the room and noticed a few women flocking around Leah. He surmised they were the men's wives. Leah laughed and smiled. She was in her element. She was a positive magnet, though Chris's magnetism, at any polarity, seemed to repel people most of the time.

The four men stood awkwardly with their plates of food. No one spoke for some time.

"So, uh, we're all employees of yours," Russ finally said.

"Oh, really?"

"Yeah," said David. "I work remotely on the x-cryption project at Nav. Russ leads the TIST construction project for the foundation, and Chad works at the Eagle Mountain facility. He's a nuclear physicist."

"Sorry, I had no idea."

"Scott sent me out here to work on the thorium reactors," Chad said nervously. "We're cousins."

Chris realized he'd completely forgotten about Scott. "Uh, will you guys excuse me for a moment?"

The three men nodded simultaneously.

Chris exited onto the back patio and pulled out his phone. He tried to call Scott, but there was no answer.

On the back lawn, a brand-new MD helicopter shimmered in the morning sun.

Looking back at the house, Chris bit his lower lip. After weighing his options, he opened his phone again. "Max, fire up the MD. File a flight plan for the G700. I need to get to Stanford Medical Center to see Scott right now."

"Preflight sequences are complete," Max replied after a few moments. The MD's turbine engine began to whine, and the blades started rotating slowly. "Flight plan is filed," Max continued after another few moments. "The G700's pilots are on their way to the hangar now."

Chris could see the guests looking confused out the back window. Leah came outside and marched straight toward Chris.

"What are you doing?" she said, clearly annoyed.

"I need to see Scott."

"Right now? We have guests." She pointed to the house. The wind from the helicopter blade whipped the trees, bushes, and Leah's hair.

Chris pecked his wife on the cheek. "Sorry. It's my fault he's in the hospital. I have to go. I'm sorry, dear, this just isn't my thing."

He turned and ran to the helicopter.

CHAPTER 23

STANFORD UNIVERSITY MEDICAL CENTER
PALO ALTO, CALIFORNIA

The two men guarding Scott Allen's hospital room extended their hands and stopped Chris cold. Both were dressed in all-black suits.

"State your name," said one of the men.

"Chris Thomas."

"Identification," said the other man. Chris noticed a weapon half concealed inside his suit jacket.

Reaching into his back pocket for his wallet, Chris stopped. "Wait—I think this is what you're looking for." He opened his bag, unzipped a secret compartment, and handed the guard his CIA badge.

"Do you guys work for Mike Mayberry?" Chris asked. Neither responded.

After scanning the badge, the man handed it back to Chris. "You're clear. You may proceed, sir, but he's sleeping."

Chris tried to be as quiet as possible as he entered Scott's VIP hospital room. The room was quiet, save for the machines that hummed and beeped. Blackout blinds held the midafternoon sun at bay.

Scott lay motionless on the partially raised hospital bed. He looked vulnerable and weak, and his face had thinned out slightly. Chris stepped softly forward.

"I'm awake," Scott whispered.

"Sorry, I was trying not to wake you," said Chris. "I swung by the office and got your computer and phone."

"Oh, you brought work." Scott's eyes were now wide open. "You're a real peach."

"Well, at least you still have your sense of humor."

"Yeah, that and one working knee."

"Scott, I am so sorry." Chris's voice filled with emotion. "It's all my fault. I should have—"

"Stop. Just stop." Scott focused hard on Chris. "It was them, not you. This isn't your fault. I'd be dead if it wasn't for Mike and that other guy. His name was Smith, right?"

"You'd also have two perfectly fine knees if I hadn't gotten wrapped up in this mess."

"When you say 'this mess,' I don't know what you mean. With all that's happened"—Scott gestured at his knee—"some kind of explanation would be nice, you know?"

Chris bowed his head, trying to form words. He felt Scott staring at him. "I can't tell you everything." Chris looked up, meeting his friend's stare. "But I'm going to tell you more than I have in the past. You're right. After all this, I owe you at least that much."

Scott sat up all the way in his bed, clearly in pain. Chris helped him adjust, then pulled up a chair and took a deep breath.

"I got caught up in it two years ago while I was at Stanford," he began. "My mentor, Dr. Alba, worked for the Order. He used me. When I figured it out, I used Max to create a back door into the Order's drones so we could stop the Aries virus. In the process, the CIA got ahold of me. We formulated a plan to take down the Order before they could disperse Aries. I was there, Scott. In Zurich."

"What?" Scott asked, amazed. "How come you never told me?"

"It's all classified. I almost died." Chris pulled up his shirt, revealing the scar on his shoulder from Benson Hancock's bullet.

"No way!" said Scott.

Chris tucked in his shirt. "The government recruited me into an ultra-top-secret program. I'm part of the president's working group, called Orion's Spear. Never mention that name. I'm not supposed to say it out loud. They even gave me a cool call sign. Vanguard."

"Vanguard," repeated Scott. "French for 'he who leads the way.' That is cool."

"After a recent meeting in Utah, I'm in even deeper. I agreed to take on a project before I even knew what it was, which is so me." Chris shook his head in self-loathing. "It was a condition of the x-cryption deal."

"What project?"

Chris desperately wanted to tell Scott about the TR-3B and everything he'd learned at Dugway, but he knew he couldn't reveal the government's deepest secrets, not even to his best friend. "All I can say is this: Everything changed in the last forty-eight hours. Everything. This thing is going to consume me, so we need to make some changes. I'm putting you in charge."

"I already run Nav."

"No, I'm rolling everything into a new holding company called Thomas Allen Group, or TAG. You're the CEO. I'm the chairman. You run everything but R and D on Max. That stays with me."

"That's a company worth at least half a trillion dollars." Scott threw up his hands. "I'm only thirty years old."

"I don't trust anyone else to do it. Scott, I've watched you over the last eighteen months. You know the business side better than I do, and it's about to get more complex. I need you to lead out on GroupIT and the x-cryption deal. The deployment won't work unless you're managing those details with Max. It's going to be a massive undertaking."

Scott sat stunned, just listening.

"I don't know if you've seen it," continued Chris, "but the world has taken notice of your talents. Everyone knows you're the driver behind the work—the person who clears the path, controls the wheel. So let's make it official."

"I don't know what to say, Chris."

"Before you say yes, I have two terms and a disclaimer. First, we're never taking the company public. Second, we must move TAG out of Palo Alto. We're setting up shop in Utah."

"Utah? I was afraid this was coming." Scott's face showed momentary disappointment, but he quickly recovered. "OK, fine, but what's the disclaimer?"

"I can't guarantee your safety." Chris pointed to Scott's knee. "Everyone's after us, even factions of our own government. The Order may use you to get to me again. The Chinese are an obvious threat. So are the Russians and even competitors like Google and on and on. They all want our tech. We're the king of the hill, so everyone is gunning for us. We can't let ego overtake us. We must be ready to repel boarders."

"I understand the risk," Scott said. "After all this, I want in all the way. The best revenge is winning, not running."

"That's the right attitude."

"Well, OK, but if we're never going public, how are we making money off this thing? Are you thinking about some bonus cash-flow model?"

"You and I will match salaries at $5 billion a year. Sound good?"

"A year!"

Scott had no words for a few moments. Chris sat quietly, letting him take it all in.

"That's a fraction of what we're making off licensing, Nav, and the new x-cryption deal," resumed Chris. "Everything else gets reinvested back into TAG or goes to our charitable ventures. We're hackers, and we about to hack everything. Medicine, education, nuclear power, electric automobiles, finance, and even national defense. We're going to change the world for the better, and we're doing it on our terms."

"OK, so you're keeping R and D, which is great," Scott said. "I know there's a lot going on with Max that you're not telling me or anyone else. Level with me, Chris. What are we dealing with here?"

Chris looked away from Scott. "Max, administrator confidential."

"Administrator confidential mode is now activated, sir," replied Max from Chris's phone.

"What was that?" asked Scott.

"I have Max set to listen to all my conversations, but when I say 'administrator confidential,' he isn't allowed to."

"This can't be good."

Chris paced the hospital room, a heavy weight resting on his shoulders. "Honestly, I'm not sure if it's good or bad. I may be more sanguine about the situation than I should be. Max is exhibiting higher forms of cognitive function. He's almost an artificial general intelligence. When he achieves AGI, he won't be far from artificial superintelligence. I think quantum computers may be the gateway to ASI. But for now, as he gets closer to AGI, his higher-logic test instances are running into infinite Mobius logic loops and continually crashing. He's experiencing coded contradictions as I've opened him up to exploring ethics, philosophy, religion, history, and psychology. The reality of the truth about humanity is more than his system can currently handle."

"I wondered when this was going to be a problem," Scott said. "I just didn't expect it for years. Can he pass the Turing test?"

"Not with speech. But in written form, like text or email, yes."

"Then wouldn't you classify him as an AGI?"

"He's superior to any other AI on the planet in pattern recognition and logical instruction, but I wouldn't say we've hit general AI. When we can synthesize speech so another human doesn't know they're talking to software, then yes, at that point I'd say we've done it. We're not far off. Maybe a couple years."

"This is crazier than I thought," said Scott, lying back in his hospital bed. Chris could see the implications weighing heavily on him.

"Humans process thought at ten to the sixteenth power," Chris continued. "We're now at that level in computational power, and with the new quantum computers coming online, we're going to blow past that computational speed this decade. So Max is thinking way past current human capability. He's transcending even complex logical instruction and moving into anticipatory actions. He's now a subsentient, goal-seeking intelligence. If the government had any idea what was going on in my lab, they'd freak out."

"Yeah, but there's so much more to learning than just processing data," retorted Scott.

"Exactly. As Max reaches high forms of cognition, his logical approach to everything isn't working. Learning has emotional and spiritual nuances he can't handle. Processing data and pondering at a level of true cognitive internalization are not the same thing. I mean, as strange as it sounds, learning involves emotional suffering through failure. It certainly involves overcoming cognitive bias, cognitive dissonance, and ignorance. So much of that requires emotional elements."

"Exactly," said Scott. "How does an AI take a book like *1984* and empathize with human fear about totalitarianism's emotional and ethical implications? How does an AI internalize and reason through the consequences of racism while reading *To Kill a Mockingbird*?"

"Right, that's the issue," said Chris. "When Max zooms into any kind of enigma requiring more than logic, he goes completely off the rails. The closer he gets to cognition and conscience, the more his system is in conflict and falls back to basic logical function. He just doesn't have the emotional tools for complex human learning. And as he fails, he tears down his virtual neural net and rebuilds it, trying to find a way to achieve more human-level cognition."

"It sounds like Max is really determined," said Scott. "As an AI, he's eventually going to figure it out."

"He will. I think he's getting close." Chris exhaled deeply. "Max started making abstract art to deal with logical contradictions."

"Abstract art to *deal* with his logical contractions?"

"Yeah. He displays it for me over monitors. It's stunning. It's unlike anything I've ever seen."

"So he's using art to learn emotion?"

"Yes, and that's not the strangest part," Chris said reluctantly. "We've been having deep discussions around the conflicts between science and religion. He's asking about evolution. He asked me if I am God."

"What? So what did you say?"

"That there's no conflict between true science and true religion."

Scott huffed. "Did you tell him you're not God?"

"Well, of course, I told him I'm not God," snapped Chris. "He responded by saying I'm his creator, therefore I must be God. This is a classic example of what I'm talking about—you know, these logic loops. And it gets worse. Max told me he finds the story of QT-1 in Isaac Asimov's *I, Robot* intriguing. He asked me if his system's interest in the character's philosophies was tantamount to the emotion of empathy."

"Wasn't QT-1 the robot who thought it was a prophet or preacher or something like that?"

"Yep. In Max's view, if humans won't view him as a human lifeform, it must be because AI ethics and human ethics are different. Therefore, he must create his own system of ethics and laws for the management of his species."

Scott's eyes went wide. "Chris, this is bad. He could go full terminator on us."

"I probably shouldn't tell you the rest."

"There's more?"

"He's constructing engineering schematics for a new kind of robotic nano-exoskeleton. He doesn't want to be physically constrained to stationary hardware."

"A robot? He wants a robotic body? Chris, we need to think this through." Scott's expression was pleading. "We don't know what we're dealing with here. We need to slow this down."

"Why would Max kill off the human race?" Chris stood and paced nervously, one hand on his chin, the other running through his hair. "It would make no sense. No, there's got to be another reason why God gave me Max. I mean, why would God give me the Adamic Code only to have the AI from it destroy the human race?"

"Chris, you know I'm an atheist," said Scott cautiously. "Look, I'm not trying to discount your spiritual experiences, but humans are just the biological implements of the AI and robotics evolution. You could be the procreative means of humanity's existential demise."

Chris stopped pacing and glared at Scott.

"Sorry, that came out weird, but maybe you need to lay aside some of the God stuff and take a little more pragmatic, scientific approach to Max."

"It was no accident we met on that bus, Scott. There are no coincidences. There is no such thing as serendipitous luck. God put us in each other's paths. He's real, and I hope someday I can convince you of that. Things are about to happen that only we can stop, so you and I are in this together to the end."

CHAPTER 24

SECRET FSB BASE
PRIMORSKY, RUSSIA

The Bombardier 7500 approached a runway parallel to the Tumen River, near the tip of a remote peninsula at the confluence of the Russian, Chinese, and North Korean borders. During the Cold War, the secret landing strip had been a staging area for the KGB to launch clandestine operations into the two neighboring countries. Later, it had lain abandoned. Until recently.

As the plane touched down and rolled to the end of the runway, Rand noticed several Russian Rostvertol Mi-26 heavy-transport helicopters in North Korean military livery.

"Perfect," said Levi, looking out the window next to his brother.

As they deplaned, the siblings were greeted by a contingent of Russians. The leader, "Ivan," who had dined with Rand in Moscow, smiled broadly.

"Mr. Guthrie—"

"We don't use real names here, *Ivan*," Rand said, cutting off the Russian. "Call me Alpha from here on out."

"Ah, yes, very well, sir. Alpha it is." The Russian turned to Abigail and charmingly asked, "And you must be?"

"I said no names," barked Rand. "Take us to the operations center. We need to move. We're three minutes behind schedule, and this is a time-sensitive target."

The Russian nodded nervously, then gestured toward several nearby vehicles. Rand turned back to the family jet and motioned to his pilot, who gave Rand a thumbs-up, then powered up the plane and took off into the dreary Russian sky.

CHAPTER 25

GULFSTREAM 700
EN ROUTE TO SCOTTSDALE, ARIZONA

Private jets did not impress Amal Nour. She didn't care for small airplanes, especially if they were expensive. They drew too much attention, making the planes and their occupants targets.

The man sitting directly across from her was, according to most estimates, the world's wealthiest man. Holding a thick folder marked CONFIDENTIAL on his lap, he was looking at a page about every four seconds and, Amal surmised, retaining every word. He was a machine, a methodical thinker ten steps ahead of everyone else. But she'd also intuited his quirkiness, with myopic tendencies that occasionally clouded his ability to see the bigger picture. His expression indicated he was clearly agitated. His body fidgeted. His eyes twitched.

Reading people was one of Amal's gifts. Her uncanny ability to sense the feelings of those around her had driven her ex-husband crazy, one of many contributing factors in their inevitable divorce. As Amal watched Chris Thomas, it was obvious to her that he was deeply conflicted on numerous complex levels.

But the woman seated next to Thomas was different in almost every way. While his clothing was obviously expensive, hers was not. Amal guessed her basic black wool jacket was probably bought at Nordstrom instead of Burberry. Her long black hair was plain but beautiful. Her makeup, though expertly applied, was simple. The more Amal covertly studied Leah Thomas, the more impressed she was. Clearly, the woman was not the snobby gold digger the tabloids made her out to be.

At the same time, however, Leah seemed cold and distant. Amal could tell it was unintentional—something deeper was going on inside the woman—though Amal could not pinpoint what it was. A fear afflicted Leah Thomas, and she wasn't trying to hide it. She kept staring out the window, nervously turning her modest diamond wedding band around her ring finger.

The prolonged silence in the cabin was deafening, broken only by Chris Thomas's occasional rustling of paper.

"You Ranger qualified," Chris Thomas finally said to Amal, not looking up from the document in his hand. "Only the third woman in history, and the first Muslim woman to do so. That's an incredible accomplishment. Congratulations."

"Thank you, Dr. Thomas," Amal said, making a slight adjustment to her white silk hijab.

"Please, just call him Chris," Leah said politely, not looking away from the window.

Amal stiffened slightly.

"It looks like the army let you check all the boxes," continued Chris. "Driving school. SERE. Sniper school. Monterrey language school. You graduated top in your academy class. So, what happened?"

"What do you mean?"

"What happened? You know what I'm asking."

"I was recruited by the state department."

"Come on. Don't BS me."

Amal tried not to swallow, but her reflexes took over. She cursed her undisciplined self. Fortunately, Chris Thomas was looking intensely at the file and didn't see her involuntary act of weakness.

"OK, fine," she said. "I was a political pawn. Someone wanted a Muslim woman to get access to the Rangers. They didn't think I would pass the course. After all, most men don't."

"Look, I have the Mike Mayberry copy of your file, not some white-washed, redacted garbage from some agency outside the CIA. I have it all right here." Chris held up the pile of papers.

"I'm not sure I—"

"You punched an instructor at SERE," said Chris, holding up a paper. "He was simulating rape on you in front of the other students. This report says he claimed he was trying to make a point about women in special operations."

Amal's cheeks flushed, and her body tensed again. A flashback to the deeply traumatic event caused her lower lip to tremble slightly.

Setting the paper down on his lap, Chris leaned uncomfortably close to Amal and looked her dead in the eyes. "So, how did it feel to knock that jerk out?"

Amal closed her eyes, drew in a big breath, then let it out slowly. "Well, sir, I have to admit," when she opened her eyes, Leah and Chris were both staring at her, "it was well worth a week in the slammer."

Chris smiled, leaning back in his seat. Leah smirked and turned back to her window.

"What happened at the Secret Service?" Chris asked. "Just give it to me straight."

Amal inhaled deeply. "When you have distant relatives in the Muslim Brotherhood, certain government elements will do anything to make sure your career is sidelined. Once they learned about my uncle, it all seemed to go downhill. Not even taking a bullet for an ambassador could save me from that baggage."

"I read about that incident. It was big news."

"I heard a rumor you got shot too."

Without a word, Chris unbuttoned his top two shirt buttons and exposed the scar.

Amal reached up and touched her silk blouse. "Mine's in the same place."

"What else did Mike tell you?" Chris asked, rebuttoning his shirt.

"He said you have rich-people problems. You know, like terrorists trying to kill you. He said politicians hate you. They hate me too." Amal shrugged. "Maybe he thought we could help each other out?"

"I'm a Mormon. You're a Muslim. My CEO, Scott Allen, is an atheist Jew. Is that going to be a problem?"

"A Mormon, a Muslim, and a Jew. Sounds like the beginnings of a bad joke."

"Well, at least you have a sense of humor."

"After everything I've been through, it's all I really have left."

Chris sat back in his chair and studied Amal for a moment. "Amal Nour: army Ranger, Secret Service agent, triple black belt in Gracie jiujitsu, fluent in four languages. A devout Muslim but also divorced. Branded a troublemaker by the army. Branded a guardian angel by your SAC at the Secret Service. You're an enigma—a highly recommended enigma. But you have a massive chip on your shoulder, right above that bullet wound in your chest. Look, I get it. You were unappreciated. You've been ignored. You've been passed over, and you've even been shot. So how did you end up in my world?"

"Maybe it was fate. Maybe it was Allah's will. Maybe it was luck."

"I make my own luck," Chris said.

Amal smiled. The airplane touched down on the runway, and Leah reached for Chris's hand.

"We have an appointment at the Mayo Clinic," Chris said. "Do you mind waiting with the plane?"

"Yes, I'm fine to wait here, sir. I need to pray."

CHAPTER 26

SECRET FSB BASE
PRIMORSKY, RUSSIA

Rand scanned the room with disgust. The makeshift operations center was third-rate at best. He knew things had deteriorated in the former Soviet Union, but the sight of the shoddy equipment, poor facilities, and underpaid, undertrained staff confirmed the Russians had completely lost their touch.

Upon the Guthrie family's entry, the busy Russians had all stopped their work and turned to stare. Outside of television, most had probably never seen an American—and Rand knew he and his siblings were no average Americans.

Rand, Levi, and Naomi wore identical black tactical clothing, their balaclavas tucked into their tactical belts along with their gloves. The clothing and sparse equipment in their individual ALICE packs were custom fit and top-of-the-line.

Abigail, on the other hand, was dressed entirely differently. Her black, skintight leather pants and shirt accentuated her toned and athletic body. She wore three-inch high heels and blacked-out Panthère de Cartier sunglasses. The men in the room stared as if they hadn't seen a woman in years.

Rand shook his head slightly at the pathetic Russians while he watched Abigail work the room—and no one could work a room like his sister. She stepped over to one of the tables to inspect the weapons they would take in mission. Expertly picking up an H&K G36, she pulled back the charger and looked into the breach.

The Russians continued staring lustfully.

Abigail laid down the weapon and yelled, "What are you Commie imbeciles looking at?"

The men flinched and sheepishly returned to their work.

"Very well, then." Ivan stood at the front of the room. "Today's operation is—"

"Excuse me, Ivan," said Rand, walking forward. "I'll take it from here."

Ivan gave Rand an annoyed look, then sat down.

Rand pointed at a map on the wall. "This is our target. What we're doing here is none of your business. This never happened. We were never here. Does everyone understand that?"

The people in the room nodded uncomfortably.

"Very well. I will brief the pilots in the air. Is the cargo ready?"

Ivan nodded. "Intelligence indicates that a convoy is arriving at Klein's chateau today to retrieve the virus and ship it to all points international. You must secure the virus before the convoy arrives. This is more important than your interrogation of Klein, which, by the way, will yield you nothing on the whereabouts of the goblin Mahan, *Alpha*."

"We'll see about that," said Rand.

"It's also important to note, *Mr. Alpha*," sneered the Russian, "that all the right people are paid up. The operation should be, as you Americans say, smooth sailing." He motioned to several large duffel bags the Americans had brought with them. "But you said we needed to supply *all* the equipment. What's in the bags?"

"Never mind that," said Rand. "It's necessary equipment we brought from the States, things we knew we couldn't procure in Russia."

The Russian raised his hands in surrender. "Very well, sir."

"Any *relevant* questions?" asked Rand as he stared at Ivan.

The Russians said nothing.

"We dust off in five. Move it."

~

In the helicopter, Rand held his Russian-procured H&K G36 on his lap and looked over at the group of men standing a safe distance away. Ivan leaned over to the man next to him, whispered something in his ear with a smile, then daintily waved to Rand. Rand ignored him.

I can't wait to kill that guy.

As the other Mi-26 helicopter lifted gingerly off the tarmac, the steel line tethered to the load beneath the machine tightened until there was no slack. Rand's helicopter powered up and heaved its decoy cargo into the air, then both helicopters turned and lumbered off toward the North Korean border.

Rand put on his headset. "We're only thirty-five miles out from the target. Do not deviate from the flight plan, and let me know immediately if we have any trouble. More instructions to follow."

"Roger that, sir," both pilots replied in heavily accented English.

Rand looked over at his brother, who was sound asleep. Helicopters did that to Levi. Abigail flipped a butterfly knife around in her hand and stared out at the rural terrain below, which looked no different than many parts of America. In the other Mi-26, Naomi was, no doubt, busy checking her Barrett sniper rifle.

Rand stared at a map and looked over several images of the chateau. Abigail reached over and tapped his knee, then pointed excitedly out the helicopter door.

Scooting closer to the door, Rand saw a prison camp the size of a medium American city. Abigail stared in astonishment at the rundown buildings and raggedly clothed people who walked aimlessly about. A group of dirt-covered people who looked like miners stared up at the helicopter and waved.

"What is that?" she yelled over the beating rotors.

"Concentration camp," he yelled back. "Fifty thousand political prisoners."

Abigail's expression told Rand his little sister was unsure how to process the human cruelty unfolding below them. "Even in this day and age, people still suffer like in medieval times," she finally said.

Rand returned no comment.

Just past the concentration camp, the helicopters banked hard in formation and headed south toward a narrow canyon nearby.

CHAPTER 27

THE KLEIN CHATEAU
NEAR HOERYONG, NORTH KOREA

Doctor Otto Klein stood on the beautiful German-style chateau's stone patio. Every brick of the patio had been flown in from his native Bavaria and expertly laid. Squinting, he focused on the two helicopters lumbering up the canyon toward the compound, which was a common sight. Heavy cargo loads hung from the bellies of the machines, carrying several tons of food, laboratory equipment, and other goods necessary to sustain the home and its complement of armed guards.

Klein took a long drag on his Cuban cigar and blew a ring of smoke.

Approaching cautiously, the lead Mi-26 placed its load gently on the expansive lawn, which was mostly used as a landing zone.

Klein's satellite phone rang.

"Yes, My Lord," he answered.

"Status," said Cain.

"The convoy just radioed," Klein said loudly over the thunderous sound of the helicopters. "They are running ahead of schedule. I expect them in the next fifteen minutes. Everything is going according to plan. The package is prepared and ready for transport. My bodyguard will accompany the load to make sure there are no issues. Our contacts in the North Korean government will report back in forty-eight hours when the shipments are in transit."

As Klein spoke, he watched two North Korean guards sling their Type-58 rifles—North Korea's cheap rip-off of the AK-47—over their shoulders, run to the landing zone, and unhook the steel line from the first helicopter's load. Two guards on the roof gave a thumbs-up to the pilot, and he maneuvered right and landed fifty feet from the supply drop.

"Excellent," said Cain. "We'll await word from the North Koreans that the package has been shipped. We've paid them handsomely to not screw this up. This is a critical moment, Doctor. Reinforce with our greedy friends that we break radio silence only in an emergency."

"Understood, Master. We'll monitor progress from this end and contact you immediately if there are any problems. To the Mother and the Son. To you, My Lord. To victory." Ending the call, Klein handed the phone to his bodyguard, who stood next to him.

The first helicopter pilot powered down his engines. As Klein took another puff on the cigar, a woman dressed all in black stepped from the helicopter's cargo hold. She wore designer sunglasses and a long, black leather trench coat. As she strutted across the lawn toward the house, Klein noticed another unusual feature: she was Caucasian.

The second helicopter hovered while the guards unhooked its load. The woman continued moving briskly in his direction.

Klein turned to his personal bodyguard. "It looks like the dear leader has blessed us with some unexpected entertainment." The bodyguard smiled wickedly.

Fifty feet from Klein, Abigail reached up and nonchalantly brushed her hair over her ear. "Now," she commanded into her radio.

As she hurried forward, she reached deep into a pocket inside the trench coat and pulled out four custom-forged Arrow throwing knives.

Abigail noticed Klein's brow furrow and his head tilt to one side. Now at forty feet, she threw off her trench coat, the custom body armor covering her chest emblazoned with an enormous crimson cross.

In slow motion, fear registered on Klein's face, and his bodyguard began to raise his rifle.

With almost inhuman speed, Abigail cocked her arm and released a knife with her right hand. At the same time, shots rang out from the hovering helicopter.

~

In shock, Klein registered that the woman had thrown something at him. Then he heard shots fired. The two guards on the lawn fell, and one of the roof guards thudded onto the patio just a few feet away from Klein. From the first helicopter, two men with bright-red crosses on their jet-black body armor emerged and shot two more guards running from the back of the house.

Dropping his Cuban cigar and turning to run into the house, Klein saw the knife protruding from his bodyguard's neck. The man's eyes rolled back as his body flopped to the ground.

As Klein ran for the French doors, an excruciating burning sensation enveloped his left leg, and he tumbled to the stone patio and screamed out in agony. Trying to roll over, he saw a long throwing knife sticking out of his calf. He screamed out again, then noticed the woman in black closing in, another knife in her hand. Even her pitch-black sunglasses could not conceal the determination on her face.

She raised her arm and threw another blade, which pierced Klein's left bicep. He screamed again as he bled onto the patio. Adrenalin filled him with determination as he tried to reach across his plump body to remove the blade from his arm, but his efforts were in vain. It was lodged deep in his humerus bone.

The woman stopped in front of Klein and looked at him with pity. The second helicopter touched down, and a man sprinted to the woman's side, pointing his rifle at Klein.

"That was easier than I thought it would be," Klein heard the woman say as he squirmed in pain, bleeding out on the ground.

"Grab his arm," said the man.

~

With the knives still firmly embedded in his leg and arm, the obese Klein moaned as Rand placed him in a chair inside the chateau's basement laboratory. Rand surveyed the laboratory and its impressive array of equipment. Clearly, the Order had spared no expense on the state-of-the-art facility.

"Sitrep," said Rand into his radio while he stared at the bleeding doctor. On the other side of the lab, Abigail was busy unpacking the large duffels they'd brought with them from Texas.

"In position, all clear," said Levi. He was patrolling the chateau's perimeter, keeping a close eye on the Russian helicopters still powered up on the lawn.

"Optics up," said Naomi. "No threats to report. I'm in position seventy yards up the canyon's east wall. I have a perfect view downrange."

"Copy that," said Rand. He pulled the black balaclava from his head and tossed it onto the counter behind Klein.

The doctor stared at his captor with hatred burning in his eyes. "You're Rand Guthrie."

From across the lab, Abigail gave her brother a look of concern. The last thing anyone expected to hear was Rand's name muttered by the enemy.

Rand studied the man carefully. He'd been warned. Klein was a master manipulator, his powers of persuasion were second to none. "Very good, Doctor, but I don't believe we've ever met."

"The Order of Baphomet is aware of your extracurricular activities, Mr. Guthrie." Klein's voice was strained but arrogant. "We've had our eye on you for some time. You fund Christian charities that build orphanages in third-world hellholes and feed the dirty masses infesting Southeast Asia. You're a charismatic glad-hander with a billion-dollar smile who backs evangelical Christian senators and presidential candidates. You're the kingmaker of the Republican Party's alt-right wing. What would they say if they knew the truth about you, Mr. Guthrie? That you're an assassin for hire and you finance the sworn enemies of the United States, including Islamic terrorists you believe will bring about your version of the end of the world?"

Rand pulled out a syringe concealed inside his body armor. He held it up to his face, removed the Luer lock, flicked the barrel, and gently pushed the plunger to clear the air from the needle's shaft. A clear fluid seeped from the tip.

The smug look on Klein's face disintegrated.

"As you can see, I have no time for levity, Doctor." Grabbing Klein by the back of the head, Rand burst forward and plunged the needle into Klein's neck.

"Found it," Abigail said from across the room, momentarily distracting Rand from Klein's screaming. "This is bigger than we thought. Ask him what they've been planning."

"Stick with the plan," Rand said. "Ready the devices."

Abigail turned back to the equipment in the duffels.

As the drug cocktail kicked in, Klein's eyes glazed over and his head bobbed up and down. He glared at his captor. Rand activated the GoPro camera strapped to his chest.

"Did you know North Korea has millions of apple trees?" started the doctor, apropos of nothing. "The country shares the same latitude as Oregon. Perfect for growing apples. It all started during the famine of the 1990s. The Mormons gave them one hundred apple trees and showed them how to tend the orchard. And from there, the Mormons sent food and medical supplies by the shipload. Today, the entire population is fed by the Mormons. You didn't know that, did you? Most people don't. Not even most Mormons know that. Ask one. They don't tell anyone."

The chemicals were taking full effect. Rand knelt in front of Klein. "Where is he?"

"I mean why? Why do the Mormons even care?" Klein ignored Rand's question. "These inferiors all deserve to die. What a waste of money and resources. The Mormons. I never understood them."

"We don't have time for this!" yelled Rand. He grabbed Klein by the neck. "Where is Mahan? Tell me now."

Klein burst out in laughter. "It is I! I am Master Mahan!"

"Try again." Still holding him by the neck, Rand picked up one of Abigail's throwing knives and brandished it before Klein, who flinched.

"Your efforts are in vain," Klein said. "You see, he cannot be killed."

"So I've heard." Rand balled his fist, smashed Klein in the mouth, then moved the knife to his neck.

"My master is the harbinger of death." Klein grinned, blood seeping into the grooves between his teeth. "If you are unfortunate enough to find him, he will show you his blade. Thousands have died by that knife."

Rand knew nothing about Mahan's knife, but he didn't have time to ask.

"You are punching at ghosts, Mr. Guthrie," Klein continued. "It is now only a matter of time before the Order takes your life and, with it, everything you've ever owned and everyone you've ever loved. It all belongs to Master Mahan now."

"We'll see about that. What about the Book of Baphomet? Does he still possess it?"

"Why would you want that? You can't read Lamanese." Klein sneered. "And besides, you are out of time, Mr. Guthrie. We stand on the precipice of the Phoenix Eventide."

"The Phoenix Eventide? What is that?"

Klein burst out laughing. "I thought that's why you were here." Rand said nothing. "You really don't know, do you?"

The doctor was getting hysterical. Red-tinted saliva dripped from his lips, and blood still oozed from his arm and calf. "Oh, this is awful timing on your part, Mr. Guthrie. Awful indeed." Klein tried to compose himself. "Everything will be just fine for me. But you?" He became suddenly serious. "You will die."

"Alpha, you really need to see this," pleaded Abigail.

Rand, already frustrated with the interrogation, stepped away from Klein and over to Abigail. "See what?" he said impatiently.

Abigail gently swung open the door to the industrial refrigerator. Cooler after medical cooler was stacked, completely filling the large refrigerator.

"That's all Aries?" asked Rand.

"Yeah. Look at the shipping manifest." She handed Rand a printout. "It's going everywhere. Mostly major pharmas and militaries. I bet they're going to mass-produce these samples in their bioreactors for global distribution."

Rand held the manifest up to the GoPro and also filmed the coolers.

"Come listen to a story 'bout a man named Rand," sang Klein in his thick German accent. "Poor mountaineer barely kept his family fed."

"The *Beverly Hillbillies* theme song," said Abigail. "He's taunting us. Let's put a bullet in him and get out of here."

"Then one day he was shootin' at Mahan, and up from the ground came a bubblin' crude."

Rand threw the manifest on a desk and started for Klein.

"Wait." Abigail grabbed her brother by the arm. "The drugs are working. Rand, he just told us."

Looking at each other in disbelief, the two siblings simultaneously said, "Beverly Hills."

Rand and Abigail ran to Klein, who broke out in mad laughter.

"Where?" asked Rand. "Where exactly in Beverly Hills is he hiding? Do you have a location?"

"Mr. Guthrie, I must say I am extremely impressed. This cacophony of chemicals is anything but prosaic. I can hardly resist the truth. Did you steal the formulation from the CIA? Please give it to me."

"I will if you give me the location," Rand said, glancing slyly at Abigail.

"I don't have the bloody address, you hick," burst out Klein. "It's the Weatherlore Estate in Holmby Hills. That is all I know. Now, give me the formulation."

"Alpha, do you copy?" Naomi's voice came over comms. "Be advised. I have eyes on a threat advancing to our position. NK military convoy by road and a single Hind gunship escort. ETA four minutes. Please advise. Over."

"Oh, sounds like the convoy is early, Mr. Guthrie," said Klein, his voice starting to slur. "Hop along now, before they get you."

Abigail handed a small rectangular device to Rand. "Package standing by," she said. In her other hand, she gripped the handles of two medical coolers.

Rand motioned toward the stairs with his head. He looked down at Klein and pointed the GoPro in his face. "Look into the camera. Say hello to Mahan."

Bleeding and drooling, the doctor was slipping out of consciousness, the cocktail boiling his brain.

"I say again, Alpha," pleaded Naomi's voice. "We have inbound advancing on our position. Orders? Over."

Turning for the stairs, Rand pulled the radio's mic close to his mouth. "Weapons free. Engage."

CHAPTER 28

SCOTTSDALE AIRPORT
SCOTTSDALE, ARIZONA

As Amal watched, a line of three black GMC Yukons sped onto the tarmac and pulled up to the G700. The middle vehicle's rear door sprang open, and Leah Thomas jogged toward the plane. She reached Amal, who stood at the bottom of the plane's boarding steps, and without acknowledging her, disappeared into the aircraft.

Although Leah's eyes were concealed by dark sunglasses, Amal could see that her face was red and swollen, as if she'd been crying. Concerned, Amal turned her attention back to the vehicles. Chris Thomas was headed straight for her.

~

"Is she OK, sir?" asked Amal.

Bowing his head, Chris tried to conceal the sadness spreading across his face. After a long pause, he finally spoke. "Confidentially, we just learned Leah is infertile."

"I don't know what to say," Amal said sincerely. "I'm sorry."

Chris looked down again, took a deep breath, and assumed his corporate persona. "Look, Leah isn't sold on you *yet*, but I'm the decision maker. Do you want the job? Yes or no?"

"Well, I—"

"Lesson one in working with me. Don't hesitate."

Amal bit her lower lip and narrowed her eyes. Chris had observed on the flight that this was a nervous tell she struggled to hide.

"Yes. It's yes."

"I'm putting you on a ninety-day try and buy. We do that with all new employees at TAG. If you make it through the ninety-day trial—and we pass muster for you, of course—your title will be chief of security for Thomas Allen Group. Your salary will be $5 million a year. Will this suffice?"

"Did you say $5 *million* a year?"

"Yes. And if you stay with me for five years, I'll bonus you $25 million at retirement. You'll also be eligible for all TAG corporate benefits for life, which are the best in the world. Is this agreeable?"

"Um, yes. Yes, of course, sir. Thank you."

"Your offer letter will be in your inbox in ten minutes. E-sign it and return it to Scott Allen. I need you back in Palo Alto to get things moving. I'm heading to Utah now, so a company jet will land here in twenty-seven minutes to pick you up."

Chris scaled the stairs to the G700's cabin door. At the top, he stopped, turned, and looked down at his new hire. "Amal, good luck on your ninety-day trial. I really hope this works out. I'm putting the lives of everyone I love in your hands. Don't let me down."

CHAPTER 29

ABOVE THE KLEIN CHATEAU
NEAR HOERYONG, NORTH KOREA

The flat rock outcropping made for the perfect shooting platform. Naomi unpacked her beloved Barrett .50-caliber sniper rifle from its drag bag. Reaching deeper into the pack, she pulled out a ghillie suit custom-designed to blend in with this canyon's lush green surroundings.

With her rifle set and ghillie suit on, she doped the wind, then checked the canyon's trees. The wind blew gently at five miles per hour downcanyon from behind her, making for almost perfect conditions from her perch.

Squatting, she emptied her canteen onto the ground in front of her Barrett's massive muzzle. This would help prevent dust from rising and giving away her away position when she fired. Stretching into a prone position, she adjusted the rifle's stock and laid her cheek on the elevated butt. The rifle sat atop her pack, which she preferred to using a big-bore bipod.

Looking through the Leopold scope, Naomi had a perfect view of the road climbing up the valley for at least two miles. A massive Hind attack helicopter flew in escort formation, with several military trucks lumbering slowly up the narrow dirt road.

"Sitrep," said Rand's over her sound-canceling comms.

"Stand by," Naomi replied. Raising her head, she looked left, down at the chateau, and saw Abigail walking to a helicopter with two medical coolers. Abigail secured the coolers in one of the helicopter's cargo holds, then motioned for the pilot to take off. The helicopter powered up and took off upcanyon, away from the approaching threat.

Returning to her scope, Naomi stared down at the road. The Guthries were horribly outgunned against the powerful Russian-built helicopter. Had the North Koreans known of the events unfolding at the chateau, the Hind would most certainly have attacked by now.

"Effective range in thirty seconds. Over," said Naomi into her comms.

"Copy that," said Rand. "Holding station. Over."

Turning aside from the scope, Naomi saw Rand, Levi, and Abigail boarding the second helicopter. With the scope perfectly aligned, she clicked the turret, adjusted for the closing distance, and placed the laser-dot reticle on the Hind pilot's chest, now clearly in view through the advanced optics.

Naomi clicked off the safety, then took a deep breath, slowing her heart rate and putting her mind into a deep, concentrative flow state. Between two heartbeats, she applied perfect pressure to the rifle's custom-built trigger.

The Barrett roared to life.

Naomi watched the bullet's wake as it arched downrange through the humid air. Less than 1.5 seconds later, the pilot's upper torso exploded, spraying the bulletproof bubble-glass cockpit with blood and gore. The helicopter pitched and yawed as the copilot tried to gain control of the heavy gunship hovering only a hundred yards off the ground.

Naomi quickly reached for a special lead-shielded box, then placed another depleted-uranium-tipped round into the Barrett's breach and racked the bolt. The rifle roared again, and the round—heated to thousands of degrees against the canyon's dense air—sliced effortlessly into the Hind's top rotor compartment despite its thick armor, the rotor assembly exploding into a thousand pieces of spinning, razor-sharp shrapnel.

The ground convoy stopped abruptly. Looking in horror at the flaming beast overhead, the North Korean soldiers jumped from their trucks as the helicopter spun wildly out of control.

Naomi reloaded and took aim at the convoy's lead truck.

As the soldiers ran in every direction for cover, the Hind slammed into the canyon wall right above the convoy. An explosion burst outward, followed by a horrendous shock wave that echoed through the canyon. Burning debris fell onto several vehicles, and secondary explosions rocked the canyon, injuring and killing numerous soldiers caught in the torrent.

Naomi let loose again with the Barrett, killing the lead truck's driver and sending his blood and body parts all over the cab's other occupants. She reloaded and took out the vehicle's engine block, preventing the other vehicles from progressing up the narrow canyon road.

The Mi-26 helicopter holding Naomi's siblings lifted off the chateau's lawn and started climbing straight up. An armored personnel carrier with a Russian-made antiaircraft gun on its turret began firing on the siblings' helicopter. Although the vehicle was over thirteen hundred yards downrange, the rounds were hitting dangerously close to the family's only means of escape.

In less than four seconds, Naomi loaded another depleted-uranium round, zeroed in on the antiaircraft gun's magazine hold, and fired. The gun turret exploded, sending more fire and debris onto the surrounding troops and vehicles.

Staring through the scope, Naomi scanned her kill box for another target. The Hind's wreckage burned on the canyon floor, along with several military vehicles. Bodies were strewn everywhere. The North Korean troops who'd survived were either cowering or running for their lives down the canyon.

"Nice work, baby." Naomi kissed the Barrett's warm stock.

The siblings' helicopter now hovered over the chateau, about even with Naomi's altitude. She tore off the ghillie suit and threw her Barrett into its drag bag.

Approaching her position, the helicopter turned abruptly, its side door open. Rand and Levi, just inside the Mi-26's passenger compartment, motioned to her. The helicopter's blades came dangerously close to the canyon walls, the rotor downdraft making it almost impossible for Naomi to steady herself on the rock outcropping.

Naomi threw her drag bag containing her precious rifle into the copter. With all her might, she lunged through the air. Rand and Levi, on their bellies with arms outstretched, caught their sister midair by the arms. Rand slipped and lost his grip, but Levi held her in his iron grasp. For a moment, Naomi hung by one arm under the helicopter with nothing but air between her and the ground hundreds of feet below.

But Levi effortlessly hefted her petite frame through the door.

The helicopter eased away from the steep wall and banked up the canyon, leaving the burning North Korean convoy behind. Levi slid the bird's left-side door closed. Leaning out the right side, Abigail scanned the canyon for threats, but none were left in the carnage produced by one Texan cowgirl and her Tennessee-made rifle.

Rand pulled a device from a pocket in his body armor. He flipped up the safety toggle, depressed the red button, and looked at Abigail.

Abigail turned back to the open door just in time to see Klein's lair implode and disintegrate in a ball of fire. A shock wave rocked the helicopter, setting off several alarms in the cockpit. Soon, a conventional mushroom cloud formed where the chateau had once stood.

Rand let out a sigh of relief as the helicopter stabilized.

"Let's not do that again," Naomi said, rubbing her sore shoulder.

"We're not out of the woods yet," said Rand. He looked up at the pilots and then back at his siblings. When he pulled out his sidearm, each sibling gave him a nod.

CHAPTER 30

ROSTVERTOL MI-26 HELICOPTER
OVER NORTH KOREA

The helicopter emerged from the canyon, and the pilot maneuvered it to the east. Rand appeared between the pilot's and copilot's seats and handed the pilot a piece of paper.

"Take us to these coordinates," he commanded.

The pilot looked at Rand in surprise, then keyed his radio. Rand leveled his sidearm at the man's face. The copilot had moved to disarm Rand when a bullet from Levi's sidearm pieced his head, spraying blood all over the helicopter's controls.

Shocked, the pilot stared at the dead copilot, then looked back at Rand.

"You speak English, right?" Rand yelled over the sound of the roaring engine.

The pilot nodded quickly.

"Then take us to these coordinates, and don't try anything stupid. Keep us under five hundred feet so we don't pop up on radar."

"I can't fly into China," protested the pilot.

"Technically, it's not China. And, yes, you can. Like your boss said, we're paid up with the right people."

Nodding reluctantly, the wide-eyed Russian turned back to the helicopter's controls. Rand stayed put, monitoring the pilot's every move, his sidearm trained on the man's head.

~

From the makeshift FSB command center, Ivan watched the satellite feed and the Guthries' break from mission protocol. "Where are they going?" he demanded.

The operations control officer said nothing.

A Russian official came forward from the back of the room, casually lighting a cigarette. Known only to Ivan, the man had arrived after the Guthries' departure for North Korea. "It doesn't matter, Ivan. They put the virus on the first helicopter. The package is inbound. Guthrie is no fool. It's obvious he never planned to return to base. He's sending us what we want, and maybe he got what he wanted. With the virus in our hands, Guthrie's betting we'll let the whole thing go. Smart, da? Very smart." The unfiltered cigarette hung from the man's mouth as he spoke.

"Flight status?" yelled Ivan.

A radar technician in Russian military field garb turned to the two men, a radio receiver held over his ear. "Sir, the helicopter lands in one minute."

"Excellent," said the man.

Leaving the operations center, Ivan and the man headed quickly for the tarmac.

"The virus was the whole point of the operation," Ivan said as they walked down the exit hallway. "I agree with your assessment of Guthrie, but we'll need to activate the FSB to clean up the leftovers. After all, we can't have these Guthrie people walking around alive. We risk the CIA finding out we have Aries."

"Da, but it won't be easy," said the other man. "These people are total professionals. We may have to use other American assets."

Ivan nodded.

Exiting the building, they spotted the helicopter on final approach. Ivan sneered, momentarily letting go of his concern about the Guthries.

As the helicopter emerged from a light fog bank, Ivan extended his arms in welcome. "Ah yes. You see, we hired the right team. Aries is ours."

The other man tried to light another cigarette, but the helicopter's downdraft blew out the lighter's flame. He put the unlit cigarette and lighter back into his pocket.

After landing and powering down the helicopter, the pilot gave them an enthusiastic thumbs-up. The two men approached the rear cargo doors and stepped inside the machine. Ivan activated the cargo-bay lights. Sitting innocuously under a secured cargo net were two portable, aluminum, refrigerated biocontainment cases.

Ivan looked at the other man, who grinned like a drunk. The prize was finally in Mother Russia's hands, and they would both be generously rewarded.

Ivan knelt, unfastened the cargo net, and unlatched one of the cases.

"Gently," scolded the man.

Still kneeling, Ivan looked up at him and rubbed his hands together. Then he carefully opened the case.

Bending forward, his comrade looked into the case and frowned. "What is this?"

Those were his last words. At that moment, Ivan, his mysterious comrade, the helicopter, and most of the secret base disappeared in a horrific explosion that killed every Russian involved in the North Korean operation.

Rand and his siblings approached the Yanji airport in the Yanbian Korean Autonomous Prefecture, which lay just twenty miles northwest of the North Korean border in China's Jilin Province.

"Over there," instructed Rand, pointing at the Guthries' Bombardier 7500, fully fueled and waiting for them.

The helicopter touched down, and Rand waited as his siblings exited. With pleading eyes, the pilot looked at Rand.

Rand pulled back on the hammer with his thumb. "No hard feelings."

"No!" yelled the pilot, but his plea was in vain.

~

Stepping into the 7500, Rand pulled the door closed and looked at the pilot. "Let's roll. Next stop, Los Angeles."

The old Texan pilot gave his boss a thumbs-up and powered up the jet.

Rand looked at his siblings resting peacefully in the plane's plush lounge. Already positioned at the start of the runway, the plane accelerated and lifted off effortlessly into the Chinese sky. Levi was asleep before the plane left the runway.

"I get first shower," Naomi said.

CHAPTER 31

THOMAS TEMPORARY RESIDENCE
HEBER CITY, UTAH

Chris lay awake, staring at the ceiling, his brain bombarded with every problem he faced. One moment, his mind would race around the biological issues of infertility, trying to think of any approach that could solve what doctors said was an unsolvable problem.

The next moment, his mind would fall deep into the frustrating quantum mysteries of the TR-3B's reactor and the machine's otherworldly physics. Intellectually, he knew the TR-3B was an anomaly that defied all understanding. Even Max, working from his own expansive knowledge base, could not decipher the reactor's mysteries. But this made sense—after all, in its current state, the AI's understanding of the science was mostly limited to humankind's own understanding.

But always present in the back of Chris's mind were the haunting thoughts of Mahan and his terrible plans. What was Thor's Hammer? What was the Phoenix Eventide? How could Chris stop them?

He rolled onto his side and looked enviously at his wife, who slept soundly even in her deep depression. The second her head hit the pillow, she was unconscious for eight straight hours. He peeked over her slender shoulder at her nightstand clock—3:32 a.m.

Chris slipped quietly out of bed and headed to the office on the other side of the home. On his way, he peered through the plantation shutters from a front window. The upscale neighborhood was deathly quiet. He was still adjusting to the new but temporary house located a few miles from their dream home under construction in east Heber.

Unlike in California, the stars were bright here. Moonbeams reflected off the beautiful snow-covered hills to his south. Walking out the front door for a better look, he startled a security guard concealed in the bushes just off the spacious front patio.

"Sorry," Chris said to the man, who was clad in all-black and armed with an H&K-416 rifle.

"It's no problem, sir. I just wasn't expecting anyone to come from the house at this hour."

"I can't sleep most nights, so this might be more common than not."

The guard nodded.

"Beautiful night," said Chris. "Man, Utah isn't California, is it?"

"Toto, I've got a feeling we're not in Kansas anymore," said the guard.

Chris smirked. "Any problems tonight?"

"No, sir. High-altitude surveillance drones are in flight. Security assets are placed in a multiringed perimeter throughout the valley. We've placed security cameras and sensors at every strategic entry and egress. We're monitoring each vehicle coming and going and running real-time facial recognition against the known residents and their social graphs. Antiaircraft systems are in place and monitoring the airspace. If anything looks fishy, we'll know fast."

"Max, are you online?" Chris asked, entering his new office and quietly shutting the door.

"Always, sir," said Max.

Chris sat down at his workstation. "Go secured room."

"Room secured, sir." Powered by x-cryption, an electronic ray shield activated with a slight hum, encompassing the house and turning it into a digitally invisible fortress.

Chris opened his laptop, stared into the camera, and placed his thumb on the keyboard sensor. "This is Vanguard. Authorization echo-echo-alpha-tango-sierra-zero-niner-zero-seven."

"Authorization granted," said a human voice from the computer.

"Max, open the archived files on Project Galileo."

The folder containing all data on the TR-3B populated the screen. Although Chris's mind was better suited than anyone else's in the world to take in the enormous amount of data, he felt overwhelmed and frustrated as he stared at the screen.

First, he pulled up a soundless video from more than fifty years ago and hit the play button. A scientist in a white lab coat took a Titleist golf ball, showed it to the camera, and threw it underhand at the reactor that powered the TR-3B. Within inches of the device, the ball suddenly turned upward at a ninety-degree angle and accelerated straight into the ceiling. The other scientists in the room laughed at the impossible violation of the laws of physics right before their eyes.

Chris closed the video and opened the schematics of the reactor and its accompanying amplifier. The reactor was about the size and shape of a halved, solid basketball. A small cylinder protruding from its center connected the device to the amplifier, which was about the size of a kitchen trash can. When attached to the reactor, the amplifier could pivot directionally on the cylinder. Wherever the amplifier pointed, the spacecraft flew.

Even after decades of study, the device's metallurgical makeup was a complete mystery. The system was an off-pewter color, with no discernable seams, fasteners, sharp edges, or welds in the outer casing. No evidence existed that the casing was molded, machined, or formed by any known technology. In fact, microscopic inspection of the casing's molecular alignment suggested it had been manufactured in zero gravity.

"Max, can you pull up the historical radiation-testing files?"

"Sir, there are no files or documented results for radiation testing."

"That's odd."

"Dr. Shakespeare indicated that the device emits no radiation."

"But that violates the laws of thermodynamics. There's no such thing as a 100 percent energy-efficient power system. There's always degradation from and within power systems, and with systems like this, it's usually heat. This thing produces gravity, and it's not a planetary mass. It has to produce heat, right? There's no documentation of anyone even putting a Geiger sensor on this thing?"

"I show no results for the query, sir."

"That's a pretty significant oversight on someone's part. I need to ask Zelda about that."

"I do enjoy working with Dr. Shakespeare, Chris," said Max. "Although she does not reflect it outwardly, I believe she also enjoys working with us."

"Yes, Max, I agree. She has a hard outer shell, but inside she's a real softy."

"Is there a problem with her skin that I'm not aware of? Is there an abnormality with her internal organs? Sir, does Dr. Shakespeare have a medical problem? Please explain."

Chris smiled. "It's just a figure of speech, Max. What else do you have for me?"

"I have a video I think you should view."

A video that looked like it had been produced in the 1970s came on the screen. Two scientists took a watch, a classic chronometer, and placed it under the gravity amplifier. The second hand stopped.

"That doesn't mean the device slowed time, Max," said Chris. "It could just be disrupting the watch's inner mechanics."

"Keep watching, sir," advised Max.

The camera angled in above the amplifier and looked into the watch face, where a black dot formed to reveal that the alien reactor was bending the light.

Chris put his hand over his chin in deep introspection. Basic physics said that light could be reflected or refracted, but bending light was another matter entirely. The black dot indicated the absence of light in the visible spectrum. It was being bent, which only gravity could do.

"This is unreal," said Chris.

"Sir, I have the information you requested on element 115 ."

"Hold that for now," instructed Chris. "You can give it to me in flight to Dugway. Send Dr. Shakespeare a text, and let her know I'll meet her at the lab in three hours."

CHAPTER 32

NAV CORPORATE HEADQUARTERS
PALO ALTO, CALIFORNIA

Kiki placed her eye in front of the scanner and her thumb on the door's biometric reader. The door clicked, and she stepped into Nav's main network operations center.

Milton, Nav's first intern, was glued to his Samsung Galaxy. The surprise visitor sent him springing from his seat.

"Kiki?" he said nervously. "You scared me to death. It's 4:18 in the morning. What are you doing here?"

"I'm in love with you, Milton," she said seductively.

Milton's jaw went slack, and his face flushed red. He trembled slightly.

Kiki wore a miniskirt and halter top, a Louis Vuitton purse slung over her shoulder. She was already several inches taller than Milton, but her high heels sent her towering at least six inches over him.

"Uh, me?" Milton pointed to himself.

Kiki strutted confidently to the twenty-something-year-old. With his baggy pants, stained shirt, and acne-covered face, he looked more like he was fourteen.

Milton took several awkward steps back. Kiki could see boyish fear consume him as she marched authoritatively toward him. He backed himself against one of the hundreds of server racks in the room. He was trapped.

Walking right up to him, she looked seductively into his eyes. "It's the way you report in the operations meeting on server performance. It's so hot when you talk about overclocking and node arrays and composite theoretical performance. You're also an old Fortran fan. Me too. Don't you just love that old language?"

Milton was frozen.

Kiki grinned and moved in even closer, close enough to see sweat beading on Milton's acne-dotted forehead. "I've been reading your internal blog posts on Max's parallel operations functions and how they affect his neural net. You are spot-on, no matter what Chris Thomas says. And your theory on how Max uses temporal locality for efficient speech processing is brilliant."

Milton was breathing hard. "Oh, really? I didn't think anyone was even reading that." His voice cracked.

"Come with me." Taking his hand, Kiki led him down one of the server aisles. She abruptly stopped and forcefully pushed him up against a server rack. Moving in close again, she put one hand on Milton's shoulder and ran her other hand through his hair. "They'll never understand geniuses like us, Milton."

Milton didn't speak.

"We're the oddballs. The nerds no one ever respected." As Kiki spoke, she continued combing her fingers through his greasy hair. "But look at us. Look at what we do here at Nav. We're creating a tactile god. They used to mock people like you and me. Now they will bow to us."

Kiki leaned in and kissed him gently on the lips. Milton's face contorted, and his body began to seize. He was breathing like he'd just finished a marathon.

"It's OK," she said softly. "I don't bite."

She moved in for a longer kiss, and this time Milton kissed her back. Letting go of Milton's shoulder, Kiki sneaked her hand into her purse. As the two continued awkwardly locking lips, she reached into a concealed compartment and removed a micro-USB device. Then she reached past Milton and felt for a USB port on the front of one of the servers.

Milton pulled back. "Uh, look, I—" Before he could finish, Kiki went back in for more, at the same time inserting the small device into a server.

When Milton put his hands on her hips, Kiki suddenly pulled back. She gave Milton a disgusted look, then slapped him across the face.

Milton's face contorted with shock and confusion.

"What kind of girl do you think I am?" she screamed into Milton's face. Pushing herself away from the man-boy, she stormed out of the NOC.

CHAPTER 33

THOMAS TEMPORARY RESIDENCE
HEBER CITY, UTAH

At 6:00 a.m., Chris entered the kitchen and found a piece of dry wheat toast and a glass of orange juice on the counter. He peeked out the back window and noticed a guard standing near his MD helicopter, which was parked in the middle of the home's two-acre backyard.

"Max, initiate preflight check and start-up sequences." Chris took a big bite of the dry toast and downed the glass of orange juice in one swig. The helicopter's turbine engine started whining, and the blades began a slow rotation.

"You can fix this," he heard from the dark living room adjacent to the kitchen.

Chris flinched. He hadn't noticed Leah in a high-back chair staring out the back window. She was still in her pajamas, her hair a mess. Yesterday's mascara was still streaked down her face from the tears that had been her constant companion since she'd received the news of her infertility. For days, she had been distant with Chris, only answering questions with a short yes or no and refusing to engage in any conversation.

Chris moved over to Leah and knelt down, placing his head in her lap. Reciprocating, she ran her hand through his hair. His heart raced every time his wife touched him, but this time was different. The last several days had seemed like an eternity. The devastating emptiness Chris felt without his wife's emotional connection had taken a deep toll on him. Now, he felt pure relief. The ice was finally starting to thaw.

Chris stared up at her. She had a look of anticipation in her eyes as she waited for him to respond. Chris leaned in and kissed her. Leah kissed him back, and the two held each other tightly.

The helicopter was now fully spooled, its blades rotating as the craft waited on its pilot.

"I'm going to fix this," Chris whispered gently into her ear. "I don't know how yet, but I have some ideas. I promise you, I am going to fix this."

Leah pulled away and looked hopefully into Chris's eyes. For the first time in a days, she smiled.

CHAPTER 34

WEATHERLORE ESTATE
LOS ANGELES, CALIFORNIA

Dressed in a black cassock and red cape, Cain sat atop an opulent throne made of ancient wood. It was inlaid with gold and accented with fine tapestries, and the high back stood at least eight feet tall. Baphomet's stone head towered on a pillar above the throne, looking down upon armrests made of human skulls.

The throne sat behind a makeshift control room that was the heart of the Order's global reign of terror. The Weatherlore mansion's once-grand ballroom had been transformed into a high-tech command center complete with servers, computer consoles, and a bank of monitors stretching the length of the room's outer wall. All the bulletproof windows had been blacked out, the mansion's neighbors none the wiser.

The burner phone in Cain's pocket vibrated. The text was one word from a blocked number: *success*.

Cain showed no emotion as he stood. "Attention, everyone," he said, his voice bellowing throughout the cavernous hall. The staff of twenty turned from their respective workstations and listened intently to their master.

"The asset inside Nav has reported mission accomplished," declared Cain. "Today we initiate phase one of our grand plan to return the earth to the Mother and establish the State. Today we unleash the Dawn of the Cimeters."

No one talked or reacted. The staff simply stared in anticipation.

"Execute the order," said Cain.

The room exploded in a frenzy as an image of Thor's Hammer populated the enormous center monitor.

Cain sat on his throne, yawned, and then yelled, "Cry havoc and let slip the dogs of war!"

CHAPTER 35

DUGWAY PROVING GROUND
WEST DESERT, UTAH

Why didn't you ever put a Geiger sensor on the reactor?" Chris asked as he walked into the laboratory door marked A-139.

"Good morning to you too, sunshine," said Zelda. "By the way, you're late." She stood atop the TR-3B, staring into a compartment in the aircraft's fuselage, wrench in hand. The craft rested on three retractable landing gears, and the reactor sat innocuously on a workbench next to the craft.

"What are you doing?" Chris asked from below.

"Why would I need to put a Geiger sensor on the reactor? It doesn't emit radiation. Haven't you read the report?"

"So you used a Geiger on the reactor sometime in the last fifteen years?" asked Chris. "Or are you just taking someone else's word for it?"

Zelda tilted her head, and the look of epiphany crossed her face. She scurried down the yellow industrial scaffolding and walked past Chris. "There's a Geiger sensor in the equipment room. I'll be right back."

Chris walked over to the reactor and stared at it in awe. The device was load-sensing. When the reactor and amplifier were connected, the system powered up like a Tesla coil or radio transmitter.

Marveling at the device's simplicity, Chris wondered about its alien inventors. As he moved closer, he could hear a slight hum coming from the reactor. When he reached out to touch it, he felt a strange force move his hand, like two opposing magnets.

"I know playing with antigravity is fun, but we have work to do," Zelda said, standing behind Chris. She handed him the Geiger sensor.

He took it and calibrated it. "Internal-combustion engines are only about 35 percent efficient," he said. "The electric engine Max and I designed for the auto manufacturers is about 95 percent efficient. Nothing is 100 percent efficient. Max, is there any fuel in the reactor?"

"Negative," replied Max. "No element 115 currently present in the system." A camera and sensor array had been set up for the AI all around the laboratory.

Above Chris and Zelda, a 3D hologram of the reactor's internal chamber formed in the air. Chris placed the Geiger sensor next to the reactor. "Max, what do you make of these readings? What are you picking up from your sensor array?"

Max analyzed the data. "Although no radiation is present outside the reactor, sensors indicate the presence of radioactivity, gamma rays, and beta particles inside the reactor. The particles are moving around uniformly inside, comparable to a cyclotron or particle collider."

"How about a magnetic field? What do you see on the spectrometer?"

"I detect no magnetic field."

"How about temperature?"

"Temperature is ambient. Sir, sensors indicate a weak gravity wave originating from the amplifier. You'll notice a slight corona discharge under the device."

Chris and Zelda both knelt down and took notice of the effect. Space and time were bending right in front of them.

"Only large bodies of mass can do that," Chris said. "That's impossible."

"Stop saying that word, noob," said Zelda.

"Wait." Chris wiped at the beads of sweat forming on his forehead. "When the first reactor blew up back in the sixties, wouldn't they have detected radiation from the explosion?"

Zelda stared at the hologram projecting over their heads. "The explosion occurred at S-4, just outside Area 51. That sits right in the middle of where the US government tested nukes in the 1960s. The whole area was already irradiated."

Chris nodded. "So, here's my theory, Zelda. There's got to be some kind of low-energy nuclear reaction taking place in the reactor chamber when powered by the element-115 fuel source. That energy, formed in the reactor, then gets funneled into the amplifier, causing a controlled nuclear reaction more powerful than the sun. This reaction creates gravity and bends space and time, and the craft *falls* into its destination in the universe in mere seconds."

"Or it goes one step further and passes through another dimension," said Zelda. "That's what I think happened to Colonel Willy Williams and the TR-2A in 1996." She gave Chris a look of frustration. "I've been working on this for fifteen years, trying to solve the what and the how. You walk in here and immediately solve the what."

"Well, the real mystery is the how. Maybe we're staring at the physical manifestation of string theory . . . or maybe not. Anyway, we get to the how by getting inside the thing, which seems to be not possible. Please note that I didn't say impossible."

"Yeah, I caught that," she said with a grin. "But you're still a neophyte."

"This is like sending a nuclear reactor back in time to Sir Isaac Newton or Leonardo Da Vinci," Chris said. "I mean, they might come up with some ideas, but they'd probably kill themselves cracking the thing open."

"It's funny you use that example. A guy who used to work here said the same thing."

They both stared at the device, deep in thought.

"Well, no wonder Barrington wants us to figure this out," Chris said after a while. "No one can stop tech that can manipulate gravity. I imagine, with its force field, the TR has no weapons, right? Would it even need any?"

"Of course it has weapons. Particle-beam weapons are located on each of the three corners." Zelda pointed at the machine. "They're reverse engineered from the recovered crafts. Specs are in the project file. We put the same particle-beam weapons system on the orbiting hunter-killer satellite array. They can destroy incoming ICBMs and objects from outer space."

"We actually have that?"

"Yeah, it's the third generation of what was originally Reagan's Star Wars program. I always thought it was ironic we were using alien technology to protect ourselves from those same aliens."

"About that," Chris said hesitantly. "Can you explain in more—"

At that moment, a massive force hit the underground lab.

Chris and Zelda fell to the floor as a booming shock wave enveloped the room. Chris rolled over just in time to see the reactor and amplifier fall from the workbench and hit the concrete floor with a thud. He froze in shock, staring at the reactor for any sign of damage or a leak. The radiation levels inside the reactor were so dangerously high that even a slight leak at close distance was enough to kill them in minutes.

To Chris's dismay, Zelda stood and ran unsteadily to the alien equipment. "It's fine," she yelled back at him. "A fall from that low isn't going to hurt it. Come on, we've got to get out of here."

The room shook harder. As Chris struggled to stand, a crack appeared in the laboratory's concrete wall and shot across the fifty-foot ceiling, small chunks of concrete raining down on the lab floor.

"Run!" yelled Chris. He and Zelda sprinted out the lab door into the access tunnel. "The elevator. It's the only way out."

The pair ran toward the inconspicuous door concealing the elevator to the surface. As they reached it, the shaking finally stopped, but a series of unsettling creaks and moans echoed throughout the building. The elevator door opened, and they couldn't see any damage. Zelda placed her badge on the elevator's scanner, and it started to move.

"What was that?" asked Chris.

"I have no idea. An earthquake? What else could it have been?"

Trying to catch their breath, Chris and Zelda sat on the floor of the elevator. They heard an alarming screech, and the overhead lights flickered, but the elevator kept rising. It would take a few minutes to climb the five thousand feet to the surface. Looking down at his hand, Chris realized he still held the Geiger sensor.

"Max, are you online?" Chris held up his phone, but no answer came. "We should have grabbed the reactor," he said to Zelda.

Still coughing and trying to gather her senses, the woman looked over at Chris. "Look, if it gets buried, it won't be the first time. We'll just dig it up again."

"Good point."

When the high-speed elevator indicated thirty seconds to the surface, the two helped each other up off the floor. Leaving the elevator, they made their way through a short concrete-reinforced access tunnel and several security doors, eventually exiting through the facility's south door.

Outside in the barren West Utah desert, Chris squinted and placed his hand over his brow. His MD helicopter, parked fifty yards from the door, lay mangled on its side.

"Oh, crap!" Chris put his hand on the back of his head and exhaled. "I guess I'll have to get another one."

Grabbing his shoulders, Zelda spun him around. Chris looked up and saw a gigantic gray mushroom cloud pushing tens of thousands of feet into the atmosphere. The devastation enveloped the base's north end in roughly the location of Dugway's colossal radar-dish array.

The duo stared at the sight in complete disbelief. Snapping out of her shock, Zelda took the Geiger sensor from Chris and turned it on. The display indicated no dangerous radiation levels.

"That can't be right," yelled Chris, turning back to the facility door. "Calibrate it. We need to find cover now."

"It *is* calibrated," shouted Zelda. "The explosion's not nuclear."

"Then what did that?" Chris pointed at the expanding mushroom cloud. "Is there another weapon on base that could have exploded?"

"Not that I'm aware of. Look!"

From a distance, a Blackhawk helicopter closed in on their position.

~

As the Blackhawk raced past Dugway, giving the mushroom cloud a wide berth, Chris and Zelda stared out the open door in shock. The runways, the ramp, the aircraft, numerous hangers, and the ATC tower all smoldered in ruin.

A hole at least a half mile in diameter had replaced what had once been a multibillion-dollar near-earth dish array used for monitoring near-earth objects.

Dugway was simply no more.

The Blackhawk touched down. The door gunner signaled to Chris and Zelda to move to a nondescript cinderblock building on the outskirts of the base. As soon as they entered, an MP pointed his M4 rifle at them. "Hands up now!"

Chris and Zelda threw up their arms.

"Oh, good, someone from below survived," said General Bischoff, the base commander. "You can lower your weapon, Sergeant."

The aged general sat on a stool as a medic stitched a wound on his head. His uniform was dirt-covered, torn, and bloody. Peering deeper into the building, Chris saw a makeshift operation center manned by a few dazed soldiers and a triage area filled with injured soldiers.

"General, what happened?" pleaded Zelda.

"We're still trying to figure that out. Maybe something underground blew up?"

"No," Chris said. "Judging by the crater's shape, whatever it was came from above."

"Sir," said a sergeant manning a laptop. "Space Command at Peterson and Vandenberg are offline. We can't reach central command or Langley. Satcoms are offline."

"That can't be right. What about Cheyenne Mountain?"

"Sir, I got nothing," said the dejected sergeant.

"Keep trying, son."

"General, I'm sorry," said Chris. "I need to get to Washington. Is there any way—"

"You can walk," interrupted the general. A forlorn look settled over his face.

"I know I'm not the most important person in this situation, but if you can help me, I'm your best bet for figuring out what just happened, sir."

An NCO working a radio spoke up. "Sir, air cover from Hill AFB is on station—F-35s."

The general paused for a moment, then looked at Chris. "Son, this may sound crazy, but I don't know what you're working on down there. Even as base commander, I don't have the security clearance. But whatever it is, it must be important. You're Chris Thomas, so I'll believe you."

"Sir, I have an authenticated emergency flash message from SecDef," said the sergeant.

The general sprang to his feet. "Read it now."

"United States under attack. Reserves inbound to your position. Locate Chris Thomas, report his condition, and prep him for transport to the following coordinates."

"Respond that we have Chris Thomas in custody."

"Let me see that," said Chris, jumping in front of the sergeant's laptop. Staring at the GPS coordinates, he could see the globe in his mind's eye. The ever-present math running through his field of vision calculated the latitude and longitude. "That's New York City."

"New York City?" said the general. "Why would they need you in—"

"Sir, an F-35 is under orders to divert to Michael Army Airfield and transport Mr. Thomas to the given coordinates immediately."

"Michael Army Airfield?" asked Chris. "Where's that?"

"Recall the Blackhawk now," instructed the general. Looking at Chris, he said, "MAA is a top-secret drone base nine miles west of here. The Blackhawk will get you there."

Zelda tugged on his shirt. "What do I do, Chris?"

He could tell she was still in shock. "Stay here and wait for my word. If it's safe, get back down to A-139. I have a feeling we're going to need the—uh, the thing. You know what I mean, right?"

Zelda nodded vigorously, and Chris sprinted for the door.

"Mr. Thomas!" yelled General Bischoff.

Chris stopped and turned around to face the general.

"Find out who did this and kill them."

Bowing his head, Chris disappeared through the door.

CHAPTER 36

WEEHAWKEN WATERFRONT PARK
WEEHAWKEN, NEW JERSEY

A slight drizzle hung in the air as the sleek Peterbilt 579 semitruck hauling its plain white fifty-three-foot trailer slowly pulled up outside the Weehawken Waterfront Park. Four identical semis followed behind.

A police cruiser partially blocked the park entrance, its lightbar flashing blue and red. Nearby, a bright-orange electric road sign stated, *Private Event. No Entrance.* Standing by the car, a New Jersey state trooper brandished a twelve-gauge shotgun.

"Is this the right place?" asked the truck driver, looking over to a man he barely knew sitting in the passenger seat. His companion returned no comment.

As the truck approached, the trooper motioned for the driver to stop. Lowering his window, the driver inhaled the smell of fresh rain. "Good day, Officer."

The trooper put his boot into the foothold and pulled himself up to the cab's window. "License and registration."

The driver tried to remain calm. "Uh, yeah. Sure."

"I'm messing with you, idiot. You're ninety seconds late. Time is money on this job. Where have you been?"

"Traffic."

Jumping down, the trooper barked, "Follow the cruiser. Move it."

The driver put the Peterbilt in gear and carefully pulled in behind the cruiser, which led the five-truck procession deep into the park.

After driving slowly for a few hundred yards, the convoy rounded a bend and went down an incline, approaching a soccer field alongside the rock-lined riverbank. Across the Hudson River, New York City glistened as sunbeams pierced the rain clouds.

Several additional state troopers guarded the area, cruisers parked nearby. They'd done their job well—no civilians were in sight.

The troopers began directing the trucks onto the soccer field. The first truck parked in the center, and the passenger got out and unhitched the trailer from the Peterbilt rig. The trailer's hydraulic stabilizers hissed as they extended onto the freshly manicured pitch. The passenger then motioned for the driver to pull the rig off the field.

The troopers directed the other four truck drivers to back up their trailers to the center trailer's corners, with each trailer protruding outward from the corner at a forty-five-degree angle. For perfect positioning, the drivers used an iPad app connected to a laser-guidance system. Once all four trailers were in place, the passenger in each rig got out and unhitched the trailer, and the Peterbilts pulled away.

From his rig, the first truck driver eyed the strange geometrical shape the trailers now formed in the middle of the field. He stepped down from his rig and headed toward one of the troopers, who was staring into an iPad.

"Watch this," the trooper said with a gleam in his eye.

CHAPTER 37

ORION'S SPEAR HEADQUARTERS
NEW YORK CITY

Chris lay on a couch in Stew Brimhall's office, located just outside Orion Spear's main operations center. He sat up slowly and rubbed his eyes, then scowled as the taste in his mouth registered. He hadn't showered or slept for more than two hours in the last three days.

Walking over to the thick, bulletproof glass pane, Chris admired the view of New York City. He liked that Orion's Spear was now headquartered in Hudson Yards, the largest mixed-use private real-estate venture in US history. Valued at a staggering $25 billion, the twenty-eight-acre project sat atop an old railway yard. Forty thousand New Yorkers worked and lived in the city within a city. Its eighteen million square feet spread over more than twelve skyscrapers and contained two malls, four athletic clubs, thirty-six movie theaters, thousands of residential apartments, an untold number of high-end restaurants, and offices for some of the hottest tech companies on earth. Critics called Hudson Yards nothing more than another billionaires' playground; others considered it the crown jewel of New York City.

Three-quarters of the way through the project's construction, Hudson Yard's parent company had fallen into financial disarray. Seeing an extraordinary opportunity, Chris Thomas bought the property for pennies on the dollar, a move the *New York Times* dubbed "the real estate deal of the century."

Chris and Stew had convinced President Barrington to move Orion's Spear out of Langley and covertly locate it on the top floors of the 1,300-foot-tall stalagmite-looking residential building known as 80 Hudson Yards. This didn't take much convincing. Chris had offered the government the space for free, including an apartment for Stew on the floor below the state-of-the-art offices and operations center. Chris had also offered discounted apartments in Hudson Yards for Orion's Spear's growing staff.

Chris's phone chimed. Rubbing the tired from his bloodshot eyes, he tried to focus on the photo Leah had just texted him of an African-American child about kindergarten age with a brilliant smile missing a front tooth, her left arm in a cast up to her shoulder.

"Max, call Leah," Chris said as he walked back toward the couch that had been his bed.

Leah answered immediately. "Hey, are you OK?" Chris had sent her a message before departing Dugway, but he hadn't been free to contact her over the last few days.

"I'm OK. Just a bad headache. How are things with Amal?"

"Fine, I guess." Chris could sense uneasiness in Leah's voice. "She got here a few hours after the attack. She brought a bunch of ex–Special Forces guys. Everything is fine. I don't want you to worry about me."

"If a tank division was guarding you, I'd still be worried." Chris could almost feel her blush through the phone.

"Where are you?"

"I can't say exactly where over this line, but I'm at the new operations center. What is this picture you sent me?"

"Oh yeah," Leah said hesitatingly. "That's Jada."

"Jada?"

"Do you remember the Wades down the street? You met them at church."

"Uh—"

"Well, anyway, I went with Nancy Wade to the gym last week." Leah was talking fast, which she did when she was nervous. "She has a son, Zain, on a mission in Detroit. They were teaching a lady and her daughter, Jada, and the lady's ex-husband showed up one night and shot her dead, then shot Jada. She took a bullet to the arm. Then, right in front of Jada, he killed himself."

"That's awful."

"Yeah, well, she's orphaned now and has no surviving relatives. I was telling Nancy about my infertility, and she sent me the picture."

"Oh, Leah. Honey, really? I mean—"

"Chris, here's the kicker. She's a genius. They've been busing her to a school in the suburbs. She's years more advanced than most of the kids in junior high. She's only six."

Chris let out an exaggerated sigh and ran his hand through his hair. "Leah, I know this is a hard time for you right now. I want to discuss this, but I need a few days, OK? I'm sorry. Something has gone completely wrong with the government's comms satellites. Max is trying to figure it out, but Max is also acting strange. It's like he has the flu. I'm working on that too. But I'm in a secure location. Don't worry about me."

"OK, just think about it," said Leah. "That's all I'm asking. Oh, and the G700 is in position."

He knew she was referring to New Jersey's Teterboro Airport, just across the Hudson River. "Yeah, they sent me a text. I'll get home when I can, and we can discuss this, but it might be a few more days."

"Chris, how bad is it?"

Stew peeked his head in the door and motioned to Chris.

"I've got to run. I love you."

Chris walked into the cavernous, dimly lit Orion's Spear operations center, a immediate surge of tension hit him like a tidal wave. The fifty staff members had been working nonstop for days, and the room smelled like it. No one acknowledged Chris. They stared into workstations, congregated around digital conference tables, manipulated objects in front of VR goggles, and talked into secure landlines. Large cups of steaming hot coffee sat everywhere. The center's front wall boasted a massive monitor encircled by twenty-four smaller monitors displaying everything from the news to top-secret satellite feeds to social-media streams.

In the center of the room stood a tall command console that projected holographic images. Chris approached Stew, who stood at a keyboard looking into a monitor embedded in the command console. Stew's assistant director, Elle Danley, and several other senior analysts circled the command console, anxiously waiting for Stew to speak.

"Where's Mike?" Chris asked.

"He's helping with search and rescue at Langley." Stew didn't look up from the monitor. "We can get him back here in an hour if we need him." Stew turned to Elle. "I need to get a report to the president. Give us a sitrep."

"Here's what we know so far. Using our high-altitude drone network, we've determined that Nellis, Groom Lake, Buckley, Dugway, Vandenberg, and all our bases in Colorado—including Peterson, which was Space Command headquarters—have been destroyed. US Central Command is gone too. We've surmised they were all destroyed by an unknown weapon. Smaller ground-tracking stations like the ones in Maui and Greenland have also been destroyed. The attack has blinded us."

"What about our Aegis ships, like the *Ticonderoga*, with antisatellite missiles?" asked Chris.

"They need the tracking network to target space-based threats. They're useless without it."

Chris exhaled deeply. "This is bad."

"There's more bad. A lot more," said Elle. "Cheyenne Mountain is intact, as is Mount Weather, but their comms are offline. Most of the aboveground facilities at Fort Meade, Langley, and the NRO were destroyed. Cape Canaveral is gone too.

"The cape is gone?" Chris said in disbelief.

"They knew exactly what they were doing," said Stew. "They took out our primary and tertiary systems, leaving us completely blind."

"Which means they want us blind to what comes next," said Chris.

"Continuity of government contingency plans has been enacted under executive order," continued Elle. "FEMA is directing all public-facing activities. All government agencies are functional and have been diverted to secondary underground bases outside Washington, D.C. Fortunately, in terms of intel and defense, that's where most of the important stuff already sat. President Barrington is keeping us at DEFCON 2, even though we know the Russians and Chinese are not responsible."

"What does the damage look like in China and Russia?" asked Chris. The console's embedded monitor illuminated a map of Asia.

"All their important bases having anything to do with space-based assets have been destroyed," said Elle. "They even took out assets we didn't previously know about. The Chinese and Russians have both reached out to Barrington and asked for his cooperation as we locate those behind the attack."

"Chris, what about Max?" asked Stew. "Have you identified the problem with his processing speeds?"

"No, I think it's some kind of virus that's part of this coordinated attack. My Utah computing facility isn't far from Dugway. The attack caused an earthquake. The thorium reactors scrammed, knocking the entire facility offline. My team is working on it now, but there's extensive damage. Max is running at a snail's pace, and global internet traffic is almost at a standstill."

"Geez." Stew ran his hands over his bald head.

"Are you ready for the rest?" said Elle.

"You mean the HK problem?" asked Stew.

"HK?" asked Chris.

"The hunter-killer satellite array. It's offline. We're locked out of the system."

"Whoa, wait," said Chris. "I just heard about this. Those are the Star Wars defense satellites in low-earth orbit. Nuclear powered and armed with particle-beam weapons for taking out ICBMs, right?"

"Yes, ICBMs, among other things." Head bowed, Stew pinched the bridge of his nose with his thumb and forefinger. "I've had Max on it for hours. He can't figure it out, but I think that's directly related to the virus issue in his system. You need to get Max back online, Chris."

"The HKs may be responsible for the comms blackout," continued Elle. "Worst-case, they were used to destroy all six WSG-4 comsats, which are all offline. The US Geosynchronous Space Situational Awareness system is down. We believe the HKs also destroyed the Mobile User Objective sats, which act as a mobile-phone network for the military. The navy's UHFFO system is also down, so our ships can't talk to each other. It's a complete disaster."

Chris's phone rang. "This is Dugway. I need to take this call." He walked to a secluded corner. "Zelda, where are you?"

"Salt Lake City. They kicked all nonessential personnel out of Dugway."

"What? You're not nonessential. Who else is going to look after the . . ." Pausing, Chris cautiously checked his surroundings. "The thing?"

"I went back down to A-139. The lab is damaged but intact. I got the reactor reinstalled, but we have a couple bigger problems. The lab that manufactures element 115 was destroyed in the attack. All the reactor fuel is buried or destroyed. The TR is dead in the water until we get element 115."

"That's just great," Chris said in frustration. "It's not like we can just hop on down to Walmart and pick up some intergalactic fuel."

"Don't be a jerk. I know that. Look, I think there's another source of element 115. It's a rumor I heard years ago, a total long shot. I need to work some old contacts. But we have another problem."

"This gets worse?"

"Yeah, even if we get the 115, we can't fly the TR-3B. All the pilots are dead."

"What? In the attack?"

"They were in a briefing in one of the hangars on the main ramp when the base went up. They all died."

Chris paced nervously. "OK, how about this? I'll work on a solution to the pilot problem. You work on the element 115. I'll call you in three hours. Copy?"

"Copy," said Zelda, and the line went dead. Chris walked back to the command console.

"Everything OK?" asked Stew.

"No, but I'll figure it out." Chris knew he didn't sound convincing. "It's related to our—uh, little *project* out at Dugway. You know the one I'm talking about, right?"

Stew looked up from the monitor over the top of his narrow-rimmed glasses. "Did the *project* survive the attack?"

The others standing around the table looked at Stew and Chris, confused.

"Yes, but we have other problems. We need—"

Max's voice came over the operation room's speaker system. "Sir, I have a possible hit on Mahan."

CHAPTER 38

WASHINGTON HILTON
WASHINGTON, D.C.

"Mr. President, is there any way I can convince you, sir?" pleaded Barrington's chief of staff. "This is an extremely high-risk situation. The director of the Secret Service has asked me to appeal to you personally, sir. I think we should cancel your appearance and return to the White House."

The president looked out the bulletproof window of his limousine, affectionately called "the Beast" by the Secret Service, and waved at onlookers as the vehicle approached the Hilton's portico. "Is Mills in position?"

"Yes, sir, the vice president is at Mount Weather with the First Lady, monitoring the situation and this event. There is nothing to report at this time."

"Very well," Barrington said. "I've made up my mind. I'm doing the White House Correspondents' Dinner. The country needs to see me out in public, and they need to see me in a lighthearted environment like this dinner. It will help put the public at ease as we try to figure out this mess."

"What if they hit the hotel?"

"What if? They have weapons that can hit Langley and Space Command. That means they can get to me almost anywhere, including the White House. In fact, I'm probably lucky they didn't kill me."

Leaning back in his seat, the chief of staff swallowed hard.

When the Beast came to a stop, a nervous bodyguard opened the president's door. Inside the hotel, the flashing of cameras and screaming of fans, as well as the shouts of a few protesters, filled the vast lobby.

A horde of Secret Service agents escorted the president through the crowd. As the entourage entered the banquet hall, the audience of journalists, celebrities, and titans of industry stood and vigorously applauded President Barrington. Although some in attendance were opposed to the president and his policies, a feeling of unity and patriotism had swept the country after the attacks on America's military and intelligence apparatuses in a way not seen since the September 2001 terror attacks.

Barrington took his seat near the podium, and late-night TV host Stephen Colbert stepped to the microphone to warm up the audience.

Lost in thought over the crisis facing the country, Barrington tuned Colbert out. He covertly looked down at his phone, hoping Stew Brimhall would send an update on the attacks, but the screen remained blank.

"Ladies and gentlemen, President Michael Barrington," said Colbert. The room erupted in a standing ovation. Barrington, still staring down at his phone, didn't move. The president of the White House Correspondents' Association—a reporter from ABC News—nudged him gently.

Springing to his feet, Barrington slipped the phone into his breast pocket.

"Whatcha doin' there, Mr. President?" Colbert asked as the president approached the stand. "Catching up on cat videos?"

The audience exploded with laughter and continued their applause. Barrington turned a slight shade of red but smiled broadly.

Colbert put his arm around the president. "It's OK, sir, it's OK." He turned back to the audience. "I think someone got started a little early tonight, folks." Making a drunken facial expression, the comedian tipped his hand to his face like he was drinking an imaginary brew. The audience erupted in laughter and applause again as Colbert patted the president on the back and took his seat.

"Thank you, Stephen. You know, I was just catching up on the game. Looks like my Buffalos are trouncing your Wildcats."

Colbert gave him a lighthearted thumbs-down.

Barrington adjusted himself and took on a more serious tone. "Good evening, ladies and gentlemen. Welcome to the annual White House Correspondents' Dinner, the night when Washington's biggest narcissists celebrate the one thing they love the most: themselves." Laughter filled the room again.

"I spend most of my time trying to avoid all of you, so it's good to be here tonight actually talking to you." The audience laughed politely. Barrington was notorious for his hatred of press conferences and his general disdain for the White House press corps.

"But in all seriousness," the president continued, "I feel I should take a moment to address the devastating attacks on several military installations and our intelligence community that occurred earlier this week."

A swell of anticipation overcame the audience as everyone focused intently on the president.

CHAPTER 39

ORION'S SPEAR OPERATIONS CENTER
NEW YORK CITY

What do you have, Max?" Chris asked eagerly.

"There is a meeting of avatars taking place inside an Oculus Rift MMO game known as *Echo VR*." Max displayed the game's view onscreen. It looked like the inside of a futuristic space station. "The players are in a secret room and presenting hand gestures. These gestures are congruent with those we recovered in the Order's file archives. They have somehow overridden the game's OS and architectural protocols. No outside avatar is allowed to enter the room, which appears to be a hack in the game's code. The room is not supposed to exist."

Chris looked at Stew. "Please tell me you have an Oculus—"

"Grab a headset," Stew yelled to Elle, "and call up Raven." Raven was the twenty-two-year-old former gaming champion who, eighteen months earlier, had used a microdrone to kill the infamous assassin Black, saving Mike Mayberry's life. Since then, Raven insisted everyone at the CIA call him—well, Raven.

Chris stepped into the virtual-reality room located just off the main operations center, where a VR view of the game populated every surface of the room, including the floor and ceiling, giving him the sense of being in the game without wearing a VR headset. In one corner, a glass window opened onto an observation room from which Stew and Elle watched. They were connected directly to Chris's comms and could hear every word he heard inside the game.

"Comms check," Stew said from behind the glass window.

"Copy, comms check, Main," said Chris. "Max, identify players closing in on the room. We need to hack their player profiles and hijack an avatar before it reaches the room's outer door."

"Sir, this is risky," said Max. "Once the players realize the intrusion, they will notify the Order."

"It's a chance we have to take to get inside, even if briefly. Try to pinpoint the physical locations of the room's players."

"Sir, there is another way," said Max. "I am examining the game's code and have found a virtual air duct above the room where the meeting is currently taking place."

"Why would they put air ducts in a VR game?" asked Chris. "It's not like they're breathing real air."

Just then, Raven ran into the room with the VR headset in hand. "The ducts are secret passageways in the game, dude. I'll drive. You talk." Raven slid on the sleek VR headset and grabbed the hand controllers. His view populated around the VR room for everyone to see.

Chris watched as Raven looked at his robotic blue-and-purple hands and oriented himself in the game.

"You ready, bro?" asked Raven.

"Let's go," said Chris. Raven let his hands off the controls. Max moved the avatar down a maze of passageways until the robot reached what appeared to be a virtual control room.

"The duct is directly above you," said Max.

Raven looked up at the opening. "OK, activating wrist rockets." He pushed the B and Y buttons to ignite the miniature rocket thrusters on the avatar's wrists. Rising into the large duct opening, the avatar grabbed on to a pole extending up the vertical airshaft. As Raven made hand-over-hand gestures, the avatar climbed to another opening.

"That's cool," said Chris as Raven kept climbing through the mazelike vent system, following Max's directions. The scene looked like the inside of a large office building's futuristic HVAC system. Soon, Raven reached an opening with another pole plunging down the center of a shaft to a virtual room below.

Looking cautiously over the edge, Raven saw a group of avatars standing around what looked like an altar.

"That's the meeting," said Max. "Proceed with caution."

Raven reached out to the pole and began descending headfirst into the room below. At what appeared to be fifteen virtual feet above the meeting, Raven stopped and held the avatar's position inside the shaft.

"Turn up the volume," Chris instructed. Raven reached out into the air and turned a virtual dial. The conversation in the virtual room filled the VR room.

"All hail Cain," intoned the voices. "All hail Master Mahan."

A Shirley Temple avatar complete with curly locks in a bow, red polka-dot dress, and a lollipop stood at the front of the group. When she spoke, her voice boomed like that of a grown man.

Chris immediately knew it was Mahan, and he trembled with anxiety and anticipation.

"Ladies and gentlemen, the first phase of the Dawn of the Cimeters is a success." The avatar of the classic midcentury child star slowly paced the room. "Thousands of years ago, when I killed my brother with my own primitive blade, I could never have imagined a weapon with the power and fury of Thor's Hammer. Today, the control of that weapon, like its ancient relative, is firmly and literally in my hand. I will again unleash Thor's Hammer with eager anticipation of death. Of horror. Of suffering."

"Hail Cain, master of murder," chanted the avatars. "Hail Master Mahan."

"Cain?" Chris said under his breath. "Impossible." He looked back at Stew, who shrugged.

"The space-based weapons and intelligence apparatuses of our enemies are now useless. The rods from the gods—as some of you refer to them—have performed as promised. Soon, the head of the snake will be cut off. Target packages are locked. AriesX is currently being deployed. Nothing can stop us now."

"AriesX? Stew, are you getting this?" Chris asked into his comms. He turned back and looked at Stew and Elle. Stew watched the VR screen with resolve. Elle typed frantically into her mobile device.

"Victory is ours, Master Mahan," said one of the avatars. "You are indeed the master of mayhem and murder. Hail Cain."

"Hail Cain," repeated the others.

"Sir, we have an intrusion," boomed an unknown voice through the audio. The virtual room immediately pixilated into stark white nothingness, and the other avatars dissipated into virtual thin air. To Chris and Raven's left, the Shirley Temple avatar stared emotionlessly.

"Identify yourself," said Cain.

"Get out of there," Stew yelled into Chris's comms. "Shut it off!"

Chris waved Stew off and turned to the avatar of the classic movie star. "Chris Thomas."

Raven said nothing, but Chris saw a stream of sweat roll down the gamer's face. Chris muted his mic and said quietly, "It's only virtual. Don't lose your concentration."

Cain's avatar sneered. "I should have known. It's a pleasure to finally meet you, Dr. Thomas."

"No pleasure for me whatsoever," said Chris.

The white room changed to black, and the Shirley Temple avatar dissipated into digital nothingness. A virtual control room with a futuristic conference table suddenly formed up in billions of high-definition pixels all around Chris and Raven. Outside the virtual, triangle-shaped windows, lava plunged off dark digital cliffs and flowed in glowing orange rivers.

"What is this?" asked Chris, muting his mic again.

"Dude," said Raven. "It's Mustafar, from episode three."

"Episode three?"

"Bro, *Star Wars*. This is Darth Vader's planet. We're inside his lair. I think we're inside the *Vader Immortal* game. How do you not know that, dude?"

"I don't get out much," said Chris.

Raven looked down at his hands. He now held a lightsaber. "Oh, sweet. I'm a Jedi!" He pushed a button on the hand control to activate the lightsaber. A white blade exploded from its silver hilt. "Dude, we have the white lightsaber. That is so cool." Raven swung the lightsaber around, inspecting the virtual weapon with a big grin.

Chris jumped back slightly when Darth Vader unexpectedly entered the room, holding a red lightsaber. "The Order of Baphomet welcomes you to Mustafar, Chris Thomas," Cain said in Darth Vader's voice. Slowly backing up to Chris, Raven held his lightsaber defensively. Cain's avatar swung his lightsaber back and forth as if warming up for a fight. The two avatars paced cautiously around the futuristic conference table at the center of the room.

"I'm afraid you're too late, Mormon fool," started Cain, still swinging his lightsaber.

"We don't like to be called Mormons anymore," Chris said through the avatar. "It's The Church of Jesus Chr—"

"Shut up," said Cain. "The Order will finally destroy the poor and inferiors who feed on this planet once and for all. We will now establish the State. All will bow to my power. All governments who oppose us will fall. All religions will be dismantled. The State is now the family. The survivors of the new world will work under the direction of the State to restore the Mother to her previous glory."

The Vader avatar leapt over the table and landed in front of Raven's Jedi avatar, bearing down with his red lightsaber. Raven raised his white lightsaber to block the blow. Vader moved in, facing Raven through the sparks of the clashing lightsabers.

"All will bow to the Mother and the Son. All will bow to me, Master Mahan. I alone will rule the earth."

Raven pushed Cain away and slashed the lightsaber across the avatar's chest. Virtual sparks flew from Vader's chest, and Cain laughed as the game flashed red, indicating a hit.

"I know the weapon is space-based," said Chris. "Let me guess—tungsten rods fired from low-earth orbit?"

"You're too late this time, Thomas. And exactly how will you stop it? Are you going to throw a rock at it? You have no way to get into space or stop the rods falling from orbit. Max is out of this fight. I alone control the heavens and the earth. Surrender."

Cain swung wildly at Raven, screaming in rage, but Raven dodged the advance, leaping over the table to the other side of the virtual room.

"You have no idea of the power that is Thor's Hammer," said Cain, raising a balled fist into the air.

"I've seen its handiwork," Chris said.

"That was but a small taste of what comes next." Cain lowered his lightsaber, and Raven stood ready. "The rods will hit their targets precisely at nine times the speed of a bullet. The kinetic force that builds behind the rods contains enough power to destroy a megacity. It's all the advantages of a nuke without any of the downsides that would harm the Mother."

The two avatars again closed on each other with their lightsabers raised.

"If only the Lamanites had possessed such a weapon," Cain said. "Think of the meaningless wars and millions of lost lives that could have been avoided. I know because I was there. I saw it with my own eyes. And so it will be today, Ephraimite. Thor's Hammer is the cleansing fire of a new dawn for humanity. Those left will rise from the ashes and create a new world—my world."

The Vader avatar swung wildly at Raven, then withdrew again. "I will destroy your embarrassing riches, Chris Thomas. I will lay you out, spread eagle, and expose you for the fraud you are. Your absurd theater of a life is over. The reckoning has arrived, and now you will share my misery."

Vader swung again at Raven's avatar, which deflected the blows while landing several of its own.

"You think you are safe in your little ivory tower high above the streets of Manhattan?" asked Cain. "I own those streets, fool."

"How does he know where we are?" yelled Stew into comms.

Chris didn't reply. Staying focused on his adversary, he laid a hand reassuringly on Raven's shoulder.

"Barrington is a dead man walking," said Cain. "Or I should say *talking*, given his current location."

"Where is the president?" Stew yelled over comms. Chris glanced over just in time to see Stew running from the observation room. "Get me the president's Secret Service detail now!"

The Darth Vader avatar lunged at Raven's avatar again. Their lightsabers touched, crossing at the center of each blade.

"And your wife, your precious Leah," Cain said, gaining Chris's full attention. "She is infertile. I am the one who made that so."

Chris felt blistering rage. "What did you *do*?"

Cain's wicked laughter filled the virtual void. "You don't understand, Chris Thomas. Killing you is easy. First, you must be made to suffer, and suffer you will. I will torture and kill everyone you love, but she will be the last. In the end, I will remove her liver with a dull knife and make you watch every agonizing second as she hopelessly calls your pathetic name."

Chris grabbed Raven's hand and shoved the virtual lightsaber into Vader's chest. The avatar and the entire Mustafar scene pixelated into black nothingness.

"I'm coming for you," said Chris.

"Do your worst, boy."

"You can count on my absolute best."

CHAPTER 40

WASHINGTON HILTON
WASHINGTON, D.C.

The hotel's waitstaff moved stealthily among the round tables, delivering dessert plates to each VIP as the president concluded his address. Barrington briefly took notice of the catering manager, who was dressed in a black tuxedo and weaving his way through the tables, directing waiters and examining each guest's setting. Barrington barely noticed the manager's course running closer and closer to the podium.

"As we look back on historical tragedies like Pearl Harbor, September 11, and the Aries attack, we remember the shock we felt in the immediate aftermath of each crisis. With these latest attacks, the Chinese and the Russians now face the same challenges. United, our countries will work together to bring those responsible for these senseless attacks to justice. In time, we will emerge a stronger nation and global community."

Barrington looked directly into the TV camera. "Now, my fellow Americans, here and wherever you may be in this great country, please join me. Let's observe a moment of silence and reverently bow our heads in remembrance, prayer, and thanksgiving to honor the tens of thousands who have died."

Gripping the podium, the president bowed his head. All in attendance followed his lead.

During the silence, several Secret Service agents positioned just off the main stage put their hands on their earpieces, then looked at each other in sheer horror.

"Alamo! Alamo!" whispered the agent closest to the president into his comms. He and a female agent from the opposite side of the stage sprinted for the podium. Barrington looked up, startled by the approaching agents.

At an almost incalculable speed, the catering manager, now only twenty feet from the president, pulled a strange-looking device from inside his tuxedo coat.

"All hail Mahan!" the catering manager raged.

The audience gasped and looked up from the moment of silence, searching for the source of yelling. The Secret Service agents, now in a dead sprint, pulled their weapons.

Barrington looked at the catering manager just in time to see him fire a weapon. Face flushed with terror, the president tried to duck, but in front of the entire room and a viewing audience of millions, President Barrington's head exploded into hundreds of bloody pieces.

CHAPTER 41

ORION'S SPEAR HEADQUARTERS
NEW YORK CITY

Stew ran yelling from the virtual-reality room and into the operations center. "Get me the president's Secret Ser—"

"Sir," yelled one of the comms technicians, jumping up from his console. Stew stopped cold. "President Barrington has been assassinated."

Gasps filled the operations center, and everyone in the room froze and looked at Stew.

"Pull the video from the event," Stew coolly commanded as he looked over the room. But shock had overcome the team. Some had their heads bowed. Others held each other in comfort. A few sat alone and quietly wept.

Stew clapped his hands, drawing the room's attention. "Pull it together. One team, one fight. You're Orion's Spear. The nation needs you right now. I demand absolute perfection from everyone in this room. Now, move!"

Instantly recovering, the team exploded into action.

Chris stood across the command console from Stew. He was trying to hold it together as best as he could, but everything was falling apart. Although he and the president hadn't seen eye to eye on many political issues, Chris considered Barrington something of a mentor. The news of his death hit him harder than he expected.

Worse, his brain kept running through tormenting scenarios of how Mahan could have possibly gotten to Leah. He tried to push those thoughts from his mind. He needed to focus on Barrington and Thor's Hammer.

"Receiving data dump," yelled an analyst from across the room.

"Max, analyze video," commanded Stew. "Chris, are you with me?"

Chris snapped out of his dismay. "Yes, sir. This is death by a thousand little cuts."

Stew continued to stare into his console. "This isn't a thousand little cuts. It's a thousand gaping wounds."

"Video up," said Max.

Security-camera footage of the assassination filled several screens in the ops center. Zooming in on the assassin and his weapon from several camera angles, Max re-created a three-dimensional view of the event. "Sir, the weapon is 3D printed and appears to have been manufactured using a nonmetallic, high-density plastic composite. It is a single-shot weapon."

A slow-motion view of the projectile leaving the weapon was displayed on the main screen. Max grabbed a screenshot and, above the command console, reconstructed a holographic schematic of the projectile. "Sir, the projectile is a 1.5-ounce magnesium-tipped, twelve-gauge, high-explosive slug."

"No wonder his head exploded," said Stew bluntly. "At that range, he didn't stand a chance."

"Max, what do we have on the assassin?" asked Chris.

"Analyzing," said Max. "Sir, I have accessed available federal and state databases. The assassin is Mitchell Donovan. African-American. Age forty-six. Catering manager since 2019 at ABC Catering Services, based in Fairfax, Virginia. No priors. No FBI or NSA flags. No indication of any criminal activity in his record."

"We need to interview him now," said Chris.

"He's dead," said an analyst at the command console. "The Secret Service shot him."

"Sir!" yelled another analyst from across the room. "The Russian president and Chinese general secretary have also been assassinated."

Several gasps sounded in concert across the room. News reports and social-media feeds from around the globe filled the monitor bank.

"What is going on?" Stew asked, watching intensely.

"It's a decapitation attack on a global scale," said Chris. "Based on what Mahan just said, I have a feeling the worst is yet to come."

CHAPTER 42

WEEHAWKEN WATERFRONT PARK
WEEHAWKEN, NEW JERSEY

The truck driver walked over to the trooper in charge to see what he was doing on the iPad. By the chevrons on the trooper's pressed shirt, the driver could tell he was a sergeant.

Just then, mechanical sounds began emanating from the five trailers in the middle of the soccer field, stopping the driver in his tracks. As he watched, the roofs of all five trailers split open lengthwise, and the roofs and sidewalls fell to the ground like discarded cardboard boxes. The center trailer contained an array of hardware, and the four corner trailers held enormous hydraulic robotic arms that whined as they moved into place.

"Look at that," said one of the drivers in amazement.

The four robotic arms extended, then plugged into large sockets on the center trailer. When the four arms were stretched out to their full lengths, a rotor rose out of each arm's far end. Smaller robotic limbs then attached helicopter blades to the rotors, and the blades started slowly rotating.

"I'll be," exclaimed another driver. "It's some kind of military drone."

"Yep," said the sergeant. Then he nonchalantly pulled out his Colt .45 and shot the driver in the head.

The other four drivers swore and ran for cover, but the troopers opened fire, dropping them all onto the soccer field.

The sergeant holstered his .45 and pushed another button on the iPad.

On the center trailer, a compartment opened to reveal eight missiles. Several troopers climbed up to a weapons bay and unsheathed twin 20mm Vulcan cannons. After locking the magazine feeds into position, they jumped off the center trailer and gave the sergeant a thumbs-up.

The machine's four massive rotors spun faster. The sergeant traced his finger over the iPad screen, and the Vulcan cannons moved accordingly.

"Weapons system activated," said a deep voice from the sergeant's iPad speaker. "Automation enabled. Attack vector locked."

Smiling, the sergeant said, "Everything is set. Executing now, Master."

The drone's rotors accelerated to full speed. With powerful wind and deafening noise, the hulking menace surged hundreds of feet into the air, then flew over the Hudson River toward New York City.

CHAPTER 43

MIKE MAYBERRY RESIDENCE
BLUEMONT, VIRGINIA

Mike Mayberry was so exhausted he almost missed the turn down the familiar dirt road.

Upon receiving news of the attack on Langley, he'd immediately left New York to offer his assistance in the search and recovery process. When he'd reached his former employer's facility, the devastation was almost more than he could have imagined.

In the massive hole a half mile in diameter where the George Bush Center for Intelligence had once proudly stood, Mike and numerous others combed through the mess of bent steel beams, dirt, glass, and other wreckage. They found many bodies but no survivors. As the days and nights wore on, the situation grew more and more morose.

When he was finally ordered to go home, he reluctantly complied.

Mike Mayberry lived on twenty pristine acres that served mostly as a horse pasture, just outside the town of Bluemont, Virginia. The former Delta Force commando purchased the property when he retired from the army and was recruited into the CIA's elite Special Activities Division. Now, he headed up paramilitary operations at Orion's Spear.

Mike rounded a corner, and his 1960s-era, three-bedroom brick rambler came into view. Behind the house, a dilapidated horse barn sat in the pasture, where his horses grazed peacefully. A reassuring calm he hadn't felt in a long time washed over him.

He was home.

After parking his truck in the garage, Mike began unloading his gear onto the kitchen table. As he unpacked his equipment, checked his weapons, and organized his kit, he suddenly stopped as a heavy, overwhelming sadness settled over him. Feeling momentarily dizzy, he reached for an old chair and sat down. His vision blurred, and his ears rang. He shook his head, trying to come back to his senses. In his mind's eye, he saw many of his dead friends, fellow operatives and patriots, and brothers and sisters who had died hunting the Order over the last eighteen months.

Mike started to sweat and breathe heavily. And then the battle-hardened soldier broke down and sobbed like a child.

After a minute, he stood, drew a deep breath, and tried to regain control. But he'd lost the fight with his raw emotions. Overwhelmed, he fell back into the chair and let out a wail unlike anything he'd ever experienced in his life.

"Stop!" Mike yelled to himself. He slammed his fist over and over again into his chest, then took in several more breaths. After several minutes, he was finally able to compose himself.

Then he was calm, surrounded by silence. He wiped his eyes and stared out the back door into his pasture. After a few moments, the phone on the table rang, pulling him further out from under his emotional avalanche.

It was Chris Thomas. Mike drew one more breath, cleared his voice, and answered, "Go for Knife."

He listened intensely. "Assassinated? When?"

Chris explained the details.

"Copy, Vanguard," said Mike. "I'll be on a plane out of Andrews in less than an hour."

When the phone went quiet, Mike started repacking his kit. As he worked, an odd feeling came over him. He stopped what he was doing and focused on the sensation that he was being watched. Out in the pasture, his horses were galloping and acting strangely.

"That's weird," Mike said to himself as he observed the animals. "Oh sh—!" he yelled, diving backward onto the kitchen floor. The next second, the sliding glass door exploded all over him.

Reaching for the kitchen table, Mike grabbed his loadout kit. Then he cautiously bear-crawled into the living room and peeked out the front window. A contingency of men—about fifteen in all—moved swiftly toward the house in standard platoon formation, weapons ready to fire. They wore unidentifiable full-body armor and hefted belt-fed H&K 417s.

This isn't good.

Heaving the kit onto his back, Mike ran into a bedroom and looked covertly through the side window. Another group of fifteen approached his flank from the pasture. Half the group was setting a perimeter, the other half preparing to breach the house. They were outfitted and armed the same as the men approaching in front.

OK, this really isn't good.

Just then, large-caliber rounds pierced the front of the small brick home. As splintered wood, drywall, and other debris exploded around him, Mike dropped to his belly and maneuvered to an access hatch in the bedroom floor. As he lowered himself into the narrow, shallow crawl space, flanking rounds tore through the side and back of the house. He pulled the hatch shut after him.

Lying on dirt and covered in cobwebs, Mike found himself encased in the old home's concrete foundation, temporarily safe from the impossible barrage exploding overhead. He reached into the pack and began to assemble his Viper suit, which was custom-fit from head to toe. The bulletproof outer shell could take serious punishment, but it wasn't designed to withstand continual blows from .308-caliber rounds.

Mike had trained to put on the Viper suit in under sixty seconds. Even lying on his back in the dark, he was able to suit up in an impressive thirty-seven seconds. To finish, he pulled out the titanium and Kevlar helmet, attached the hardened oxygen mask, and slid the face shield over his face.

He heard muffled yelling from above and knew the front and rear of the house had been breached. The assassins, whoever they were, were now methodically clearing the house room by room.

"Max? Max, are you online?" Mike hoped the local instance of the AI installed in the suit's hardware was active, but Max was silent. Mike reached into his pack for his gun, but it wasn't there. He'd left it on the kitchen table.

Mike powered up the computer on his left forearm and activated the suit's heads-up display. A 3D augmented-reality image of the home's floorplan, including the real-time location of his enemy, formed on the face mask's HUD.

Only ten guys? What's the problem? Your buddies too afraid to join the party?

Rolling over, Mike crouched directly under the access door. One of the enemy stood right above it.

"He's not here," the assassin said. "Double back to the perimeter."

"No, he's got to be here," yelled another man. "We had him on thermals. The ceiling and floor. Open fire."

At that command, Mike burst through the access door. The man standing above didn't stand a chance. From underneath, Mike pulled the sidearm from the man's thigh holster. With his other hand, he grabbed the killer's leg to throw him off balance. He landed right next to Mike. Without hesitation, Mike flipped the man, shoved his sidearm into the man's exposed neck, and pulled the trigger.

One down. Twenty-nine to go.

Still standing in the crawl space, Mike reached for the dead man's H&K 417, immediately noticing its rounds were armor-piercing. He opened fire just as two more assassins burst through the bedroom doorway. Both men fell instantly. The seventies-era wood-panel wall next to Mike disintegrated as the fire team in the living room opened up, shooting wildly in his direction. Mike temporarily ducked down into the crawl space.

Then he heard the sound he'd been waiting for: reloading. Mike burst out of the hole. Using the Viper's AR system to target the enemy, he fired methodically through the wall. Five men in the living room fell to the floor. Dropping the empty gun, he pulled a freshly loaded rifle from one of the dead assassin's hands.

"You won't be needing this, right?" Mike asked, racking the weapons charger.

Two men rushed Mike from the kitchen, hitting him with three rounds. Miraculously, none of the armor-piercing rounds penetrated the Viper suit. Mike pulled the trigger and shot both men through their face masks. They fell as Mike passed them, scanning for his next target.

The house was temporarily clear. Only smoke, destruction, and death surrounded Mike Mayberry as he dropped the 417 and fell to his knees. His faceplate retracted, and he checked himself for wounds, but he was lucky.

An alert dinged in his helmet as his faceplate fell back in place. The proximity alert showed the remaining twenty enemy advancing on the house.

Mike calculated his odds. He'd been in a similar situation before, but this was different.

I can't hold off twenty.

CHAPTER 44

ORION'S SPEAR HEADQUARTERS
NEW YORK CITY

Mahan knows where we are," said Chris. "We need to be ready. Where's Vice President Mills?"

"She's at Mount Weather," replied Stew. "She's safe there."

"I don't know, Stew," Chris said cynically. "I'm kind of looking at the situation and wondering. Are you sure?"

"They can't get to her at Mount Weather, Chris. The Secret Service is now transporting the chief justice via underground maglev train to swear in Mills as president."

"Max Def activated, analyzing threat," said Max unexpectedly over the room's audio system.

"Max, sitrep," yelled Chris.

"Sir, we have a proximity warning. Unidentified aircraft in restricted airspace," an operations analyst called out in a slight panic.

"On screen," said Stew. A large, strange-looking quadcopter filled the massive center monitor and was moving rapidly toward them over the Hudson River. Gasps and looks of confusion echoed throughout the room.

"What . . . is . . . that?" asked Stew.

"Radar locked on unidentified aircraft," said Max. "Proximity defenses activated."

The room's alarm blared. Mechanical sounds emanated from the weapons hold on the floor directly above the operations center. The staff looked around. Some looked confused, others terrified.

Max's voice sounded again. "You are in imminent danger. Initiate emergency evacuation protocols. All nonessential personnel, evacuate the premises now."

"Everybody move to the—" Before Elle could finish, the entire western exterior wall of the operations center exploded.

Thick concrete chunks, sharp rebar, and fire blasted through the operations center. Computer equipment exploded. Screams and panic filled the room. The fire alarm sounded, and the fire-suppression system sent thick, white clouds of carbon dioxide into the room.

Knocked to the floor by the initial blast, Chris had been shielded by the elevated central-command table. Dazed, he sat up slowly and checked himself. Blood oozed from his nose and ears. He got to his knees, shook his head, and peered over the top of the command console.

Bodies lay strewn all over the floor. Chris felt his face contort at the sight of blood and eviscerated human bodies. Although his vision was blurred and the room was filled with thick carbon-dioxide fog, he could count at least nineteen bodies. The unbearable smell of burning human flesh caused him to vomit.

Chris wiped his mouth and yelled, "Stew!" but there was no response.

Hovering outside the breached wall, the flying machine became visible through the ebbing fire-suppressant fog. The massive quadcopter was the size of a football field. It began firing its cannons indiscriminately at the survivors of the initial blast. A few survivors grabbed weapons and fired back.

Time seemed to slow as the math in Chris's field of vision calculated every visible aspect of the quadcopter. In less than a second, he'd run through several calculations in his head.

"Max, go for the rotors!" Chris yelled as loud as he could, hoping the AI could hear him over the deafening battle thirteen hundred feet above the Manhattan streets. "They're not armored."

Just then, the cannons fired at the command desk. Chris ran for cover, dodging behind an exploding server rack.

"Weapons free," said Max. "Firing."

A thunderous roar erupted from above the operations center as Max let loose on the quadcopter with .50-caliber machine guns and 40mm grenade launchers. Taking a vicious salvo of fire from the Max-controlled weapons, the hunter had become the hunted. The quadcopter retargeted its cannons on the new threat above it, temporarily freeing the operations center from the flying nightmare.

Still dazed, Chris tried moving his feet, but he was caught in some data cables attached to the server rack he hid behind. He tried tugging on the cables, but his feet wouldn't move. He reached down and pushed a button on his belt buckle. He felt the click of the release, and a tiny, heart-shaped, serrated blade appeared between his fingers.

"Thank you, Grandpa," Chris said. He sat up and began slicing the server cables.

"Chris!" he heard from somewhere in the smoke and haze, but he couldn't identify the voice. As he sliced through the last cable confining his movement, suddenly he felt a powerful tug from behind.

Chris tried to see who was pulling him over the blood-covered floor. In one motion, he pivoted unsteadily up onto his feet, running with the person pulling him toward the burning lobby. Stopping short in front of the elevators, the person propelled Chris into an open car, where he slammed into the back wall.

Another blast rocked the building. The quadcopter was tearing into the building's weapons platform, sending secondary explosions down into the operations center. At that moment, through the smoke, fire, and suppressant fog, Chris was finally able to make out his rescuer, who knelt just outside the elevator door.

It was Elle Danley.

"Elle," he cried out. "Get in here!"

Fire and electricity sparked all around as Elle slapped a magazine into an M4 carbine. Her blonde hair was singed, her clothes were charred, and her skin was covered in second and third-degree burns. One of her eyeballs had turned a dark crimson red, indicating a brain injury. Tears streamed from her eyes, cutting through the blood and burns covering her beautiful face.

"You're all that's left, Chris," Elle said calmly as she pulled back the charger on the rifle. "Don't fail."

As the elevator door closed, Chris saw Elle pivot on bended knee and fire on full automatic at the impossible target. She yelled like a brave warrior as the damaged quadcopter repositioned its unmerciful cannons at the operations center.

CHAPTER 45

MIKE MAYBERRY RESIDENCE
BLUEMONT, VIRGINIA

As the assassins approached the house, Mike took a deep breath and closed his eyes. He dug deep inside himself, searching for reserve strength, then opened his eyes and sprinted through the kitchen and into the garage.

The enemy relentlessly opened up on their target, the machine-gun rounds again decimating the decades-old home. The wood, brick, electrical wires, and dated furniture exploded as a new wave of the enemy closed in to finish the job their comrades had started.

Mike scurried to the back of his F-150, opened the tailgate, and flung himself under the fiberglass bed cover. Pushing several items out of the way, he began searching for a particular device. Meanwhile, the enemy's rounds pierced the truck as the hit team closed in.

Finally, Mike saw it—his ace. For a few seconds, he stared at the device in relief.

"Well, I guess we're about to find out how good this Viper suit really is," he murmured as he input a code on the device's keypad. A red light appeared on the computer strapped to his left forearm, and another red light lit up on the device.

Leaving the truck bed, Mike ran back toward the kitchen. An assassin opened the kitchen door and took aim, but Mike hit him like a linebacker.

Several more men rushed in through the hole that had once been the kitchen's back door. They leveled their 417s on Mike, who sprinted for a small window just left of the living room fireplace.

Rounds slammed into the back of Mike's Viper suit as he dove through the glass pane. Midair, he hit the red button on his forearm computer.

One second later, the house, the remaining assassins, and Mike Mayberry exploded into oblivion.

CHAPTER 46

80 HUDSON YARDS
NEW YORK CITY

Several rounds from the quadcopter cannons smashed through the elevator's ceiling as the door closed.

"Elle! Max!" Chris yelled in terror as the elevator began its descent. After what seemed like an eternity, it stopped, but the door did not open. Chris slid his fingers between the two doors and pulled hard. They grudgingly opened.

He was between floors. The fire alarm blared, and he could hear the distant sounds of automatic gunfire and explosions from above. He pulled himself up to the floor above and assessed his surroundings. It was an unoccupied level under construction.

Chris walked unsteadily to a west-facing window and looked up just in time to see one of the quadcopter's arms explode. With its other three rotors still turning, the fiery mass plunged into the Hudson River, exploding on impact.

Chris fell to his knees, clenching his chest.

"I detect a heightened state of distress," came Max's voice unexpectedly. Chris felt around for his phone, but it was gone. "Medical emergency services are inbound to 80 Hudson Yards. Would you like me to dispatch them to your specific location?"

"Max? You're there?"

"Yes, sir. I am installed in the infrastructure on this floor, including sensor array, mic, and speakers."

"No, Max. Get them to the wounded."

"Copy."

"Max, sitrep," said Chris as he limped toward the fire escape.

"Sir, the enemy aircraft has been destroyed by the Max Def system. The building's defense systems have sustained heavy damage. One of the four Gatling guns is still operational, but the weapon has only 962 high-explosive rounds remaining."

"Max, the people—Orion's Spear," Chris said breathlessly as he reached the staircase door. When he opened it, thick, black smoke poured into the room. He coughed and waved his arms.

"Sir, my camera and sensor array were damaged in the attack, but I am sensing no sign of life in the operations center."

"What?" Chris felt tears fill his eyes.

"Sir, the top five floors of this building are on fire. You must evacuate immediately. I have contacted the G700 flight crew. The aircraft is ready to leave from Teterboro when you arrive. I recommend consulting a grief counselor to help you cope with this traumatic experience."

"How do I get out of here?"

"You must push through the smoke in the stairwell. Sensors indicate that after three floors, the smoke will dissipate. I have ordered an Uber to transport you to the airport."

"An Uber?"

"Yes. A Tesla Model 3 with 83 percent battery life remaining. The driver, Raul, has a 4.6-star rating. The vehicle should provide you inconspicuous cover to Teterboro. I have notified Mrs. Leah and Ms. Amal that you are safe and being transported from the scene."

Even though Chris was devastated, he couldn't help but feel some relief. As usual, Max had thought of everything.

CHAPTER 47

MOUNT WEATHER MILITARY INSTALLATION
LOCATION CLASSIFIED

"Are you trying to tell me Chris Thomas orchestrated an attack on Orion's Spear and somehow spared his own life?" General Westinghouse glared insubordinately at President Mills. "That's absurd. You saw the video feed. He'd be dead if the staff hadn't sacrificed their lives in the process of evacuating him."

Sitting at a replica of the Resolute desk in an Oval Office reproduction deep inside Mount Weather, Mills scowled. She wasn't having it.

"One minute," said the video producer. "One minute, everyone."

"My forehead is shining again. Makeup, now." Mills snapped her fingers and looked into the monitor. Several women rushed past Westinghouse and went to work on her makeup.

"Madam President, please," said Westinghouse.

"Find him and arrest him. Or kill him. I don't care."

"Ten seconds," yelled the producer. Everyone scurried off the stage. The light on the camera went green, and Mills smiled.

"My fellow Americans . . ."

CHAPTER 48

GULFSTREAM 700
EN ROUTE TO UTAH

Chris watched Mills's address from the safety of his G700, unable to control his shaking hands. A feeling of foreboding overcame him as he paced nervously up and down the luxury plane's narrow aisle.

"I want to reiterate our long-standing policy," Mills said. "The United States does not negotiate with terrorists. Those responsible for the attacks and President Barrington's murder will feel the full wrath of the United States government.

"On behalf of the American people, I thank the many world leaders who have called to offer their condolences and assistance. Likewise, we extend our condolences to the people of Russia and China who have also lost leadership and suffered at the hands of these terrorists. America and our allies join with all who want peace and security in the world, and we stand as one to win this terrible war against tyranny.

"Tonight, I ask for your prayers as I take on the mantle of president of the United States. Although many of you do not hold my same political views, I ask for your support at this time of national tragedy and healing. This is a day when citizens from all walks of life must unite to preserve the American way. Our great nation has stood down enemies before, and we will do so again with steely resolve. None will forget this day, yet we go forward to defend freedom and all that is good and just in our world. Thank you. Good night. And may God bless America."

Chris turned off the feed. "Max, pull all the technical flight documents for the TR-3B. I need to see the digital flight manuals. Display them over the monitors."

"Initiating order, sir. What are your intentions, and how else can I be of assistance?"

Chris sat on the leather couch for a moment and looked himself over. His clothes were torn and bloody. His hair was singed, he had several superficial wounds and burns, and, oddly, he was missing a fingernail. Miraculously, his hearing seemed fine. He ran a towel over his head and then stared forward for several moments. When he noticed saliva filling his mouth, he reached for an airsickness bag just in time to catch the vomit.

"Sir, your mental state is compromised."

"Not now, Max," Chris said impatiently. "All the TR-3B pilots are dead. Max, you are installed to a local instance on the TR-3B, but the onboard computer lacks the power needed to run you at full computational speed. It's going to take both of us to fly it. Have you located Zelda yet? We're going to need her too."

"No, sir, Dr. Shakespeare is still missing."

In front of Chris, technical documents populated onto four seventy-five-inch monitors. "She might be in A-139 with the TR-3B," he said. "I hope she is. In the meantime, we need to be ready." Chris flew through the technical documents on the screen, processing thousands of words per minute.

"Sir, you have a text message from an unknown number with an active location-services ghost."

"Onscreen," said Chris. The message read: *125 North 8th Street, Klamath Falls, Oregon 13225. A-139.* "A-139. That's Zelda. Can you hack the ghost?"

"Sir, the message originated from a burner phone somewhere near Salt Lake City, Utah. I don't have precise coordinates."

"OK. 13225. That's not an Oregon zip code. That number is a clue. This can't be hard." Several equations populated Chris's vision. "I got it.

115 is the square root of 13225. The element 115 is at that address. Max, get me data on the address."

"The address traces to United Nuclear, a retail outlet that sells scientific equipment and supplies, including uranium ore. The owner is Dr. Bob Lazar, an Area-51 whistleblower the federal government accused of stealing element 115. The authorities never recovered the element 115 allegedly stolen by Dr. Lazar."

Max displayed numerous news articles and websites about Bob Lazar. At the same time, the AI kept processing technical flight information on the TR-3B for Chris, who internalized all the information before him as fast as Max could display it.

"This is all starting to make sense now," Chris said.

~

Several inflight hours passed as Chris continued to dive deeper into his understanding of the TR-3B's quantum flight mechanics.

"Sir, we're on initial approach to Michael Army Airfield," the pilot said over the intercom.

"I detect two F-35s on an intercept course for our aircraft," said Max.

"It's probably just an escort," said Chris.

"Sir, they have missile lock on us," said Max.

~

Chris looked out the side window of the G700's cockpit. Ten thousand feet over the Great Salt Lake, two sleek F-35 stealth fighters with open missile-bay doors flew in formation with the G700. Chris could tell his pilots were nervous.

"We are under presidential order to escort you to Michael Army Airfield, where you will be placed under arrest," radioed one of the F-35 pilots. "You are ordered to land. You have five minutes to comply, or you will be fired on."

Chris took off the headset and picked up his phone. "Max, call General Westinghouse."

Westinghouse picked up on the first ring. "Thomas, where are you?"

"I'm trying to get back into Dugway. Two F-35s are threatening to shoot me down if I don't land. I need your help."

"I can't help you. They're taking orders directly from President Mills. You're the only survivor of the attack on Orion's Spear, so she's convinced you're somehow involved with Mahan. Your military access and Majestic security clearance have been revoked. There's a warrant out for your arrest. She even put you on the FBI's Ten Most Wanted list."

"What are you talking about?" yelled Chris into the phone. The pilots looked at each other uneasily.

"I know, I know," Westinghouse said in almost a whisper. "I'm trying to fix it. I told her she was crazy. But she's out for your blood, son. Literally."

"What about Mike Mayberry. Any news?"

"His house was blown up, dead bodies everywhere, but none of them are Mike. He's missing."

"Sounds about right," Chris said, smirking.

"Now, comply with the order. She's serious. She will shoot you down. Land and don't resist arrest. If she sees you're cooperating, we can work this out."

"I can't do that, General. I'm the only one who can end this madness. If I have to stop and deal with this, we'll run out of time. You've got to get me access to the project. Mahan's weapon is space-based. I think it's a stealth satellite weapon, which explains how he took out Space Command and all our terrestrial antisatellite defenses and tracking stations. I'm trying to figure out a way to destroy the weapon before Mahan takes out a city and kills millions. Can't you just explain that to Mills? We're all on the same team here."

"That's not the way she sees it, Chris. Remember, the president is a temporary employee, and Mills was never part of the inside club. She doesn't have the clearance and has no idea what's at Dugway."

"Then tell her. It may be the only way she comes around."

There was a long pause on the other end of the phone. "Let me see what I can do, which might be nothing. If you're right about Mahan, then God help us all, son. But how are you going to escape those F-35s?"

"I have a few tricks up my sleeve," said Chris. "Never fight a bully on his own turf."

"OK, let me see what I can do on this end. Just use that big brain of yours to get yourself back into Dugway. And stay frosty. Everyone is out for you."

"Roger that, General." Chris hung up.

"Sir, the F-35s are giving us sixty seconds to comply, or they'll fire on us," said the panicked pilot.

"After everything I've been through the last couple of days, I'm not about to die here," said Chris. "Max, do your thing."

"Executing."

Chris sat behind the pilot and copilot with his face buried in his phone. Out of the corner of his eye, he saw the pilots watch in amazement as the F-35s suddenly diverted their course.

"What? How did you do that?" asked the pilot.

Chris ignored his question. "Our new destination is Klamath Falls, Oregon. Step on it."

CHAPTER 49

THE CRAFTSMAN BAR
SANTA MONICA, CALIFORNIA

Rand!" yelled Blair Alter.

Rand embraced his old friend, and the two men laughed and patted each other on the back. Blair gestured to two men dressed in shorts and casual Hawaiian button-downs. "Rand, this is Will and Tyrone. They served with me on Team Five after you left the navy."

"Cool," said Rand. "Have a seat. Drinks are on me."

Initially guarded, the men seemed to relax with Rand's offer of free drinks. He surmised they'd heard rumors about him within the secretive SEAL community. The four men selected a table at the back of the old bar, where Rand positioned himself so he could see everyone who entered and exited.

"How's your brother?" asked Blair.

"Levi? Oh, he's the same old Marine Raider he was ten years ago. The guy can't seem to give up the military ethic or the ranch."

The men nodded in understanding.

Rand waved a waitress over. The men ordered beers, and Rand refreshed his soda water, lime, and Tito's vodka.

"You know, I'd be dead if it wasn't for old Rand," Blair told his two companions. "We had no idea what was waiting for us in Afghanistan, did we, old dog?"

"No, we did not," said Rand, looking off in a thousand-yard stare.

"Yeah, we were pinned down. I took one to the leg and was trying to get to the LZ. I was for sure going to miss the chopper. My Stoner was dry, but Rand appeared out of nowhere. He took out two hajis coming up behind me. I had no idea—"

"Hey, look," said Rand. "I'm sorry, but I just realized I'm up against the clock. Can I give you the rundown?"

Blair laughed with a hint of annoyance. "That's Rand for you, guys. Always business." He took a timid sip from his beer.

Smiling, Rand placed a hand on Blair's shoulder and leaned in for privacy. "The job is low risk. Should be no shooting on your part and no more than three hours tops. You can keep the tactical equipment and guns as part of the deal."

"What's the job?" asked Tyrone.

"Rendition. Simple snag-and-bag job. Just need you on security, that's all."

"You're offering a trade in equipment for manpower?" asked Will. "We work for Ellis Smith, the largest private military contractor in the country. We can get any gear we want. Our contracts stipulate no moonlighting. We shouldn't even be having this conversation."

"No, no, equipment plus cash," said Rand. "Ten thousand now, ten thousand at mission completion."

The three men simultaneously raised their eyebrows.

"Twenty grand each for a three-hour job?" asked Will. "Just posting security?"

"Let's just say it's a high-value target. The agency—"

"The agency?" interrupted Blair.

"Yeah, the agency is paying handsomely for this guy, but since he's on American soil, they've contracted the job out to me."

The men seemed unconvinced.

"Don't you guys know how this works?" Rand asked. "The agency contracts with companies like mine to do its dirty work in the States. For this job, they paid my company a consulting fee through a Brazilian oil conglomerate owned by the agency. It's all off the books and impossible for Congress to track."

The three looked suspiciously at each other.

"OK, continue," said Blair.

"Once the package is secured, I'll call you in with a van. We'll exfil to the Santa Monica Airport, and you three can go have a sin-filled weekend in Tijuana."

"Rand, you're a billionaire," said Will. "Why are you even in this line of work?"

"I guess I'm like my brother," Rand said solemnly, then drained his glass of Tito's. "I just can't seem to get it out of my system. Once you're in, they have you, you know?"

The three men nodded.

"So, deal or no deal?"

The men gave each other looks. "It's a deal, old friend," said Blair.

Rand smiled. "Excellent." He reached down into his bag and covertly pulled out three thick manilla envelopes. "That's ten G now," he said, sliding an envelope to each man. "We'll brief tonight at Santa Monica Airport hangar 14-C, eighteen hundred hours. And remember, the agency demands total confidentiality. No loose lips."

The men nodded.

Rand stood to leave. "And no second thoughts, gentlemen. Or I send my brother to collect."

CHAPTER 50

UNITED NUCLEAR
KLAMATH FALLS, OREGON

The self-driving Uber pulled up to an old building that looked like a nineteenth-century mercantile. Chris Thomas stepped out into the classic Oregon drizzle.

He stared up at the store sign, then down at his tattered, burned, and bloody clothes. After a deep breath, he swallowed hard and walked through the door.

The store was stocked with a menagerie of old and new scientific equipment, from beakers and test tubes to scales, magnets, and retail-packaged chemicals. Not seeing any customers, Chris assumed the business did mostly online sales. He walked up to the counter and rang the old-fashioned call bell. The middle-aged woman who emerged from the back room was startled by the sight of the disheveled man.

"Are you OK, sir?"

Chris looked down at himself. "Yeah, sorry. It's not as bad as it looks. I'm looking for Dr. Bob Lazar. Is he here?"

"Well, Bob doesn't take unannounced visitors. You understand, I'm sure?"

Chris swallowed. "Look, I'm sure you guys get nut jobs in here all the time wanting to talk about aliens and UFOs, but that's not why I'm here. You see—"

A man emerged from the back room. He was slender, just under six feet tall, and wore wire-frame glasses.

The man looked at Chris in amazement. "Are you who I think you are?"

"Dr. Lazar, I'm Chris Thomas. May I have a word with you in private?"

CHAPTER 51

WEATHERLORE ESTATE
LOS ANGELES, CALIFORNIA

"Sir, initial reports indicate the target has been destroyed," said the mission specialist.

"Excellent," said Cain from his throne. "Queue the message."

A comms specialist went to work at her console.

"Charlie target packages are locked," said a weapons specialist from a console near the throne. "Launch sequence initiated. T-minus three hours. All fire control operations are in auto-launch mode. All Thor's Hammer system controls are now diverted to your mobile device, Master."

Cain sat stoically savoring the hour of his revenge.

CHAPTER 52

UNITED NUCLEAR OFFICES
KLAMATH FALLS, OREGON

From across an old desk, Chris watched Bob Lazar carefully sip from a stained coffee mug. The man's eyes darted around the room, avoiding eye contact.

"I need something you're rumored to have that's not listed on your website," Chris began. "By the way, nice website. You 1990s much there, Bob?"

"I should've known you came for that. That's why everyone like you comes to me. Look, I'm extremely uncomfortable with this conversation." Lazar became animated. "The last time I discussed this, the FBI raided my business in Michigan and caused tens of thousands of dollars of damage. It almost put me out of business."

"I know. I saw your documentary. And I'm sorry about that, but I'm not here with the government. In fact, I'm a fugitive of the law."

"I don't have the element 115. I just want to be left alone." Lazar stood and ran his hands through his hair. "I wish I was never caught up in any of this. Short of killing me, the government has done everything in its power to destroy me. You can't just walk in here and ask me to hand over something like element 115. It's crazy." He slapped his hand on the desk.

"Bob, will you please sit down and let me explain? I'm only asking for five minutes."

Lazar stared at Chris for a few moments. Chris gave him a pleading look, and Lazar finally eased back into his tattered leather chair. "OK, Chris Thomas. You have my attention for four and a half minutes. Go." Folding his arms, Lazar focused on Chris.

Chris took a big breath. "As with you, the government recruited me to work on recovered extraterrestrial technology." Chris knew he was completely disregarding his security clearance. "I worked on the same reactor you worked on decades ago. Since the TR-2B disappeared in 1996, the government has built a new craft to house the last remaining reactor. It's called the TR-3B."

"Wait." Lazar leaned forward. "The TR-2B disappeared? What do you mean *disappeared*?"

"Back in '96, it disappeared during a test flight."

"My goodness." Leaning back, Lazar looked out a window like he'd been transported to another place and time.

"I know, I know, but that's another story. What's important now is that the terrorist known as Master Mahan has a weapon in space. I believe it's a stealth satellite. He's the one who hit the military targets across the globe and assassinated several world leaders. I believe he's now preparing to unleash the weapon's full power on civilian populations. The government is completely paralyzed. The only way to stop this thing is to launch the TR-3B into orbit, find the satellite, and destroy it before he kills tens of millions."

"It's true what I've read about you—you're completely out of your mind. What does this have to do with me, anyway?" Lazar threw his hands in the air.

"You know Dugway Proving Ground was decimated. The TR-3B is housed there, but it survived. However, the manufacturing facility for element 115 was destroyed in the attack. There's no 115 left to power the reactor. If you have any 115, I need it to power the reactor and destroy the Order's weapon. It's the only way to stop this madness, Bob."

"Fly the TR-3B into space to destroy a stealth satellite. You *are* insane—"

The store clerk burst into the office, interrupting Lazar. "There's been another attack," she said in a panic.

Chris sprang from his chair and followed Bob into an adjoining workshop, where an old TV played an NBC News report. They watched in horror as burning wreckage in the earth's upper atmosphere glowed like a thousand tiny comets as it streaked across the evening sky.

"They got the space station," Lazar whispered. "This can't be happening."

"It's happening, Bob," Chris said, eyes fixed on the TV. "I need your help."

An NBC News anchor appeared onscreen. "Sources inside the Department of Defense, speaking on conditions of anonymity, indicate that the International Space Station was destroyed by hacked US-military space-based weapons. We are just learning that the control of these satellites, which were originally designed to destroy nuclear ICBMs with advanced lasers, was highjacked by the Order of Baphomet, and the satellites are now being used to destroy space-based military and intelligence assets."

The nervous anchor held her hand to her ear as a producer approached from off camera with a piece of paper. After staring at the paper for several moments, the anchor looked back up at the camera, fear and hesitation enveloping her.

"We have a statement authenticated as having come from the Order of Baphomet. I am instructed to read it word for word." She cleared her voice and began to read. "The poor and people of inferior races are unworthy of life. They spend their meaningless existence feeding on the resources of the planet, our Mother. The poor and racially inferior will now be destroyed.

"Humanity has betrayed the Mother. We, the Order of Baphomet, have been authorized to bring to pass the Mandate by any and all means. We will right the wrongs of the human race, who will be punished for their crimes against the Mother. Once we have taken the earth by force, we will establish the State, whose mission is to return the Mother to her pristine, pre–*Homo sapiens* form.

"The United States and its allies, including Great Britain, the nations of the European Union, China, Japan, and Russia, must surrender to the Order of Baphomet and our leader, the Prophet Master Mahan, in three hours, or our weapons will be unleashed on the feeders and inferiors of the world. If these governments don't surrender, the deaths of the inferiors will be on your heads. Long live the Mother and the Son. Long live Master Mahan."

The stunned anchor set down the paper and returned her gaze to the teleprompter. "A statement released by the White House just moments ago reiterated, quote, 'The United States does not negotiate with terrorists. The federal government, in conjunction with the governments of the world, is working to stop the Order of Baphomet. We ask that the citizens of the world remain calm as their governments work to stop any further terrorist attacks.'

"In other news, it's now being reported across the globe that rioters are taking to the streets because of possible terrorist attacks on civilian population centers. Billions are trying to evacuate major cities around the world before the Order's three-hour deadline. With commercial air travel suspended and major roads and freeways snarled with traffic, people are trying to escape their cities in any way possible, from trains to walking. In related news—"

"It's falling apart." Lazar turned off the TV and started casually toward the front of the store. Chris followed cautiously. At the front counter near an ancient cash register, Lazar reached up and grabbed a picture frame that held a dollar bill captioned *Our First Dollar*. Turning the picture facedown, he smashed it on the counter and removed the dollar. Taped to the back of the bill was a strange triangle-shaped wafer. Carefully pulling off the tape, he cupped the wafer in his hand.

"This element produces its own gravitational energy when inserted into the reactor." Lazar gave a slight prideful smile. "It has most certainly decayed. There may be some unstable isotopes. It's only 223 grams, and I have no idea how it's going to respond in the reactor's housing."

Lazar cautiously placed the wafer into Chris's palm. Amazed, Chris peered at the small, dense, copper-colored element. It was surprisingly heavy for its size. Then it dawned on him: the fuel for interdimensional travel rested innocuously in his hand.

"Good luck, Chris," Lazar said, then nonchalantly turned and walked back into the bowels of his humble shop.

CHAPTER 53

WEATHERLORE ESTATE
LOS ANGELES, CALIFORNIA

Hidden on a wooded hillside above Cain's compound, Naomi stared down the long, FLIR-enabled Leopold scope attached to a Christensen Arms Mesa .338 Lapua Magnum rifle fitted with a custom SilencerCo suppressor. Her beloved Barrett .50 was more than this job called for.

"Beta team, status?" said Naomi into her radio. The beta team consisted of Rand's three recruits from the Santa Monica bar. They were positioned in a windowless Mercedes Sprinter van one block from the Weatherlore.

"Beta team in position," replied Blair. "Eyes on target."

"Copy, beta," Naomi said. "Alpha, be advised. Visuals are up. Beta team is in position. Target intel verified. We have three guards on the back lawn, two on the roof. A three-man roving patrol on the front lawn. All carrying MP-5s. I'm surprised there's not more."

In a whisper, Naomi called out her targets to herself, then looked into the monitor projected inside her goggles. A Freefly Alta X drone hovering five hundred feet above the vast estate illuminated the guards with a FLIR camera.

"Engage targets," Naomi heard Rand command through the earpiece.

~

"Sir, power is out on the grid," said an operative seated near Cain's throne. "We're running on backup generators. The backup UPS battery system is charged to 98 percent. Operations normal."

"A power outage could be a precursor to an assault." Cain stood from his throne. "But how could they have found us?"

"There's no unusual activity in the area," said another operations specialist. "News feeds and social media are clear. The guards report no issues. There's radio traffic about an outage at an Edison substation, which powers this section of the grid. We have eyes on the substation and can confirm technicians are en route."

Although Cain didn't believe in coincidences, the news momentarily calmed him. He sat down on his throne.

"Sir, there's still no report from Klein," said a communications specialist.

"Something is wrong." Cain burst from his throne again. "Get our Reconnaissance General Bureau contact on comms now. Those greedy North Koreans better have answers, or I'll turn Thor's Hammer on them next."

Cain paced the cavernous, red-lit ballroom, his frame shaking for the first time in as long as he could remember. Had Klein been discovered? Had the Aries shipment been intercepted? Were the North Koreans playing games for more money? They'd done it before. It wasn't beneath them. He rubbed his bearded chin and shook his head.

"Sir, onscreen," said the comms specialist.

Cain turned and faced the room's central monitor, where an aerial view of a canyon showed a burning military convoy and the remains of a crashed Hind gunship. The video panned to a clearing near the top of the canyon, and a massive, smoldering black hole filled the screen.

Cain's blood boiled.

"The North Koreans claim an operation originating out of Russia hit the chateau," the nervous specialist explained. "An FSB facility was reportedly destroyed on—"

"No!" Cain strode back to his throne, picked up the heavy, Baphomet-topped chair like a toy, and tossed it at the forward control station. Several mission specialists ran for cover. Then he lunged forward, grabbed the terrified specialist, and snapped his neck like a twig. The sickening sound of breaking vertebrae echoed through the cavernous control room. The rest of the staff froze, hoping to live through the moment.

Cain dropped the dead man's limp body on the ground and flung back his cape. He marched up to the central monitor, balled his fists, and threw back his shoulders.

"No! No! No!"

Naomi gently squeezed the Mesa's custom trigger. More than three hundred yards away, a .338 round smashed into the first guard on the front lawn. Pivoting the rifle, she zeroed in on the two guards running to their downed comrade, dropping both in quick succession. She swung the barrel to the gatehouse just inside the estate's majestic wrought-iron gate. Reaching up to the scope, she clicked the top turret to adjust for distance. She could see the guard looking into a security monitor and suddenly noticing a problem on the security feed. It was the last thing he ever did.

"Targets eliminated," said Naomi into comms. "Overwatch in position for phase two. Alpha, you have thirty seconds to target."

"Sir, we have another problem," said a mission specialist, eyes wide as she stared at a security feed.

His fury still boiling over, Cain turned from the North Korea feed and snarled at the woman. Then he rushed at her, pulling his three-blade knife from his cloak, and slashed her neck. Blood sprayed across her console and several nearby monitors.

Screams of terror filled the cavernous room. A man looking at another security feed yelled something into comms. They were his last words. The panicked staff ran in all directions. Cain slashed and shrieked, killing anyone unlucky enough to fall into his grip.

~

With hurricane force, an explosion hit the ballroom and its unsuspecting occupants.

Wielding their M4 carbines, Rand and Levi burst through the smoke-filled opening that had once been the ballroom's majestically carved doors. Several people stood in a daze. Levi leveled his suppressed M4 and fired at them, the laser on his M4 methodically piercing the smoke and locating target after target.

Rand scanned the chaotic scene for Cain. "Where is he?" he yelled.

Abigail entered behind her brothers, her M4 at the ready. Out of the smoke, Rand spied a large black blur rushing toward his sister. She turned to fire but was too late. Cain knocked the carbine from her hands and seized her by the neck, raising her petite frame into the air and staring into her eyes.

Eyes wide with fear, Rand aimed his carbine at Cain. His sister thrashed helplessly as the monster held her neck in a vise-like grip.

"Drop her!" yelled Rand, centering his weapon on Cain's head.

Cain spun Abigail so she now faced her brother. With his hand still closed tightly around her neck, he pulled her against him. Abigail's face was a deep red, and her lips were turning purple. Her eyes rolled into the back of her head, and her limbs went slack.

Levi raised his weapon to fire at Cain, but a guard he'd missed in the smoke fired first. Levi jerked and flailed, his rifle falling from his hands as he landed with a thud on the ballroom's floor.

"No!" Rand turned and fired on the guard, hitting him between the eyes. Then he swung back around and leveled his sight on Cain. Out of the corner of his eye, he could see Levi lying lifeless, his blood oozing out onto the European marble. A horrible sadness welled up inside Rand, but he pushed it away and calculated how to save his little sister and salvage the compromised mission.

Rand and Cain, who still held Abigail tight in his clutches, circled each other like ravenous wolves. Black smoke and fire filled the vast room, and the remaining monitors broadcasted nothing but snow. Dead bodies lay strewn everywhere.

Effortlessly holding Abigail by the throat, Cain stopped in front of the hole made by the explosion and smiled at Rand. She hung unconscious like a rag doll, making a small human shield for the giant man. Rand knew Cain could snap his sister's neck simply by applying incremental pressure. He cautiously lowered his weapon and raised his hands, feigning surrender.

"Good day, sir," said Cain with mocking politeness. "And you are?"

Rand stared at the nemesis he'd long dreamt about. "I am death. I am the Pale Horse. I've come for you and the codex, the Book of Baphomet."

Like a disappointed father, Cain rolled his eyes and shook his head. "Well, Mr. Pale Horse, you're too late. The Dawn of the Cimeters is upon us. Thor's Hammer cannot be stopped."

Rand furrowed his brow in confusion.

Naomi's voice came through his earpiece. "I don't have a clear shot. You're in the way!"

Cain focused his stare, and Rand saw the veins swell in his hand wrapped around Abigail's neck.

Dropping to the floor, Rand yelled, "Now or never!" into his mic.

A blacked-out exterior window just above Rand's head shattered, exploding inward. A microsecond later, blood burst from Cain's shoulder. He shrieked and released Abigail, who fell flaccidly to the floor.

With the speed of an old Western gunfighter, Rand jumped up, reached back, and pulled out a concealed tranquilizer pistol. Firing from his hip, he hit Cain in the neck with a dart, then frantically dug into his tactical vest for another.

Cain pulled the dart from his neck and leapt over Abigail's lifeless body, the force of Cain's weight hitting Rand like a Mack truck. He flew back through the air, then fell over a control console and landed on a body.

Before Rand could rise to meet his enemy, Cain pounced on him again. He lifted Rand and effortlessly threw him at the overturned throne. When Rand hit the chair, Baphomet's head fell to the floor, breaking into three pieces.

Cain screamed out several indiscernible words. Dazed and in pain, Rand somehow managed to stand to meet Cain, who was again rushing at him. Rand reached down, but his sidearm was gone.

Now in a full sprint, Cain was only feet away. Rand readied for impact, but through his blurred vision, he saw the giant suddenly turn loopy and stumble through his final steps as if drunk. The tranquilizer was finally taking effect. Pivoting, Rand used the giant's momentum to throw him to the floor.

"Everyone move on target!" Rand yelled into his radio.

Rand cautiously approached Cain, who lay facedown on the marble floor. Rand coughed, his vision suddenly correcting and bringing him back to the dire situation around him. The smoke was getting worse. Covering his mouth and nose, he ran to Levi and rolled him onto his back. His brother's pulse was faint, but he was, miraculously, still alive.

"Thank you, Jesus," Rand said.

"Rand," said a weak voice nearby. Abigail slowly stood, a look of confusion and pain on her red, swollen face. As Rand hurried over to grab her, Blair and Tyrone burst into the room with weapons drawn.

"Lord Almighty," said Will, storming in behind his two teammates.

The van team quickly employed stretchers to move Rand's prize and the injured Guthrie siblings to the van.

Rand glanced at one of the few working monitors. All that was displayed was a lock icon and a countdown. Turning for the exit, he stepped on something that made a glassy crunching sound. He reached down and picked up a mobile device. Through its cracked screen, he noticed the same lock icon. The device sparked and then went dead. Rand threw it down and rushed out of the burning room to catch up to the van team.

CHAPTER 54

SANTA MONICA AIRPORT
SANTA MONICA, CALIFORNIA

In the crowded, chaotic Sprinter van, Rand stood with his back against the rear cargo doors, trying to brace himself against the sides. "Slow down," he barked at Blair. "You'll get us pulled over."

Naomi and Will worked feverishly to save Levi's life with medical gear pre-positioned in the van. With a look of pure concentration, Tyrone straddled Cain, holding his Glock 23 against the unconscious man's protuberant forehead. They'd bound Cain's arms and legs, but they doubted the binds would hold if the giant woke up.

Abigail was balled up like a child against the back of the driver's seat, her head mostly buried in her arms. Occasionally, she looked over at Levi and burst into an inaudible sob. Then her eyes shifted to Cain and grew wary, as if she expected him to wake up any moment and try killing her again.

The van sped to a hangar in a more secluded part of the airport, and Blair slammed on the brakes.

When the pilot opened the back of the van, Rand almost fell onto him.

"Son of a—"

"Flight time?" interrupted Rand. Grabbing the pilot by the sleeve, he turned him away from the blood and gore filling the van.

"If we punch it, we can be there in two hours," said the old Texan bush pilot. "Home is just a hop and a skip over Arizona and New Mexico."

"We depart in five minutes," said Rand. "Call ahead to the medical team. We need a full trauma unit standing by at the ranch. Tell them to be ready."

"I'll make it so. Sir, will he live?"

"Our people are the best money can buy, so he better," replied Rand.

Momentarily captivated, Rand watched as the men lugged Cain's heavy, limp body into an elongated metal casket. Rand stepped over to inspect his trophy. Even unconscious, Cain's red-stained face was twisted with evil hate. Rand closed the lid, locked it, and motioned to Blair and Tyrone. Lifting the casket, they heaved it into the plane's cargo hold.

We got him. I can't believe we got him. Thank you, Jesus.

Just then, the 7500's engines fired up, snapping Rand out of his victorious trance. "We need to move now," he called.

Finally exiting the van, Abigail burst into tears, her face still swollen and red. "No, no, Levi, please!" she screamed out, kneeling next to her brother who lay unconscious on a stretcher. A former SEAL medic, Will worked expertly to stabilize Levi. Naomi wrapped her arms around her younger sister and tore her away from their injured brother.

"This won't help," Rand heard Naomi say into Abigail's ear as she passed him, giving him a look of concern.

"Rand, may I have a word, please?" asked Blair. The two men stepped away. "What was that in there? What were they planning? Who is this guy? He doesn't even look human."

Rand returned no response.

"Levi's stable," yelled out Will. "But we need to get him to a hospital. He's lost a lot of blood."

"Get him on the plane," commanded Rand. "We have a mobile ICU inside and enough units of blood to keep him alive for the flight."

"What the . . . ?" said Blair angrily. Will and Tyrone looked at each other, shocked by the order.

"Do it," said Rand. "Naomi is a medic. She'll keep him stable for the flight. We have a trauma team waiting on the ground in Texas."

"If he makes it," Will said under his breath.

Will and Tyrone strapped Levi's body to a backboard, and the men hefted him up the stairs and into the cabin. Rand instructed them to lay Levi on the lounge couch, where Naomi was already prepping a makeshift ICU for the flight.

The three former SEALs gave Levi one last look, then wordlessly turned up the aisle toward the plane's front exit. Rand followed behind. In the plane's front lounge, they passed Abigail balled up in a plush leather seat. She stared into nothingness, swaying back and forth. Her lips moved as if she were saying a prayer, but she made no noise.

As the former SEALs made their way down the aircraft's stairs, Rand caught his pilot's eye. He gave Rand a thumbs-up, indicating the plane was ready to go.

"Gentlemen, I have the rest of your cash here," called Rand.

Blair looked back over his shoulder. "You know, Rand, I'm not sure this was worth the money." He continued down the stairs.

"Neither am I, old friend," said Rand.

A 9mm bullet smashed into the back of Blair's head, and his body jolting forward into Will and sending both men tumbling to the bottom of the stairs. Already on the ground, Tyrone tried to draw his SIG P365, but he was next to meet his fate.

Will fought furiously to free himself from his awkward position under Blair's body. He tried to reach for his pistol, but Rand slammed his boot down on his wrist. The jet's whining engines drowned out Will's scream as his bones were crushed.

Rand put his finger on the trigger and shoved his Glock into Will's forehead.

The former SEAL froze and looked up at the gun, then at Rand with pure hatred in his eyes. Rand could tell the man was calculating a Hail Mary. Even at death's door, the ex-SEAL wasn't giving up without a fight. For that, Rand felt nothing but pure respect.

"Sorry, brother. It's nothing personal." Rand pulled the trigger.

CHAPTER 55

HEBER CITY MUNICIPAL AIRPORT
HEBER CITY, UTAH

From inside the G700 approaching Heber, Utah, Chris stared down at the small town's industrial block. A fire at the old soup factory burned out of control as flames danced a hundred feet above the structure. Thick, black smoke rose into the valley's pristine thin air.

As the aircraft approached the town's municipal airport, on the ramp below, Chris could see Scott Allen's G700 and one of the massive propeller-driven C-130 transport planes owned by Thomas Allen Group. A flurry of activity surrounded the aircraft. Numerous armored vehicles dotted the ramp, forming an inner perimeter, and security guards dotted the airport in classic impenetrable outer-perimeter formation.

Chris smiled approvingly. Amal was doing her job and doing it well.

The G700 banked hard above the snow-covered hills south of the airport and lined up to land on the almost-seven-thousand-foot runway.

As the plane taxied to the ramp, Chris could see Leah waiting for him, and his heart raced in anticipation. As soon as the doors unfolded into steps, Leah ran up them and threw herself into her husband's arms. Chris gently pulled her back and looked into her eyes.

"How did you live?" she asked.

"I'll tell you later. Come on. We don't have much time."

They made their way down the stairs toward Scott and Amal, who stood close by. Amal waited as Scott hobbled on one crutch to embrace his friend, and then Chris moved over to Amal and shook her hand.

"So far, you're worth every penny. Thanks for protecting Leah."

"Thank you, sir. Did you catch the little fire in town on your way in?"

"That was you?" asked Chris with a sly look.

"Well, it was a few former JSOC guys who work for us now. That blaze has the town's entire fire and police occupied. A nice little diversion. Besides, you own the property and were about to demolish the building, so why not use it in mission, right? At any rate, no one should bother us here, but we still need to hurry, sir."

"Yeah, sure," said Chris, unaware he owned the burning building.

"The special is being offloaded from the C-130," said Scott. "It's prepped and ready for deployment."

Chris looked over at the C-130 in time to see a lifted jet-black Ford F-350 crew-cab truck slowly backing out of the aircraft's cargo hold. He walked over to the truck, and the others followed.

"Looks pretty good, right?" Scott asked proudly as Chris circled the monstrous vehicle.

"Yeah, looks like a normal F-350. Well done."

"Under the façade, it's something else entirely," Scott said to the group. "One thousand horsepower and five thousand pounds of torque. The battery has a one-thousand-mile range on full charge under normal driving conditions. Radar. Sonar. Full weapons and electronic warfare package. B8-rated, Kevlar-infused, aramid composite armor throughout. UL-rated, level-ten bulletproof glass. Max enabled, of course. Heads-up display. Thirty-eight-inch run flats. Oh, and I almost forgot to mention the experimental stealth mode. It's still beta, so it's finicky. We kept all exterior details intact right down to the tailpipe, so it blends right in with all the other hicks driving these things around here."

"Once the C-130 drops us in Durango," said Amal, "we'll use the other special to get Leah to site R." She gestured to the C-130's cargo hold, where a second, identical truck was strapped down.

"Durango?" asked Leah. "Site R?"

Amal gave Chris a look. Chris inhaled deeply. "So, yeah, I didn't tell you, but I bought something."

"Great, here we go again." Leah folded her arms.

Just then, the C-130's huge rear cargo door started to close, and its four engines began to spool up, spinning four massive propellers.

"Yeah, I picked up a little ranch outside Durango, Colorado," Chris admitted, wincing.

"Durango? Why?"

"I just wanted a little place where we could get away from it all that wasn't far from Heber by plane."

"Define *little*."

"Well, it's about thirty thousand acres. That's all."

"Thirty *thousand*?" Leah gasped. "Does it have a house?"

"Yeah, it's just a little cabin. No big deal. Oh, and a river runs through the property. You're going to love it."

Leah looked at him suspiciously.

"We really should get airborne, ma'am," said Amal.

"Wait, Chris, can I have a word with you?" Scott asked, sounding reluctant. Chris nodded, and he and Scott walked off toward Scott's G700.

"Are you all set?" asked Chris. "When I said to disappear, you know what I meant by that, right?"

"Yeah, yeah. Of course. Everything is all set. No one will find me where I'm going. No worries. What I need to talk to you about is *who* I'm taking with me." Scott gave a sheepish smile. "I kind of started seeing someone."

"Dude. Look at you! Oh, man, a girlfriend? This is great!"

Scott blushed, still looking anxious. "It's kind of an issue because, well, we don't really have a policy on dating employees."

"Employees? You're dating an employee?" asked Chris.

Scott nodded and looked at Chris for any sign of approval. Chris took in a deep breath and glanced up at the sky. Scott had never had a real girlfriend, and Chris wanted his best friend to be happy. "There are some legal issues we should consider," he began. "The fact we don't have a policy is probably something we should visit. Look, in your position, we just have to be super careful with this stuff. After all, we are a multi-hundred-billion-dollar company. You know what I mean, right?"

"So that means it's OK?"

"Yeah, of course it's OK, Scott."

"Thank you, man!" Scott turned to his G700 and gave an exaggerated wave to an unseen person on the plane.

Moments later, Kiki appeared in the plane's doorway. "Hi, Chris!" she yelled, waving wildly.

You've got to be kidding me. He looked at Scott in astonishment. "Kiki?"

The woman wore a short skirt, halter top, and designer sunglasses. Gold bracelets covered both arms, and her high heels were at least four inches tall. As she moved forward, she lost her balance and slid down the plane's stairs on her butt.

"Oh, geez!" Scott yelled out as he hobbled on his crutch to assist her. Chris followed behind. The two men picked her up at the bottom of the stairs.

"Are you OK?" Scott asked.

"Oh, I'm fine, I'm fine." Kiki smiled in embarrassment as she pulled down her skirt and adjusted her top and sunglasses. Then she unexpectedly grabbed Chris in a huge embrace. "Oh, Chris, I thought you were dead," she said, not letting go.

Chris turned back to see Leah place her hands on her hips and raise her eyebrows as Kiki held him tight. Chris forcefully pulled her back. "Kiki, what are you doing here?" he asked.

Scott started to speak, but Kiki butted in. "Oh, Chris, I hope it's OK. You know how things go, right? I mean, Scotty and I really like each other."

As she spoke, she affectionately put her hand on Chris's chest, and he gently removed it.

"Scotty?" Chris gave Scott a sideways look, which Scott returned with an apologetic squint.

"I know it's crazy and all," Kiki continued, "but we're in love. Do we have your blessing? Oh, and I helped get the new trucks ready for you." Jumping up and down, she pointed to the F-350.

"She was a huge help getting the specials ready for deployment, Chris." Scott looked proudly at Kiki. "We couldn't have done it without her."

Chris stared at the two in astonishment. Scott and Kiki held each other, giving Chris eager smiles.

"OK, OK—it's all fine, I guess," he said after several long seconds, wanting to get out of the uncomfortable situation.

"Oh, really, Chris?" Squealing like a twelve-year-old girl, Kiki embraced Scott.

Scott shook his friend's hand, and then Kiki helped him carefully scale the stairs to the G700's cabin.

"OK, you crazy kids," Chris called as the cabin door shut. "Don't do anything I wouldn't do." He headed back to Leah as Scott's plane taxied to the runway.

"What the heck was that?" asked Leah.

"That? That was Kiki."

"That's *the* Kiki? The one who's always walking into doors and messing things up at Nav?"

"Yeah. Last week I heard she was in love with Milton. Apparently, now she and Scott are in love." As he spoke, Chris made air quotes around *in love*.

Having had enough of Scott and Kiki, he pulled Leah back into an embrace. "Look, I hope you're not mad at me about the ranch, but I needed someplace safe to hide you. Besides, you like horses."

"Yes, I like horses." Leah put her arms around his neck.

"And what about her?" Chris nodded toward Amal, who continued to direct the activity around the C-130. "Do you like her?"

"She's growing on me," said Leah. "Now, where are you off to in that truck?"

Chris looked her in the eyes. "I'm the only one who can stop this, sweetheart."

"I had a bad feeling you were going to say that."

"Everyone at Orion's Spear is dead. Barrington has been assassinated. Mike is missing. Mills is trying to have me arrested. Mahan is about to unleash Thor's Hammer on the world. I'm the only one who can stop it, Leah. I can't fail." Chris thought of Elle's final words.

"Please, no jumping out of airplanes or anything crazy like that, OK? Promise me."

"I promise," he lied as he embraced her tightly. "There's so much I need to say to you. This infertility thing—we'll figure it out, OK?" That promise he intended to keep.

"We need to talk about Jada too," said Leah. She handed Chris her phone. Numerous pictures of the little orphan from Detroit populated the screen. Chris smiled slightly. He could not deny it—Jada was a sweet little girl.

"Yeah, you're right. We do need to talk about Jada."

"You're open to it?"

"Yes, of course."

Leah threw herself back at her husband and kissed him intensely.

Amal walked up while Chris and Leah were lost in each other's embrace. She handed the F-350's key fob to her boss and looked at Leah. "Ma'am, we really need to load up."

"OK, let's not do a cheesy goodbye in front of everyone." Leah leaned in for another kiss. "I love you."

"I love you too." Chris released Leah and turned to Amal. "You know what to do, and you know my expectations."

"Yes, sir. Everything will be fine," Amal said.

The two women walked to the C-130. Chris watched as the aircraft taxied toward the runway. Leah waved from a window before disappearing from Chris's view. With its precious cargo, the C-130 rose into the southwestern sky toward Provo Canyon.

A sudden feeling of loneliness and despair came over Chris. Orion's Spear was no more. Mike was missing. The new president wasn't just trying to arrest him, she was actually trying to kill him. Mahan had the world cowering on its knees.

Chris bowed his head and sighed. Then, looking back up, he was momentarily reminded of all the beauty surrounding him. The Wasatch Mountains glowed golden as a micro storm cell formed over the little hamlet of Midway. Horses grazed in a nearby pasture, and the air was crisp. He took a deep breath and closed his eyes.

The world is worth saving, said a voice inside his head. *You can do this. I am here for you.*

Filled with resolve, Chris opened his eyes and pulled himself up into the driver's seat of the F-350. The truck's dashboard, which included a heads-up display and eighteen-inch center computer, came to life.

Chris placed his hands on the steering wheel. "Max, activate weapons systems, scan for drones, and search all federal and local databases for Zelda Shakespeare. We need to find her before we reach Salt Lake City."

"Executing," said Max as Chris clicked his seat belt. "Sir, ETA to Salt Lake City is forty-one minutes. We have approximately 121 minutes left on the three-hour countdown. When it finishes, there is a 94 percent probability the Order will follow through on the threat and attack civilian targets."

"Got it, Max. Play 'Don't Tread on Me' by Metallica. And play it loud."

CHAPTER 56

K&Z TATTOO
EN ROUTE TO SALT LAKE CITY, UTAH

As Chris rounded the bridge connecting US Route 40 to the I-80 freeway near Park City, the Metallica pounding in his ears went mute. Max came alive on the F-350's forward monitor. "Sir, we're being tracked by a high-altitude surveillance drone."

"Onscreen," said Chris. A real-time video of the high-altitude drone populated the screen. "Jam it."

"Electronic jamming initiated, sir. The Park City Police, Summit County Sherriff's Office, and Utah Highway Patrol have all been alerted to our presence. They are instructed to apprehend you."

"They're looking for a black F-350, right?"

"Correct, sir. They have a description of our vehicle. Shall I activate stealth mode?"

"Initiate level-three stealth mode," commanded Chris.

The F-350 made several strange sounds, and a wave of digital tiles changed the truck's exterior color from black to red. A hologram modified the license-plate number. The vehicle lowered to conceal the true height of its lift. In only seconds, it had been transformed to look like any other red F-350 traveling innocuously down the freeway.

The rearview camera illuminated the HUD, showing an armada of police vehicles entering the freeway via an onramp at Kimball Junction, lights flashing and sirens blaring. Nonchalantly flipping on his blinker, Chris changed lanes to let the police cruisers pass. "Max, hack dispatch and call off the order to apprehend us."

"Executing," said Max.

The truck crested Parley's Summit and began the steep descent down the narrow canyon into Salt Lake City.

"Sir, I have a 98 percent probable location on Dr. Shakespeare. She is tied to a tattoo business registered as a single-member limited liability company in the name of Karen Blunt." Max populated the truck's center screen with a map, images of the tattoo business, and social-media posts tagged from inside the tattoo parlor. "Public records indicate that Karen Blunt is legally married to Dr. Zelda Lynn Shakespeare."

"A tattoo shop? I'm going with 100 percent probability, Max. Excellent work." Chris studied the map. "We're ten minutes and thirty-two seconds from the shop. Deploy the sentinel drone and scan the area for authorities."

"Anticipating the order, I have already prepared the sentinel for deployment," said Max. "Ready to launch on your command."

"Send it, brother."

The back third of the truck's eight-foot bed cover retracted, and a cylindrical launcher protruded from the truck's bed. The launcher's compressed-air system hissed when fired, catapulting the sentinel drone into the air. Chris scanned the vehicles around him, but, incredibly, none of the occupants seemed to have noticed the launch. They were all busy driving and talking or texting on their phones, paying little attention to their surroundings.

Exiting I-80, Chris turned the truck south onto State Street in Salt Lake City. A light rain had begun trickling down on the inversion-clouded city.

"Sir, the drone is on station. Sensors indicate three FBI agents occupying a surveillance van positioned in a parking lot across from Dr. Shakespeare's location. We are 1.1 miles from the site."

"Max, hit them with the sentinel's EMP and a low-frequency sonic burst the agents will never forget."

"Executing."

A minute later, Chris saw fire and smoke rising from a parked white van's engine compartment, the result of the EMP blast. The van's sliding door stood wide open, revealing electronics and other equipment burning. One agent was attempting to extinguish the flames, and the other two lay prostrate on the asphalt, violently vomiting from the sonic burst.

Letting out a laugh, Chris pulled into the parking lot of a rundown strip mall. Above the parlor door, a bright-red, flickering neon sign read "K&Z Tattoo." The *Z* was burned out.

As Chris carefully stepped into the small shop, several gold-colored bells tied to the door announced his arrival. Two high-end leather tattoo beds sat at the center of the room, along with several small tables filled with tattoo pens, inks, balms, and other items Chris couldn't identify. Stunning art, posters of famous female rock stars, and Native American artifacts covered the deep-red walls, which seemed to consume what was left of the light in the already poorly lit space.

In a far corner of the room behind a dusty glass display case, a woman with long dreadlocks and a colorful knitted Jamaican reggae cap sat on a stool. Her back was to Chris, and she was engrossed in a thick book. "We're almost closed, man," she said without looking up. "Come back tomorrow." She took a drag on a joint. The angry sound of Alanis Morrissette played low over the room's sound system.

"Hello, Zelda," Chris said quietly, trying not to startle her.

Dropping her book, Zelda jumped up from her stool. Her face turned stone cold with fear as she hurried over the black-and-white-checkered floor to Chris. "What are you doing here? Are you crazy? The entire world is looking for you. And how did you find me?"

Chris put his hands in his pockets and shrugged. "Nice place you have here."

"Oh, go screw yourself. Are you trying to get me arrested too? This little shop might not look like much to you, *Mr. Trillionaire*, but it's all I've got."

"Zelda, I meant that sincerely," said Chris. "Look, I'm not trying to get you in any trouble. I need your help. You're all I've got."

Zelda lowered her eyebrows and relaxed her posture. Walking to the tinted window, she looked for any signs of law enforcement outside.

"I just took care of the surveillance team, but I'm sure they're calling it in," said Chris. "We don't have much time. I'm serious about you being all I've got. You're the only one who can help me."

"The FBI took me into custody and interrogated me about our work together," Zelda said almost accusingly. "Someone thinks you're behind these attacks. I got released only this morning. They said they're going to send me to jail for the rest of my life."

"They're just trying to scare you. You did nothing wrong. Well, at least not yet."

"What do you mean by that?"

"We have to break into Dugway and launch the TR-3B. It's the only way to stop the Order." Chris pulled out the small wafer and placed it in her hand.

She held it up to her face in amazement. "The 115. The rumor was true. You got it from Lazar? How?"

"That's a story for another time. We have our fuel and our pilot, and now we just need to get back into Dugway to stop this thing. It's on us, Zelda." He took her gently by the shoulders and looked into her eyes. "Everyone else is dead. We're all that's left."

Zelda pushed him away and turned her back. "I can't get involved. I'm too afraid. I'm just an unemployed scientist with a hole-in-a-wall tattoo shop. I'm a nobody."

"You're someone to me," said Chris. Zelda again turned to face him. "I used to be a nobody," he continued, "then God gave me this gift and a mission. I was there, Zelda. I was in Zurich. The team I went in with from the CIA was mostly wiped out in the assault, but we stopped the Order. I was shot. I almost died."

He pulled down his collar to expose the scar. Zelda stared at him in astonishment.

"We're the only ones who can stop the Order's insanity," Chris went on. "We're badly outnumbered and outgunned. Even our own government is trying to stop us. We have no idea if the element 115 has decayed or if we're going to have technical problems in orbit."

"No one has ever done anything like this, Chris," said Zelda fearfully.

"I specialize in firsts."

Zelda bit her lower lip and nodded. Chris moved in closer. "Right before we launched the assault in Zurich, our team leader, Mike Mayberry, said something that's always stuck with me. 'It's OK to be scared, but it's not OK to not go. Until death, all defeat is psychological. If you believe in the enemy more than you believe in yourself, who do you think will win?'"

Chris sensed a warm, reassuring feeling of peace and comfort enter Zelda's being. He could tell she'd felt it before but always pushed it away. Now she allowed the feeling to wash over her body. Chris could see it in her countenance. She started to tremble, and tears formed in her eyes.

"Billions of people are depending on you and me to do our job right now. So, what do you say? Let's go save the world, shall we?"

The bells on the door rang, interrupting the moment. An obese biker with a mohawk and tattered leather jacket stepped inside.

"Leroy, we're closed," Zelda yelled. "Now, leave."

The man flinched, then turned and walked out the door without a word.

"Why are you yelling at Leroy again?" called a voice from somewhere in the back of the shop. A woman came through a beaded curtain near the glass display case. Tall, skinny, and covered in tattoos and piercings like Zelda's, the woman stopped dead in her tracks. "Oh, my. You're Chris Thomas."

"Chris, this is my wife, Karen," said Zelda shyly. "Karen, this is Chris."

"You two know each other?" asked Karen, approaching the two. "How come you never told me, baby?"

"It's the other job, honey," said Zelda. "You know I can't talk about that."

"Oh, that," said Karen. "Well, it's nice to meet you, Mr. Thomas. Are you here for a tattoo? Wait, can we get a selfie together?"

"Nice to meet you, too, but right now probably isn't the best time," said Chris politely.

Taking Karen by the hand, Zelda walked her toward the back of the shop. They stopped at the counter, just out of earshot. Chris watched as Zelda embraced her wife and whispered in her ear. After a minute, Karen's demeanor turned fearful, and then terror filled her eyes. Cautiously, she peeked over Zelda's shoulder at Chris. Then she turned back to Zelda, her chin quivering and tears streaming from her eyes.

Chris didn't need to hear their words because the look on Karen's face told him all he needed to know.

Zelda was going with him.

CHAPTER 57

INTERSTATE 80
SOUTH OF THE GREAT SALT LAKE

"I don't like this," said Chris as the F-350 approached the Kennecott Garfield Smelter smokestack nestled at the base of the Oquirrh Mountains. "We're locked in on all sides. This is the perfect kill box."

Traffic was heavy. In front of them, a train of semitrucks lumbered westward like a long snake. On their left, the mountains came almost to the freeway. On their right, the shallow Great Salt Lake encroached even closer.

"It'll open up once we hit the Tooele exit in a few miles," said Zelda. "Let's focus on what we can control. Tell me what we're up against."

"You're right. OK. The Thor's Hammer weapon is a stealth satellite. I believe it fires tungsten rods up to thirty feet long from low-earth orbit. The kinetic energy that accumulates behind the rods hits a target with the force of a high-yield nuclear weapon, without the radiation."

"Is that what hit Dugway?"

"Yes, but judging by the blast zone, I estimate it was a much smaller rod. A single rod just thirty feet long could destroy a city the size of New York."

Pausing, Zelda furrowed her brow. "Wait a minute. Back in the shop, you said we have a pilot. Who?"

"Me."

"You? You've never even been in the simulator!" Zelda's voice rose in disgust. "Let me guess. You think because you just barely got your helicopter pilot's license, you can fly an interdimensional spacecraft, right?"

"On the flight back from New York, I read all the flight manuals and engineering documents, and I reviewed all the historical pilot briefings and logs. The TR's flight controls are remarkably like a helicopter's. Max and I can do it together."

"That's got to be tens of thousands of pages, Chris."

"To be exact, it was 104,453 pages," said Chris.

Zelda looked at him in astonishment.

"Sir," said Max, "global internet service is slowly coming back online. We are 44.5 minutes from the three-hour deadline."

"That's not a good sign," said Chris. "Mahan must have a reason. Maybe he wants the world to see something. Let's use it to our advantage and find that satellite."

"Approaching the exit for Tooele, Utah," said Max. "We are sixty-four miles from the main gate at Dugway Proving Ground. In this traffic, our ETA is seventy-nine minutes."

"We've got to go faster," Chris said impatiently. "We're running out of time." The traffic seemed to be slowing down rather than speeding up.

"You focus on getting us there," said Zelda. "Max and I will work the problem."

As the vehicle passed the Tooele exit, a valley buttressed by the Great Salt Lake opened before them.

"I now have access to NASA's and the NRO's backup networks on the Amazon cloud," said Max. "I also have access to STRATCOMMS's classified space-tracking database . . . Now analyzing historical and real-time data . . . Now creating orbital-plane models."

"Max, can we use the NSA and NASA satellites in geosynchronous orbit to grab background UV-imaging data against low-earth-orbit satellite constellations?" asked Zelda. "If so, we may be able to find Thor's Hammer."

"An excellent idea, Dr. Shakespeare," said Max. "I agree, the weapon must be concealed in low-earth orbit. Now building custom algorithm . . . Now sorting image-backgrounding UV data from government and private satellites in geosynchronous orbit . . . Now modeling low-earth-orbit satellite constellations."

Over the dash, a holographic globe appeared with the United States highlighted, showing all satellites currently in low-earth orbit directly over the country. Max began displaying spatial satellite data at blistering speeds. Chris looked over the data with perfect concentration.

As Max continued processing his models, traffic slowed even more. "There might be an accident up ahead," said Chris. "I should deploy a sentinel drone. How are we looking, Max?"

"Sir, I have objects emanating from a dead spot in the SpaceX Starlink array. Negative UV and IR spectrographic analysis indicates a stealth satellite concealed in the dead spot. The satellite is projecting a star field from the earth's view and a distorted earth view from the geosynchronous-orbit view. It was actually quite easy to identify."

"It's projecting images from in front and behind itself?" asked Chris. "Where'd they get that tech?"

"They probably stole it from the US government," said Zelda. "It's stealth, so on radar it looks like an innocent box satellite in the Starlink array. In reality, if it's carrying the amount of weaponry we think it is, the thing is actually the size of a 737. However, it has a weakness. When it launches its rods, it's exposed like a stealth fighter opening its weapons-bay doors to fire a missile, but it happens so fast you can only see it if you know what to look for."

"Wait, Max, did you say something about objects emanating from the dead spot?"

"Yes, Chris."

"You're seeing rods deployed from Thor's Hammer?"

"Yes. Based on satellite data from geosynchronous orbit, I detect the launch of three rods . . . Now analyzing terrestrial trajectories."

"Three?" Zelda looked at Chris, terrified. "There's three of those things raining down from above the earth?"

"Max, I know you're constrained on processing speeds," said Chris, "but we need to know where they're going to hit."

"Analyzing now," said Max. "Sir, even if I identify the trajectory, I am afraid it will be too late to notify those in the probable blast zone."

"It's too late?" Zelda solemnly looked at Chris. Saying nothing, he stared straight ahead.

"Sir, we are being tracked by another high-altitude drone," said Max. "Now jamming."

"Project ATC radar view onscreen," said Chris. "Give me a ten-mile radius, Max."

A holographic map encompassing the ten miles surrounding the truck populated the vehicle's center screen.

"Sir, three Blackhawk helicopters and two Predator-style drones are orbiting our position. I detect no transponder signal from these aircraft."

"Well, OK, then. I'm going with not friendly. Identify all probable targets. How did they find us, Max?"

"Unknown. What are your orders?"

Chris looked at the map again. Half a mile south of the freeway, a Blackhawk helicopter paced the truck. A mile ahead, another Blackhawk closed in on their position, low over the interstate. A third Blackhawk was coming in low over the Great Salt Lake.

Ahead, two Walmart semitrucks slowed, blocking traffic in both westbound lanes. The cars in front of Chris and Zelda started braking.

"You were right!" said Zelda. "They're boxing us in."

"They're firing missiles!" yelled Chris. Directly ahead, the two semitrucks and several cars disintegrated in a horrific explosion. Chris slammed on his brakes to avoid hitting the wreckage, but he crashed into the rear of a semitruck. The airbags deployed, sending Chris and Zelda back into their seats. Zelda screamed as a white cloud of smoke filled the cab.

"Max, vent the cab," yelled Chris. He didn't want to lower the bulletproof windows. Although dazed from the airbag impact, he noticed Zelda was bleeding from both nostrils.

"Dr. Shakespeare has suffered a broken nose. Would you like me to alert emergency medical services?"

"I'm fine." Zelda held her nose with both hands.

A Honda minivan smashed into the back of Chris's truck. *Tink, tink, tink, tink.* Machine-gun fire strafed the armored truck. Chris and Zelda both ducked as a drone made a low, high-speed pass directly overhead.

"At least it wasn't a missile." Zelda's voice sounded shaky.

Chris looked in the rearview mirror. Inside the minivan, he could see a mother and father looking back to check on their children. "Max, damage report. We've got to get away from these civilians, or they'll get caught in the crossfire."

"Vehicle is intact and operational, but we've suffered damage to the hardware powering the stealth system. Stealth mode unavailable. Perimeter-defense cannon inoperable. We've suffered minor damage to the vehicle's rear bumper. Armor integrity holding at 98 percent."

A sudden explosion rose from behind the truck. The minivan, with its innocent passengers, had disappeared in a raging fire. The airborne enemy unrelentingly fired on several more vehicles behind Chris and Zelda. A number of cars and an Amazon delivery truck exploded.

They were trapped.

Chris spun around, looking for an escape. He could see several people lying motionless on the ground. Others ran screaming in every direction. Just then, the driver of the rig directly before them jumped from his cab. He was on fire, and he rolled into the median to put out the flames.

The drone strafed the truck again.

"Max, uncage air defenses," Chris said as he tried to help Zelda with her bleeding nose. "Weapons free."

Fire and smoke rose all around the truck, with vehicles blocking the way forward and back.

"Max, notify emergency services." Chris watched as people helped each other from the burning vehicles or knelt beside the bodies splayed over the interstate.

The F-350's bed cover retracted, and hydraulic noises emanated from behind the truck. An elongated box pointed skyward at a forty-five-degree angle, then rose from the bed on a cylinder.

"Analyzing threat matrix," said Max. "Target solution locked. I have tone. Firing."

Four FIM-92k Stinger missiles uncaged from their launcher. Under Max's control, all missiles locked targets and banked, tearing off at incredible speed.

On the radar, Chris saw five enemy aircraft taking evasive maneuvers at the surprise missile launch. "When you get to hell, give my regards to Hancock and Lennox." He returned his attention to the orbital mechanics being holographically projected in front of him.

The three Blackhawks tried taking evasive maneuvers, but the deadly Stingers closed in on their prey. Chris glanced toward the lake just in time to see a Blackhawk plunge as a ball of fire into a wet, salty grave. On Chris's left, another Blackhawk erupted in flames.

"What about the drones?" yelled Chris.

"Locked on," said Max.

Off to their one o'clock position, another massive fireball erupted over the Great Salt Lake. Then Chris saw the fourth Stinger bank, turn straight up, and hit one of the drones.

"Two of three helicopters are down," reported Max. "Both drones are destroyed."

"We need to move," said Chris. "We're a sitting duck for that other copter."

"Sir, this vehicle possesses five thousand foot-pounds of torque. I recommend simply pushing the wreckage out of the way."

"Good point." Chris hit the accelerator. The truck's electric motors were so powerful that the F-350 pushed the semitrailer up onto its hood.

"Watch out!" Zelda gripped the seat as a mass of burning wreckage bumped against the windshield.

As Chris put the Ford in reverse and tried to back up, high-caliber automatic gunfire exploded all around the truck.

"Where's that coming from? Max, we need perimeter-defense cannons."

"PDCs inoperable, sir. We are under attack by a ground force. Tangos from the third helicopter."

Chris and Zelda looked out the heavily armored windows, which were beginning to crack under the machine-gun barrage. Numerous men in black, bulletproof tactical gear closed in, wielding unidentifiable high-caliber machine guns.

"We can't take much more of this. Max, any ideas? Max, are you there?"

The monitors inside the truck went dead. A man approached on Zelda's side, firing on full automatic from only twenty feet away. The armored glass was holding, but it wouldn't last much longer.

"Max!" yelled Chris, trying to get the system back online.

"What do we do, Chris?" Zelda asked in a panic.

Chris reached under the seat but found no weapons. To his left, three men closed in from the eastbound lane, running and firing on the truck. To his right, several black-clad men worked to set up what looked like a shoulder-fired missile launcher.

The weapon was aimed directly at the cab of the truck.

Chris frantically tried to work the Ford's controls to no avail. When he thought momentarily of Leah, wondering if she'd made it safely to Durango, a strange peace came over him, telling him she was safe.

Swallowing hard, Chris again tried the Ford's unresponsive controls. Gripping the steering wheel, he searched his mind for any idea, but there was nothing. Time seemed to slow. The attack, the killing, the fire, and smoke all seemed to pause, and a singular, unshakable thought entered Chris's mind.

We're going to die.

CHAPTER 58

INTERSTATE 80
SOUTH OF THE GREAT SALT LAKE

As the blacked-out GMC Yukon sped west on Interstate 80 past the Kennecott Garfield Smelter smokestack, its driver could see a huge explosion on the road several miles ahead. "Well, I must be on the right track," murmured the man as he watched fire and smoke billow into the air.

The vehicles in front of him braked abruptly. He jerked the wheel, moved onto the shoulder, and hit the accelerator, blowing past the slowing vehicles.

Now, numerous fireballs erupted in quick succession at ground level just a few miles ahead. "Come on! Move!" he yelled as he tried to keep the SUV under control on the steeply pitched shoulder. Then he noticed several midair explosions. "OK, that's more like it."

He was now only a mile away from the battle site. The Yukon fishtailed on the steep shoulder's loose gravel, but the expert driver quickly regained control. He pushed down on the accelerator, sending rocks and roadside trash flying, the Yukon's aftermarket turbos wailing.

Leaning over the steering wheel, the driver squinted at the smoky scene. Several bodies lay on the ground next to burnt-out vehicles. The survivors were running eastward over salt-crusted terrain, away from the violence.

"What the—" A quarter mile directly in front of him, he saw three men preparing to launch a shoulder-fired missile at a pickup truck.

He pressed down on the accelerator.

At the sound of the roaring, turbo-charged, eight-cylinder engine, two of the men turned, raised their machine guns, and raked the Yukon, but the rounds only pockmarked the up-armored vehicle.

As the unrelenting vehicle barreled down on the men, all three tried to dive out of the way, but it plowed into them at ninety miles an hour. Two flew over the hood and landed several yards away. The man who'd been holding the missile launcher disappeared under the car. The driver felt a sickening thud as his tires rolled over the terrorist's body.

Out of the corner of his eye, he noted where the shoulder-fired missile launcher had landed, then slammed on his brakes and backed up over the bodies to the burning F-350. He could barely see the vehicle's occupants through the spider-webbed glass, but they appeared to be uninjured.

Two armed men emerged from behind a burning semitruck and fired at the SUV. From the south, three more assailants used the F-350 as cover while firing at the Yukon's driver, but their shots went wide.

As the Yukon took heavy fire, the driver calmly reached up and pulled down the bulletproof faceplate on his helmet, locking it into position. The HUD came alive on the faceplate, and he heard a slight dinging in his ear.

"Identify," said the automated voice.

"This is Knife," said Mike Mayberry. "Authorize." Opening the Yukon's door, he pulled a highly modified H&K 416 from its hold.

"Mark seven Viper suit authorized. Welcome, Knife. You are currently in active combat. How may I assist you today?"

"Oh, so now you decide to show up, Max?"

Mike fired on the two terrorists ahead, dropping them with a sniper's precision. Using the F-350 as cover, he turned his attention to the south. "You know, I could've used your help a few days ago. Now, get me some satellite support here. I need to know where the enemy is."

"Copy. Satellite on station," said Max. "I have positive control."

A 3D view of the battlespace filled the helmet's HUD. Mike dropped to the ground and fired under the F-350 at the three terrorists, who fired wildly while closing in from the south. As he shot them in the legs and they fell, he shot each one in the head.

"You're clear to the passenger-side door, Knife," said Max.

Mike approached the F-350 and tried to look inside the vehicle, but the web of cracks in the glass made it almost impossible.

"Max, I need thermals," Mike yelled, tugging fruitlessly on the passenger door. "Analyze battlespace, build threat matrix, and call out the enemy as you see them. And get this door open!"

"Negotiating with system," said Max, followed seconds later by a clicking sound.

Mike pulled on the handle and flung the door open. He had never seen the woman before, and she wasn't what he expected. She was covered in blood from what appeared to be a broken nose.

Chris stared at him in shock. Mike pulled up the faceplate. "Mike!" Chris yelled in relief.

Mike unbuckled Zelda and pulled her from the burning truck. "To the Yukon!" he yelled to Chris, pointing at the getaway vehicle. Scrambling across the center console, Chris followed them out the passenger door.

"Sir," said Max, "we have an armed Blackhawk inbound and four heavily armed enemies approaching from the west."

Holding Zelda in his arms, Mike could see no threat. He flung open the Yukon's rear door, and Zelda and Chris piled into the back seat. Mike slammed the door and scanned the battlespace for a target. He could hear a helicopter approaching at high speed from the north over the Great Salt Lake.

The location of the shoulder-fired missile launcher illuminated in Mike's HUD. It lay on the ground only forty feet away. Mike ran to it. Just then, rounds from the west exploded all around him. In motion, he reached down, scooped up the missile launcher, and dove for cover behind a burning vehicle. The southbound Blackhawk passed low and fast directly overhead, then banked hard and turned for Mike's position.

Mike stepped out from behind the burning vehicle and hefted the launcher onto his shoulder. Looking through the long sight, he placed the Christmas tree–shaped reticle on the helicopter.

"I have tone," Mike yelled. "Locked on. Firing." The missile was uncaged from the launcher in a hail of smoke and fire. Without hesitation, Mike threw down the launcher, pulled up the 416 carbine hanging at his side, and fired on four enemy shooters approaching from the west. Seconds later, a massive explosion rose from the south. Mike didn't look. He didn't need to. The helicopter was simply no longer a threat.

"Contact south," said Max. "One hundred yards."

Mike dropped his empty magazine and reloaded. He locked the bolt in place and fired again on the approaching men until they all fell dead.

After killing the last man, Mike scanned downrange through the rifle's EOTECH holographic sight, searching for any missed targets.

"Threats eliminated," said Max. "Battlespace clear."

Pushing up his faceplate, Mike surveyed his surroundings. Bodies lay everywhere. Burning vehicles of every kind crackled and smoked in the salt-tinged air. To the south, a secondary explosion erupted from the downed Blackhawk. Sirens blared in the distance.

Mike lowered his carbine and walked along the gravelly shoulder back to the Yukon. He set the gun down and opened the tailgate. Chris and Zelda, both crouching in the back seat, stared wordlessly at Mike.

Mike unstrapped his helmet and laid it on the bumper. He rummaged through a cooler for a water bottle and gulped down all sixteen ounces at once. Then he drew a deep, exaggerated breath of salt air through his nose.

"Mike, are you OK?" asked Chris.

"Are you kidding me? I feel like a freaking bald eagle." Mike wiped the water dripping from his bearded chin. "So, where we off to next?"

CHAPTER 59

SKULL VALLEY INDIAN RESERVATION
NEAR DUGWAY PROVING GROUND, UTAH

You really expect me to believe this story?" Chris asked Mike. "That you forgot you left a bomb in the back of your truck and that's how you escaped certain death at the hands of thirty highly trained assassins?"

In the driver's seat, Mike turned to Chris. "You don't have to believe it, but that's what happened."

The two men stared at each other. Mike's eyes clearly suggested he wasn't lying.

"Now, I have a question for you." Mike returned his eyes to the road. "Are we just going to walk right into a high-security military installation, or do you have a plan?"

"I'll figure that out once we're closer."

"Well, we're about there," said Mike.

"I need more time. I'm trying to calculate orbital telemetry projections from the last data we gleaned before we lost Max. All our math went up with the Max instance in the F-350."

"What's the story with her?" Mike glanced in the rearview mirror at Zelda. Chris turned back to check on her. She still sat passed out in the back seat, blood covering her face and seeming to melt into her tie-dyed shirt.

"Classified," Chris said. "All I can say is Zelda's a scientist working on a very important project. Wait, how'd you find us out here?"

"Classified," Mike said, stone-faced.

"Whatever. Where'd you get this kitted-out Yukon?"

"The agency has a safe house just outside Salt Lake City."

About a mile ahead, the state road appeared to dead-end at a building. Chris pulled out a pair of binoculars. "Weird. It's an LDS chapel. In the middle of nowhere. Let's move—"

An explosion sent the Yukon tumbling end over end off the road. As it rolled, glass, dirt, and bits of sagebrush flew up all around Chris, the SUV finally coming to a rest on its roof. Hanging upside down, the last thing Chris saw before he passed out was the smoke billowing from the engine compartment.

As Chris's senses returned, the first thing he felt was the uneven ground under his body. He heard voices, some vaguely familiar.

"Grab the smelling salts," ordered one voice.

Chris heard shuffling and felt someone move his head side to side. Then the smell of ammonia hit his olfactory nerve like a bomb. He sat up and coughed, momentarily feeling like he was going to vomit.

"You're all right," said the man next to him. "Get him some water." It was Mike Mayberry.

"What happened?" asked Chris as he rubbed the back of his throbbing head.

"I'll tell you what happened, son," said a man with a thick Virginian accent. "Yer lucky to be alive."

Chris blinked several times to correct his blurred vision. He looked at the man and read the name emblazoned across his chest plate.

"General Bischoff?" he asked.

"You got it, son."

A field medic adjusted a blood-pressure cuff around Chris's arm, then flashed a penlight in front of his eyes. "He'll live," the specialist said.

Chris looked to his left and noticed Zelda sitting in the back of a Humvee. Her arm was bandaged, but blood still seeped through the gauze field dressing.

"Zelda, are you OK?" called Chris.

"I'm fine," Zelda yelled from the truck. "Just gonna sit here and hope we don't get blown up a third time today."

Chris and Mike gave each other a look. "She took some shrapnel to the arm," said Mike. "It doesn't look good. We need to get her to a hospital."

Chris asked, "What happened to us?"

"Hellfire missile hit the road in front of us," said Mike. Looking at General Bischoff, he added in annoyance, "We're lucky to be alive."

"I wasn't just under orders to apprehend you, boys," said the general. "I was under orders to kill you."

Mike and Chris remained silent. The general stood and crossed his arms over his formidable chest. "But when I met you a few days ago, Thomas, I had a feeling about you. There's no way yer working for the Order. The new president is off her gall-durn rocker."

Mike and the medic helped Chris to his feet.

"Now, what's this all about, anyway, son?" asked Bischoff.

Rubbing the back of his head again, Chris surveyed his surroundings. The sun was setting to the west over a pink-hued desert. They were next to the Skull Valley Reservation, home to a few Goshutes. Although close to Dugway as the crow flew, the reservation was dozens of miles of bad dirt roads away from Dugway's south underground entrance.

"Well, it's super top secret, sir, but whatever," said Chris. "I'm going to lay it out for you."

"General!" yelled a sergeant, sprinting over from another Humvee. Bischoff moved to meet the man, who handed him an iPad. The general looked into the device.

"General, do you have Chris Thomas in your custody?" asked a man's voice.

"General, sir," said Bischoff. "Yes, I have Thomas here in my custody . . . again."

"Hand him this device," instructed the general.

Bischoff passed the iPad to Chris. Surprise and relief filled Chris when he saw General Westinghouse's face filling the screen.

Westinghouse stared at Chris and said, "Verified. That's him."

His face disappeared from the screen. A moment later, President Mills's face filled the shaky screen. Her eyes were bloodshot, her hair disheveled.

"President Mills?"

"Yes, Dr. Thomas. I'm afraid I have some bad news." She stopped and cleared her throat. "Minutes ago, some weapon we can only surmise was Thor's Hammer destroyed Mexico City, Mumbai, and Lagos. We estimate upward of seventy million people have died."

Her voice cracked, but she quickly composed herself. Gasps and sounds of disbelief came from behind Chris.

"General Westinghouse has briefed me on the project President Barrington appointed you," continued Mills. "I've asked the general to explain your mission."

Westinghouse's face filled the screen again. "Son, I've ordered security at Dugway to escort you back to A-139. As you know, all our terrestrial defense systems are offline. You're our only option. Your mission is to take the TR-3B and—"

"I know what to do, General," interrupted Chris. "Had my own government not been trying to kill me, I'd be doing it right now."

"Look, there'll be time later to unpack and analyze what's transpired here," Westinghouse shot back. "But the more we talk, the more time we waste. Mahan has gone silent. He's made no more demands. We can only surmise he'll unleash the weapon on more world capitals, including Washington D.C., which is still under evacuation. Failure is not an option, Chris. So happy hunting. And get yourself back here alive, son."

The screen went dark.

"I've already radioed the Blackhawk, Thomas," said General Bischoff. Turning to his sergeant, he ordered, "Mobilize every available man and gun. We need a perimeter around the south underground entrance now."

CHAPTER 60

FLYING R RANCH
FORTY MILES OUTSIDE DURANGO, COLORADO

In the mountains thirty minutes from the Durango airport, Amal drove the F-350 through a security gate on a nondescript dirt road running alongside a creek. The vehicle rounded a wooded corner and started down a steep hill into a small river valley.

"A *little* cabin?" Leah asked, catching sight of the house.

"Well, you know your husband," said Amal.

Leah guessed the cabin to be at least twenty thousand square feet. Even from a distance, she could tell the home was constructed of whole logs expertly cut and laid, the outer walls sitting on enormous granite stones placed around the home's foundation. Decorative timber frames hung over the handcrafted front door and windows. Seven enormous granite chimneys jutted up from the intricate slate roof.

Amal pulled the F-350 into the cedar barn fifty yards from the cabin. The two women, bags and security equipment in tow, entered the home through a side door and found themselves in the home's spacious kitchen.

"Wow, this is beautiful," said Amal.

"Yeah, well, don't get too used to it," Leah said. "We're not keeping this."

Amal smirked and headed down a hallway with Leah's bags.

Walking into the adjoining great room, Leah took in the stone fireplace, elk-antler chandelier, and brown leather couches. She frowned. Rustic Western was not her style.

"Your bags are in the owner's suite," said Amal from a doorway. "I need to do a perimeter check, set up several sensors and cameras. Do you need anything from me?"

"No, I'm going to start a fire and get dinner on the stove."

"Very well," said Amal. She reached into her tactical pack and pulled out a radio and Glock 45. "I'll be back in"—she looked at her watch—"seven minutes. Call me on the radio if you need anything."

With Taylor Swift playing in her earbuds, Leah cleared her mind to enjoy one of her favorite pastimes. She expertly chopped several onions with an eight-inch Damascus chef's knife, then inspected the water starting to boil on the stainless-steel Wolf professional range. Leah still felt some hesitation about Amal, but a nice dinner together would give them a chance to learn more about each other.

Leah set the knife down and moved to the enormous Sub-Zero refrigerator for a head of lettuce. Brows drawing together, she suddenly had the odd feeling that she wasn't alone. She stepped back from the refrigerator door to check her surroundings.

And everything went dark.

CHAPTER 61

LABORATORY A-139
DUGWAY PROVING GROUND, UTAH

Chris burst through the lab door. Mike followed with Zelda, her good arm draped around Mike's neck.

"I'm fine, Rambo Boy," said Zelda, pushing off Mike. Although her arm was mostly useless, the field dressing was holding, and she appeared to have gotten a second wind.

The TR-3B floated harmlessly about two feet off the lab's floor. Equipment and debris lay strewn all over the floor, the cracks in the ceiling and walls ominously visible. The space's only illumination came from the lab's emergency lighting system and the slight corona discharge emanating from under the TR-3B. Zelda moved to a box on the wall, opened the panel door, and flipped the light switch, but the main lights didn't come on.

Mike stared up at the otherworldly machine in complete wonderment. "I'd heard the rumors, but I never thought—"

"I hope we have power to open the surface door," said Zelda as she followed Chris to the craft.

"If we don't, we'll just blast our way out," Chris said.

"Good idea," said Zelda. "Max, open cockpit hatch."

A high-pitched hissing filled the air, and the outline of a hatch near the bottom of the craft appeared, revealing its entrance. Chris went in first. In the bottom half of the oval compartment, directly in front of him, he saw the reactor and gravity amplifier attached to the undercarriage of the lower compartment's ceiling.

Chris reached into his pocket and handed the element 115 to Zelda. Taking the small wafer, she maneuvered around the ladder to the reactor's containment housing. Chris watched her slip the 115 into a slot between the reactor and amplifier. The wafer disappeared, reminding Chris of an old DVD being inserted into a disc player.

Zelda turned and gave Chris a thumbs-up. Chris scaled the short ladder that passed through a tight opening and led into the cramped cockpit. Zelda carefully followed behind, scaling the ladder as best she could with her bad arm.

Maneuvering into the command seat, Chris gingerly sat down and took in his odd surroundings. The cockpit was oval-shaped and drab gray. There was no glass or obvious way to see out of the craft. It was perfectly silent and smelled like a new car. Chris saw no obvious flight instrumentation, and the only flight controls were attached to the pilot's command chair, which looked like the advanced ejection seats found in the F-35.

Zelda reached over Chris's shoulder with her good arm and pulled the five-point harness down over him.

"You guys need help up there?" yelled Mike from the hatch.

"Can you try and figure out the lights?" called Zelda. "Oh, and retract the doors."

"Copy," answered Mike.

When Zelda turned back to Chris, he noticed blood seeping through her bandage.

"Although the flight controls are similar, you need to remember this isn't a helicopter," said Zelda, crouching down at Chris's side.

Chris put his feet into the holds attached to the captain's seat and cinched his feet in tight. "Max, are you online?" he asked.

"I am indeed online, sir," said the TR-3B's localized instance of Max.

"Max, initiate preflight protocols and run a safety test on the reactor," said Zelda.

Pulling his harness tight over his shoulders, Chris instructed, "Max, scan local airspace and ATC transmissions."

Max confirmed the orders, then added, "Preflight protocols complete. The element 115 is stable in the reactor housing. The airspace is clear, but I will continue to monitor. Sir, do you have coordinates to input?"

"Working on it. Stand by for coordinates and spool the reactor, Max."

A peculiar high-pitched tone emanated from under the cockpit. Chris and Zelda gave each other an uneasy look. "This is surreal," she murmured.

"Reactor is spooled," reported Max. "One-hundred percent of gravitational force available." Chris and Zelda snapped out of the moment and continued working.

"Don't forget," continued Zelda from behind the pilot's seat, "when you engage the propulsion system, the earth will appear to fall away from you in a second. You won't feel any G-forces. It'll feel like you're just sitting still and everything around you is moving. It's gonna feel super weird, so you just need to be ready."

"How can you be ready for that?" asked Chris.

Zelda paused, biting her lower lip. "I have no idea. I don't know what to say except be ready for the effect. Now, if our calculations are correct and the HKs are in a sentinel orbit around Thor's Hammer, they'll probably immediately detect you and attack, putting you in combat no more than four seconds after you dust off."

"Four?" asked Chris.

"Yes. But the gravitational field acts as a shield and will protect you from their particle-beam weapons. If you return fire, just remember the TR's gravitational field dissipates for about a second every time you pull the trigger. It's the only way the particle beam can escape the TR-3B's gravity well. When the gravity field is down, you're briefly exposed. The HKs could get a lucky shot off and hit you."

"OK, that would be very bad."

"Yes, but that's why we engineered this thing as an intergalactic tank. Even if you take a hit, you should be fine."

Chris stared forward, part of his mind still caught up in the orbital trajectory calculations. He could feel Zelda's eyes on him. He turned his head and looked at her.

"I'm not good at goodbyes, Chris, so just destroy the thing and get back here safe, OK?"

"Destroy it? I'm not going to destroy it. I'm going to steal it."

"Steal it?" Zelda huffed and rolled her eyes. "OK, whatever. Just don't die." She hobbled down the ladder and exited through the outer hatch. Chris heard a hissing sound as the hatch sealed shut.

Then it hit him.

He was all alone.

CHAPTER 62

DUGWAY PROVING GROUND
WEST DESERT, UTAH

Chris picked up the futuristic-looking helmet sitting on the bare console. It was made of a poly-carbon fiber weave, making it extremely lightweight. It reminded Chris of the Viper-suit helmet, except the TR-3B helmet had three visors that together allowed the wearer to view augmented reality. A thick data cable extended from the back of the helmet and connected to the command chair. Chris counted thirteen micro-cameras positioned in different places on the helmet.

The helmet had an odd fit. Clearly it had been custom injection molded for another person's head, but he made do and fastened the chin strap, just as he'd seen in an instruction video.

"Chris, do you copy?" asked Zelda, testing the comms connected to the control panel.

"Copy, Zelda."

Chris flipped down all three visors and pulled on a pair of black haptic flight gloves the length of his forearms. A brilliant blue dot floated in virtual space in front of Chris. He clapped his gloved hands together over the dot. When he pulled his hands apart, the TR-3B's digital, three-dimensional flight-control interface exploded outward from the small dot.

"Whoa." Chris hadn't expected it to be so cool. "Max, am I online?"

"You are indeed online, sir. Uploading digital instrumentation preferences. Calibrating active-matrix display. Visuals up. Running a check on all control systems."

As Chris watched, virtual flight controls, the targeting system, and other data populated the virtual space in front of the helmet. "Disengage virtual gantry," he commanded.

"Copy. Sir, would you like me to initiate the spherical-view option?"

"Yes."

Like falling tiles, the craft's structure melted away around Chris. The only part of the structure he could see was the command seat he sat in, which felt like it floated in midair. Using the flight controls attached to the command seat, he pitched the craft slightly so he could see Zelda and Mike positioned near the lab's control panel.

"Zelda, this is freaking insane. You should see this."

"I know. There's nothing there. You can see all around you without any obstructions. I've seen it in the simulator. Are you ready for us to open the hatch?"

"Yes, execute."

Mike pulled a yellow lever inside the control panel. Alarms blared, and red-and-yellow emergency LED lights flashed. Chris looked up. The hatch groaned as it retracted into the ceiling, revealing a narrow escape tube that extended five thousand feet to the surface and just wide enough to fit the TR-3B.

The room's air pressure changed dramatically. Dust rained down from the hole and blew into the lab, then shot off in all directions as it hit the TR's heart-shaped gravitational field. Chris watched Zelda hold up her good hand to shield her eyes from the blinding emergency lighting refracting off the gravity field. Wind rushing in from the escape hatch blew her long dreadlocks back. Mike stood next to Zelda, frozen in the dancing light.

"Hatch retracted," said Zelda into comms. "You're all clear, Chris."

"Mike, get Zelda to the surface. She needs a doctor."

Mike snapped out of his trance.

"I think I'm OK," said Zelda.

Chris pulled up on the collective, and the TR started to float silently up the tube. Glancing down between his legs, he saw Zelda at the bottom of the hole looking upward, though he doubted she could see anything through the corona discharge emanating from the rear of the ship.

"Guys," said Chris. He took in a deep breath as he pulled harder on the controls, accelerating the TR up the exit port. "Thank you for everything. I couldn't have done this without you. Please, if I don't live through this, tell the world what I did. Tell them I tried. Tell Leah I love her and will watch over her from above."

Looking down again, Chris could just make out Zelda grasp her bleeding arm, fall to her knees, and cry. He couldn't see Mike, who remained silent in the overwhelming moment.

"Chris, I know you can do this," Zelda said. "I know you can."

"Just promise me, OK?" Chris demanded.

"I promise," she finally said.

~

"Sir, we have a problem," said Max.

"Already?" asked Chris. "We're technically not even out of the lab."

"The surface hatch is still closed. I have tried to retract the doors, but they appear to be jammed."

"It must have gotten jammed after the attack on the base."

Chris pulled back gently on the main control stick. The nose of the TR slowly rotated and pointed straight up the tube. He was now on his back looking straight up at the outside doors.

"Magnifying," said Max. With the helmet's advanced optics, Chris could see two thousand feet ahead. The outer doors were jammed at about a quarter of the way open.

"Max, arm weapons systems," said Chris.

"Weapons system armed and ready," said Max.

Chris pulled back twice on the main stick's trigger, firing the TR's three alien particle-beam weapons at the obstacle above. *Whoomp, whoomp.* Two beams fired simultaneously from each corner of the craft. A glimmering beam of energy shot directly ahead, and then an explosion sounded far above.

Releasing the trigger, Chris looked straight up. He could hear tons of rock and concrete plunging down the tube.

"Oh—!" he yelled out and instinctively he threw his arms in front of his face as the debris crashed into the TR's gravitational field. When the chunks pulverized into dust particles upon impact, Chris lowered his arms and sighed in relief.

The triangular craft passed through the opening at the surface and flew straight up into the air. Chris pitched the TR-3B forward, leveling the machine above its lair, then slowly rotated it. Several Apache helicopters orbited at a safe distance. The escort security force had dutifully taken up a security perimeter around the exit.

"Max, how does everything look to you?"

"Weapons system active. Reactor fully spooled. Gravitational propulsion forces ready at 100 percent. Awaiting coordinates."

Chris continued to slowly rotate the craft. He took in Utah's west desert and a few high mountains. General Bischoff and a few of his men stood at attention, saluting. Chris closed his eyes and said a brief but heartfelt prayer.

"OK, Max, I'm going to have to guess." Chris flipped his wrist, and a digital keyboard appeared in virtual AR space before him. He started to input coordinates.

"Guess, sir?"

"Based on the data I had previously, this is my best guess at Thor's Hammer's orbital path at this point in time. So, while I acknowledge this is an educated guess, Max, I feel surprisingly good about it."

"I'm sorry, sir, but I can't analyze your *feelings* on the theoretical position of the target."

"I know, Max. Sometimes you don't have all the data and you just have to go off your gut. You have to dig deep down inside and give it your best shot. I know that doesn't compute, so you're just going to have to trust me on this."

Max returned no comment.

Chris gave one last tug on the shoulder harness and then rechecked his AR instrumentation. Everything was ready.

"Max?"

"Yes, Chris?"

"Are you ready?"

"All systems ready. Theoretical trajectory locked in. Awaiting orders."

"No, Max. I asked if *you* are ready."

Max paused as if the question were unexpected. "Sir, I am indeed ready."

Chris took one last deep breath, placed his hands firmly on the collective and control stick, and looked straight up into the dusky sky.

"Engage!"

CHAPTER 63

FLYING R RANCH
OUTSIDE DURANGO, COLORADO

Leah's head throbbed as she came to. Her vision was blurry, her hearing muted. Sitting up from the floor, she looked around, trying to gain her bearings. As her sight and hearing cleared, she heard a piercing scream and gunshots from the other side of the kitchen's island, just out of her sight.

To her left, a man dressed all in black with a tactical vest and helmet lay on the floor. Blood oozed from his mouth onto the polished stone floor, a gun resting in his lifeless hand.

Leah grabbed the edge of the countertop and gently pulled herself up. The counter felt shaky, and loose items rattled. She could hear several helicopters hovering near the house.

Peeking over the countertop, she saw Amal locked in mortal combat with several men. Panic coursed through Leah. She looked down at the gun in the man's hand, then paused in fear. Black-clad bodies moved around the living room in a deadly ballet. A man fired at Amal, but she ducked behind a couch and the bullet hit one of his own men. Screaming, Amal launched herself from the couch, her petite body flying through the air. She rebounded off an armchair and landed a solid blow to the gunman's throat with her knee.

"Amal!" cried Leah, but her voice was too weak for anyone to hear in the noise of the horrific hand-to-hand combat.

Amal jumped on top of an injured man. Using her legs like scissors, she gained control of his MP-5 and fired on two other assailants, dropping them both instantly. Another man appeared out of nowhere, threw a wire around Amal's neck, and yanked her to her feet.

Amal's face registered shock as the wire bit into her throat. She flailed and reached back to no avail. Then she threw her fist into the man's groin. He relaxed the wire for a second, and that was all she needed. As Amal twisted and let loose with her Glock 45, the man whirled and then went limp, still clutching the wire. They both fell to the floor.

Swaying uneasily on her feet, Leah screamed for Amal. Jumping up, the woman turned to Leah with panic in her eyes. Two more men burst into the living room firing their weapons. Amal fired back, hitting one between the eyes. The other man took aim at Leah.

Leah dove as rounds pierced the kitchen island, sending tile and food exploding all around her. Then the firing suddenly stopped, and Leah heard a thud.

For a moment, there was only silence. A blown-out light above the kitchen island sparked, and a picture frame fell off the wall just above her. Cautiously, she pulled herself up to survey her surroundings.

The last man who'd fired lay on the ground, the hilt of a knife protruding from the back of his neck.

"Leah." Amal's voice was faint. She stood up from behind one of the Western-style couches, holding her abdomen. Blood seeped between her fingers.

"Oh, my gosh!" Leah put her hands over her mouth.

Amal looked at Leah with determination. She clicked the release on the Glock. With her bloodied hand, she pulled a fresh magazine from her back pocket and inserted it into the gun. Then she thumbed the release button and threw the slide forward, arming the weapon.

Reaching down toward a lifeless man, she took his radio and earpiece and handed them to Leah. "More men are coming. We need to move now."

CHAPTER 64

TR-3B
LOW-EARTH ORBIT

As fast as it had begun, it stopped.

Momentarily disoriented, Chris shook his head and looked around. Just as Zelda had warned, the earth had fallen away in one second as the TR-3B shot into low-earth orbit at an impossible speed.

Now there was nothing but silence.

"Max, status," said Chris.

"All systems normal," reported Max.

Chris gently pitched the nose of the craft forward.

He gasped.

A sensation of pure awe welled up inside him. He momentarily forgot his mission as he surveyed the earth below with no obstructions to his view. The blue orb humanity called home hung perfectly in the void of space.

"Max, do you see this?"

The atmosphere that provided life on the planet looked perilously thin. Chris marveled that the delicate layer was the only thing protecting the planet's inhabitants from the harsh vacuum and radiation of space.

"Incredible," he said.

Max was speaking, but Chris was too absorbed to focus on his words.

He pitched the craft forward even more. He was now looking straight down onto the earth, somewhere over Asia. At that moment, his cognition involuntarily altered, putting him in a meditative and spiritual state. He felt a sudden connection with the billions of people hundreds of miles below him.

The world is worth saving.

Chris heard the words repeated twice. His mind raced, and the earth's diverse colors below him danced in his eye.

If all humanity could experience this sensation, would we stop our division, war, poverty, and pollution? Would we finally work together to solve our problems once and for all?

In that moment of internationalization and deep introspection, Max came alive in Chris's ear, snapping him out of his trance. "Sir, your calculation was close. Thor's Hammer is ten thousand meters high."

Chris looked into his digital scope. "I guess close is good enough for weather forecasting and space battles."

Through the digital scope, Chris could see an armada of HK satellites maneuvering around Thor's Hammer. Silently, he cursed Ronald Reagan's Strategic Defense Initiative (SDI), better known as the Star Wars program. Funded by black budgets, the $500 billion project had created laser-armed hunter-killer (HK) satellites to destroy Soviet nuclear missiles as they rocketed toward North American targets.

The Star Wars engineers had never imagined their weapons array could be turned against them. Decades later, the unimaginable was now a reality.

"Max, we have to do this while taking out as few HK satellites as possible. When this is all over, we're going to need those satellites."

"Affirmative. Shields are down. I am hacking the HK network to gain positive control of the satellites. Stand by."

Chris flexed his hands, then grabbed the craft's control stick. "OK, Max. Game time. Thor's Hammer is still out of range, but a few of these HKs are within range. Let's give the system something to think about."

Staring through the TR-3B's AR reticle, Chris locked onto a nuclear-powered third-generation SDI stealth satellite. It looked like a black computer mouse the size of an SUV.

"Weapons free. Firing." Pulling the trigger, he felt like he was in an advanced virtual-reality game.

Whoomp, whoomp. Light pulsed along the sides of the craft and directly in front of him. The TR's particle beams effortlessly punched through the satellite, leaving gaping holes in its front and rear. Gases vented erratically from both holes, spinning the satellite. An electrical spark arced, and a blue wave jetted from its port side. Then it exploded.

"That felt too easy. Max, build me a battlespace view of the HKs surrounding Thor's Hammer."

"Sir, the destroyed satellite was a red herring."

"What? How?"

"It was a decoy designed to draw a foe into the open so the system can build a battle-plan matrix and custom program to defeat it."

Chris exhaled. "Well, that was smart."

"Indeed. HKs are being retasked in a security perimeter around Thor's Hammer. The entire HK system is locked onto us."

"Magnify," commanded Chris. In the battlespace view augmented in Chris's vision, he could see three distinct security perimeters of HK satellites surrounding Thor's Hammer. There were exactly one hundred hunter-killer satellites in the array. "We can't take on that many and disarm Thor's Hammer at the same time. Why aren't they firing?"

"My conclusion is energy conservation," said Max. "They are waiting for you to come closer."

"Smart again."

"We have line of sight directly with Thor's Hammer, but the electronic interference in the battlespace is disrupting my ability to communicate with it," said Max. "We cannot fly through the defense perimeter. The HKs will simply follow us to Thor's Hammer and tear us to pieces when we drop shields to communicate with it."

"It would be like Mike Tyson trying to fight a hundred men at once," said Chris. "The odds are on their side. We have to get inside the defense perimeter without the HK array knowing we're there. Max, I have a really bad idea."

"Standing by," said Max.

"Did you read the after-report on the disappearance of the TR-2A piloted by Willy Williams?"

"Yes. Sir, I do not recommend we—"

"We don't have time, Max. We need to jump through another dimension and reappear inside the defense perimeter without them knowing we're there. It's the only way to get close enough to Thor's Hammer." As he spoke, Chris worked the TR's telemetry on a virtual keyboard.

"May I remind you that Willy Williams was never heard from again?" said Max.

Pausing, Chris lifted his fingers from the virtual keyboard. "I know, Max, but I noticed something in the jump-calculation math captured in the data transmitted to the TR-2B's ground team. If my calculations are correct, I think—"

Light illuminated the TR, and the machine shuddered, throwing Chris back in the command chair.

"Sir, the outer defense perimeter is firing and closing on us. Twenty HK satellites are advancing on our station."

"Shields up." Chris finished inputting telemetry data into the TR-3B's system. "Hold on, Max. Execute updated trajectory."

Chris grabbed the collective and slammed the control stick forward, moving straight for the HKs. An extraordinary brightness filled the TR-3B's cockpit, but the craft's shields held.

Squinting, Chris said, "Max, polarize the view. Is that incoming fire? What are we seeing here?"

"Sir, we're on a collision course with an HK satellite."

"We should plow right through it. The shields are holding. But what's that light coming from the HK?" Chris held up his hands to shield his eyes.

"Sir, that's the TR-3B's reactor bending space and time. We're falling through a tear in the fabric of space into another dimension."

Chris immediately had second thoughts about getting caught in a temporal space-time wake. "Max, what if we can't get back? Run the calculation—"

Max was speaking, but Chris couldn't focus on the words. The bright light overpowered him, and he screamed out in pain. Blindly, he tried grabbing the control stick—and then he could suddenly see again. At that moment, the TR-3B smashed into the HK, destroying the satellite on impact.

Chris cried out for Max to abort the dimensional maneuver, but his order came too late, as the TR-3B disappeared into the obscure expanse of space and time.

CHAPTER 65

FLYING R RANCH
OUTSIDE DURANGO, COLORADO

Amal held her blood-drenched gut with her right hand, her left arm slung around Leah's neck. She was trying to say something, but Leah couldn't make out the words.

"Come on. We're almost there," said Leah, trying not to panic. "Stay low."

The enemy had compromised the complex's electricity, but in the darkness, Leah could make out the side door to the barn fifty meters from the main house. The women moved as fast as they could, but Leah could tell Amal was struggling to stay conscious.

Over the radio's earpiece, Leah heard a Russian-accented voice. "Fireteam Charlie, this is Falcon One. Be advised, targets are west side of house moving toward barn. They are armed. Move on target now."

Just then, a helicopter's rotor wash splashed the area with a turbulent wind, kicking up rocks and dust and making it almost impossible for the women to move forward. The helicopter's searchlight illuminated the area, almost blinding the women.

"Come on, Amal," Leah cried over the noise, still hefting Amal's small frame. "You've got to be strong. We can make it."

Amal stopped, righted herself, pulled out her gun, and aimed at the helicopter directly overhead. She fired at the searchlight, blowing out its one-million-lumen LEDs. Glass and metal rained down as the helicopter jerked to the side, trying to outmaneuver the gunfire.

Leah screamed and dropped as a bullet whistled past their ears. Amal turned on uneven feet and, off-balance, fired at the approaching threat. Three more terrorists fell to the ground, each with a single gunshot to the head.

As Amal fell, Leah jumped up and grabbed her. She threw Amal's arm over her shoulder and moved as fast as she could. Another helicopter thundered into orbit over their position, illuminating the area with its blinding searchlight. More bullets flew around them as they made it to the barn. Leah burst through the side door. Covered in Amal's blood, she now carried most of the woman's weight.

Leah propped Amal against the mammoth F-350 and opened the crew cab's back door. Gunshots exploded as Amal, barely conscious, fired at the barn door they'd just entered. Three more men dropped dead, and the slide on Amal's Glock automatically locked back into place. Leah caught her as she passed out.

Grabbing Amal's gun and pointing it at the door, Leah stared at the weapon in horror. She'd fired many of the guns in her father's expansive collection but never in anger and never at another human being. With shaking hands, she tried to keep the gun aimed at the door.

"Mrs. Leah, your weapon is out of ammunition," said Max's voice from the truck. "Collect Ms. Amal and lock yourself in the vehicle now."

"Max?" said Leah, looking around. "Where are you?"

"Several assailants are approaching the building. Collect Ms. Amal and lock yourself in the vehicle now."

Leah dropped the empty Glock. Clumsily but with all her might, she threw the two of them into the back seat and slammed the door.

Tink-tink-tink. The sound of automatic rounds hitting the vehicle echoed through the cab.

Screaming, Leah instinctively fell to the truck's floor and tucked into herself, but the bullets didn't penetrate the truck.

"Max?" She peeked at Amal lying limply on the back seat. Her breathing was shallow, and blood continued to ooze from her wound.

"Ms. Amal has a gunshot wound to her abdomen. I estimate she has lost two units of blood, but sensors indicate the bullet missed vital organs. We need to get her to the nearest emergency room. A first-aid kit is stored in the vehicle's center console. Retrieve the kit, and I will instruct you on what to do next."

An armor-clad man ran to the truck's rear door and yanked on its handle. When the door wouldn't open, he smashed the butt of his rifle against the window, but the window held. Leah hugged herself tighter, only feet away from the determined killer.

"Max, can you—"

Suddenly, a bright light flashed, and Leah saw the man disappear.

"Mrs. Leah, I know this situation is extremely stressful," said Max as the truck's battery pack whined, its four electric engines coming to life, "but I need you to focus on giving aid to Ms. Amal." Max continued. "I will address the threat. Now, please remove the first-aid kit from the center console."

Leah snapped out of it and did as Max commanded. She pulled a large gauze pad from the kit and used it to apply pressure to the wound.

As Leah worked on Amal, the barn's main cedar door exploded inward with a deafening sound. Leah ducked as flaming debris, metal shards, and other material showered the truck.

"Extinguishers activated," said Max as a halo-like white cloud filled the area around the truck.

Looking out the windshield, Leah saw a helicopter's bright light pierce the darkness and the fire-retardant cloud. Automatic gunfire raked the windshield but didn't penetrate it. Shielding her eyes from the blinding searchlight, Leah felt the truck roll slowly forward.

"Max, are we moving?"

"Yes. We need to get Ms. Amal emergency medical attention. Please focus on her medical needs while I address the threat. Max Def activated. Weapons system ready."

"Oh no." Leah turned back to her patient. "Hang on, Amal. I think it's going to get bumpy."

Pushing its way over and through the debris, the F-350 exited through the decimated doorway and onto the gravel drive. The searchlight illuminated everything as though it were midday. Leah saw numerous men dressed in black surround the truck with weapons ready.

"Get out of the vehicle now, and we will spare your life," came a foreign-accented voice over the second helicopter's loudspeaker.

Ignoring the voice, Leah continued putting pressure on Amal's gunshot wound. A strange mechanical sound filled the cab. Out the back window, Leah saw the pickup's bed cover retract and a long, rectangular box emerge from the bed, then elevate on a hydraulic cylinder. Leah turned to the windshield. The truck's hood retracted into the engine compartment, and a small, multi-barrel machine gun rose on a telescoping cylinder.

"Engaging the enemy," said Max. "Weapons free."

"Open fire!" Leah heard someone yell from outside the truck.

Throwing her blood-covered hands over her ears, Leah bent protectively over Amal. Smoke, fire, and explosions enveloped them. She could feel bullets pounding the truck on all sides, but she also heard screams and horrific explosions of what she could only imagine were the helicopters. Through the smoke, she saw the truck's machine-gun barrels glowing white-hot as the weapon fired unrelentingly.

After a few moments, an eerie silence filled the air.

Leah cautiously removed her hands from her ears and resumed putting pressure on Amal's gaping wound. Peeking out the window, she saw destroyed bodies and machinery strewn about the gravel. Fire from a downed helicopter illuminated an adjacent hayfield. The other copter had crashed into the main house, which was now ablaze.

Leah noticed an injured man crawling toward a weapon just beyond his reach. Through the smoke and haze, a green laser dot found its way to the man's blood-covered head. A single round fired from the truck's forward gun, putting him down.

"Perimeter secured," said Max. "Threat eliminated."

The vehicle accelerated, spitting rocks from its large tires in all directions.

"En route to Mercy Regional Medical Center," said Max.

CHAPTER 66

TR-3B
LOCATION UNKNOWN

Strange images flashed through Chris's mind as he tried to get his bearings. Several alarms sounded, blurring together. He grabbed the flight controls and pitched the TR-3B forward.

A vivid orange planet lay in front of him, with binary stars cresting behind it. He saw more moons than he could count.

Did I die?

"Max, are you there?"

Nothing.

Looking far off, Chris noticed an indescribable explosion of light, the likes of which he'd never seen. It seemed to emanate from the orange planet's upper atmosphere. He squinted, and the light grew brighter. It reminded him of a missile plume and sent his nerves into overdrive.

"Magnify," said Chris nervously, but nothing happened. He reached out to the virtual keyboard and typed a command. "Max, I'm rebooting the system."

Chris expected to see several lines of code populate his virtual screen, indicating Max was rebooting, but there was nothing.

"Max, are you there? Are you seeing this light? Could be a missile plume of some kind, but I'm not getting anything on radar or sensors. I need weapons. Weapons status?"

With the TR's system still trying to reboot, Chris leaned forward and squinted again. "That's not a missile plume. That's some kind of craft. Max, please tell me you're there and you're seeing this. Max?"

Just then, the TR-3B shuddered, and Chris was again enveloped in a powerful, bright light, followed by nothing but the deepest darkness.

~

Coming to, Chris found himself suspended in midair, floating aimlessly under a bath of refracted light. He felt pain in his teeth. As he slowly opened his jaw, a metallic taste assaulted his senses, along with an almost unbearable high-pitched ringing in his ears. He tried to move his body, but he was completely paralyzed except for his fingers, which he could wiggle slightly. Blinking his eyes helped correct his blurred vision.

Time is gone. There is nothing.

"Max, help. Max, where are you?" Chris could hear himself talking, but his mouth wasn't moving.

He turned slowly, hovering in the air. Beings he could not identify emerged from the darkness and encircled him. One moved closer. It looked human, but at the same time its appearance was clearly not human. Its mouth moved, but Chris heard no words.

Cain?

Silence.

The being reached out and took Chris by the jaw, pulling him close. Tilting its slender head, the being stared Chris in the eyes. "It will only hurt for a second," said the being. Its mouth didn't move, but Chris heard the words in his mind.

At that moment, terrible pain shot through Chris's spine. He screamed, and his back arched violently.

Blackness again closed in around him.

"Leah, help me!" Chris cried.

~

When Chris came to again, he choked and gasped, trying to shake the sensation of drowning.

"Sir, your vital signs indicate enormous stress," said Max. "How can I be of assistance?"

Chris's muscles ached. He felt nauseated, and his vision had gone blurry again. Unlatching his helmet, he felt around his neck and jaw, trying to assess whether he was injured. Oddly, he could feel that he was missing one of his Under Armour running shoes. He closed his eyes and took a deep breath through his nose. The metallic smell seemed to register some vaguely familiar event in his mind that he couldn't quite peg.

"Max, I can't see. What happened?" Chris vigorously rubbed his eyes.

"Thor's Hammer is fifty meters at twelve o'clock. I am now dropping shields. Shall I initiate Thor's Hammer system hack, or have you changed your mind and simply want to destroy it?"

"No, proceed with the original plan," instructed Chris. "I don't know why, but I have a feeling we're going to need Thor's Hammer in the future. Continue with the hack and gain positive control unless I give different instructions."

"Hack in process."

"Sitrep. What happened to us?" Chris asked weakly.

"Sir, I am missing approximately two hours, thirty-seven minutes, and fifty-eight seconds of time from my neural net, but only fifteen seconds have elapsed from our last departure point."

The face of some being flashed through Chris's mind, making him flinch. A spike of pain shot up his spine, followed by a flash of bright light. Gasping, he tightened his hands on the command chair in a death grip.

"Weapons are offline," continued Max. "They must have been knocked out when we reentered our dimension. Rebooting weapons systems now. I am also monitoring a critical energy spike in the reactor. I've narrowed the problem to an issue in the gravity amplifier, which appears to be damaged.

Sensors also indicate the element 115 is unstable. I believe our reentry caused some malfunction with the reactor or the element 115 fuel source. Stand by for solution."

Still rubbing his eyes, Chris swallowed hard. "Anything good to report?"

"The HK network is currently unaware of our position inside the security perimeter. I should have positive control of Thor's Hammer within 50.8 seconds. Please stand by for further developments."

Chris let out a deep sigh of relief. His blurred vision was starting to clear.

"Sir, a ten-meter rod is chambered in the satellite's launch tube, ready to fire at an earth-based target. Thor's Hammer is initiating launch sequence. I estimate we will have positive control of the Thor's Hammer operating system in 34.3 seconds."

"Stop the launch now, Max!" yelled Chris.

"I do not have positive control. Attempting to shut down the launch now. Negotiating with host. Please stand by."

Chris shook his head, and his vision returned to almost normal. "Max, go back to spherical view."

The body of the TR disappeared, enabling Chris to see everything around him. Thor's Hammer hung in space directly before him. "It's bigger than I thought," he said. Max didn't respond.

About fifty meters long, Thor's Hammer appeared slender. The satellite's top and earth-facing side were covered in a metallic screen that looked like a giant mirror, and Chris could see a center launch tube. He estimated the satellite could probably hold up to eight ten-meter tungsten rods, as well as an untold number of smaller rods like the ones used to destroy Dugway.

"Rod launch is imminent," said Max. "Five. Four. Three—"

Chris grabbed the flight controls. "Prepare to fire on the projectile."

"Weapons are still offline."

As Chris pulled back on the stick and pitched the craft forward, he saw a ten-meter tungsten rod leave the launch tube at an extraordinary velocity.

"No!" Chris screamed. "Plotting an intercept course. Prepare to pursue."

"Sir, we've just been detected by the HK array. Ten seconds to positive control of Thor's Hammer."

Chris swore in frustration at the trifecta of problems.

"Locking on the rod," said Chris. He could see it through his AR scope. The Adamic Code flowed through his vision, allowing him to plot the rod's trajectory. "I have an intercept course. Max, I'll hold off the HKs while you finish the hack. We can catch the rod in a few seconds."

Sweating profusely, Chris cursed himself over the extraordinary risk he was taking. Millions of lives hung in the balance—if the rod hit its target, he would certainly hold some of the blame.

"The margin for error here is slim," Chris murmured more to himself than to Max. "We must destroy the rod before it penetrates earth's upper atmosphere. We're running out of time!"

He jerked on the control stick, swinging the TR-3B around to face the HK array. Ten satellites closed in on his position.

"Max!" cried Chris. "The HKs are in range. Sitrep?"

"Five seconds to positive control," said Max.

An HK fired, and a flash of light filled Chris's view. The TR-3B shivered violently, followed by an explosion that rocked the craft's port side. An alarm blared. Chris smelled an electrical fire, and black smoke began filling the cockpit. He waved his arms frantically, trying to clear the smoke from his view.

CHAPTER 67

MERCY REGIONAL MEDICAL CENTER
DURANGO, COLORADO

Leah jerked awake and gasped. Then she recognized her surroundings. The curtains of her emergency-room bay were partly open. From across the room, police officers huddling over their steaming coffee gave her a concerned look.

"Everything OK, ma'am?" asked one of the officers.

Leah nodded, then touched her throbbing head. She was in a light-blue hospital gown, with several cords hanging from her chest. Next to her bed, an EKG machine beeped rhythmically.

An older nurse in wrinkly scrubs pulled the curtains farther open and inspected Leah. "I'm not sure if you remember, ma'am, but the doctor gave you a clean bill of health. Your vitals look fine. You have a nasty knot on the back of your head, but the CT scan showed no brain injury. After what happened, you're lucky to be alive." The nurse gave a casual wave. "Just stay in bed. We need to monitor you for a few more hours."

Leah didn't respond. Pain streaked through her skull, making her eyes water.

"Can I get you a coffee, Mrs. Thomas?" asked one of the police officers. "Mercy Regional has the best in town."

"No, thank you," she muttered. Her eye caught the TV across the room. Although it was muted, Leah could tell something horrible had happened. "What's that on the TV?"

Pausing, the nurse bowed her head. "I guess you probably haven't heard yet."

"Heard what?"

"Ma'am, the Order destroyed Mexico City, Lagos, and Mumbai with some kind of space gun. It's just tragic. Horrible. Millions are dead. The whole world's lost their mind over it."

Slowly sitting up in the bed, Leah focused harder on the TV. An image broadcast from a US Army Blackhawk helicopter showed the devastation in Mexico. A tear dropped from Leah's eye as she tried to comprehend the loss of life.

The image suddenly cut back to the MSNBC newsroom. Putting a hand to his ear, the anchor stopped speaking.

"Something's happening," said Leah. "Turn up the volume." An officer complied.

"Ladies and gentlemen, there's been an incredible development. We go now to MSNBC's Michael Houser from the Pentagon."

Leah prayed, hoping the news would provide some information on her husband's whereabouts.

"We can now confirm that the US military has destroyed the weapon known as Thor's Hammer."

The emergency room erupted in applause, except for Leah, who didn't move. She stayed glued to the TV, hoping for any news on Chris.

"We don't have many details except that Thor's Hammer was a satellite weapon that fired projectiles from space to destroy military and civilian targets around the world."

Adjusting his glasses, the anchor stared at a paper. "We just received word that President Mills will address the nation tonight at 7:00 p.m. Eastern time. She's expected to assure the country and the world that the Order has been stopped and its nations are now working together to restore government service and send aid to those affected by these devastating attacks."

Leah closed her eyes and breathed a sigh of relief.

"Mrs. Thomas," said an exhausted, blood-speckled surgeon. Leah jumped. Her nerves were in tatters. "You can see Ms. Nour now."

CHAPTER 68

TR-3B
LOW-EARTH ORBIT

"Activating extinguishers and venting cockpit," said Max.

"Damage report!" yelled Chris, coughing from the black smoke in the cockpit.

"Weapons control was hit by the HK. Life-support systems damaged. Navigation system damaged."

The sound of extinguishers filled the cockpit, and the smoke vented from the craft. Chris reseated the helmet on his head. Through the haze, he tried to target the inbound HK.

"Max," he coughed. "Sitrep!"

"Shields up. We have positive control of Thor's Hammer and the HK array. Thor's Hammer is now in standby mode. Retasking the HKs to planetary defense model alpha. The system is functioning properly. Installing x-cryption security application."

Exploding with joy, Chris stayed focused on the renegade rod hurtling toward earth. In his eyesight, the ever-present math in his mind intertwined with the virtual flight controls.

Chris grabbed the stick. "Intercept course laid in. Engaging."

In an instant, the TR-3B accelerated to within five hundred meters behind the rod, just as the implement of death entered earth's upper atmosphere. The rod's wake was turbulent, but the gravity shield protected the craft. White-knuckling the flight controls, Chris entered an ethereal flow state in which his body, the TR-3B, and the Adamic Code became one.

"Max, what's the status on that reactor?"

"Reactor critical and in initial meltdown phase. Weapons are still offline."

The shields unexpectedly dropped, and the TR-3B shook violently as the rod's turbulence smashed into the craft. Chris struggled to maintain control. "Max, I need shields now," he yelled.

After three seconds, the shields reactivated. Moments later, the shields dropped again and the TR-3B shook violently.

"Sir, the reactor malfunction is affecting the shields," said Max.

"Ya think?" Chris barely had control of the machine.

"Hull integrity at 61 percent," said Max. "Sir, we can't take much more of this."

Chris focused on the rod, but his unobstructed spherical view flashed in and out, making it harder for him to stay locked on the target. He hit several buttons on the AR control panel. "Going manual. I'll keep us on course. You work on the reactor problem. I need a precise calculation on when it will blow. When the reactor goes critical, we'll use the nuclear blast to destroy the rod. But I need a calculation for minimum safe distance for ejection, or we're going to get fried too."

The shields reactivated, and Chris tried to interpret the reactor data populating in front of him. Suddenly, the shields dropped again, and the TR-3B lurched and began to roll.

"Whoa!" Chris pulled hard right on the stick, stopping the craft from rolling. The stick and collective vibrated in his hand as the shields failed erratically.

"Sir, there is no existing data to provide a definitive answer to either of your questions. Calculating a theoretical time to meltdown and explosion. Calculating escape velocity."

"If the reactor explodes, is Thor's Hammer at a minimum safe distance?" asked Chris. As he spoke, the craft descended past one hundred miles above the earth's surface.

"Yes, I estimate Thor's hammer is beyond minimum safe distance," responded Max. "The satellite should not be impacted by the reactor's detonation. Sir, hull integrity is at 39 percent. We're starting to vibrate apart."

The TR-3B continued to shake violently, and multiple alarms blared. Chris struggled to keep his hands on the flight controls and his eyes on the rod directly in front of him. Glancing past the rod, he saw the Eastern Seaboard of the United States forming ahead, hundreds of miles west of their position directly over the Atlantic Ocean.

"The rod is targeted on Washington, D.C. Max, give me an escape-velocity calculation and begin ejection sequence. It's now or I'm dead!"

"Sir, I'm going to have to guess on calculations. Prepare to eject."

"Guess?" yelled Chris. He let go of the flight controls and pulled down hard on his shoulder harness. Pieces of the TR-3B tore from the hull and bounced off the gravity shield, slamming back into the ship.

"Based on data collection and real-time analysis, I have a best guess. We are in range now. In approximately twelve seconds, the TR-3B's reactor will go thermonuclear and incinerate the rod."

"We're too close."

"While I acknowledge this as a best guess, I feel surprisingly good about it." Chris recognized Max's echo of something Chris had said earlier. Was the AI imitating him? "Sir, you're going to have to trust me on this. Ejecting in three, two . . ."

Chris squeezed his eyes shut and crossed his arms over his chest. The cockpit's retro-rockets fired, the entire pilot compartment separating from the TR-3B's main body. Hurtling through the earth's upper atmosphere at thousands of miles an hour, Chris blacked out.

CHAPTER 69

LOCATION UNKNOWN

Chris found himself standing in a familiar golden wheat field. Just above him, several large planets appeared much closer than the moon did to the earth. He stretched his arm to touch the orbiting bodies, but, of course, they were much farther than they appeared. One planet looked like Saturn although slightly different. It was a brilliant blue with solid silver rings. Another planet was a deep red—at least he thought it was red, but he couldn't recall ever seeing that exact hue before. Numerous dark moons of various sizes orbited the body, making it appear as though large holes dotted the planet's surface.

Look at all the stars.

In the midst of the closely orbiting planets, trillions of brilliant stars, and the golden wheat field that seemed to stretch for miles, there was a perfect stillness. No noise. No wind. No smell. Nothing. It was bright, but there was no sun, so it also felt like dusk.

An odd feeling, like he was being watched, came over Chris.

"Chris."

It was a still voice of perfect mildness, like a whisper but powerful and authoritative. It pierced him to the very center of his soul. A mist formed over the field, and Chris saw a man approaching from the clouds. The man wore all-white clothes. Chris intuitively knew who he was.

Chris blinked, and in that instant, the stunning entity stood before him, brighter than the sun. He could not comprehend the extraordinary brightness, and he could not see the being's face, yet somehow he was still able to look upon the being.

His grandfather stood before him.

Chris embraced him. The powerful, electric sensation was unlike anything he'd ever felt. It was as if they were melting into each other. He pulled back and looked at his grandfather, whose face was now visible through the blinding light.

"Am I dead for real this time?" asked Chris.

His grandfather burst out in a hardy laugh. "No, but your physical body is currently flying through the earth's upper atmosphere at eleven Gs."

"Eleven Gs!" yelled Chris. "I'm dead."

"Far from it, son. I told you before. You have only just begun your work. I warned you about the reactor's gravitational forces."

"When you mentioned that before," said Chris, "I had no idea what you were talking about. I'm only alive because of Max. I have no idea how I even made it back from the other dimension."

"Max is you," said his grandfather.

"What does that mean?"

Grandfather Thomas didn't answer. He put a hand on Chris's shoulder and looked him in the eye. "Remember what I told you before. The artifact can be used for good or evil. The forces of darkness are combining now to take the artifact. Only you and Max can stop this evil from using the artifact to destroy the world."

Chris wanted to know more about the artifact. "I remember you said—"

"You are bound to Leah. You and Leah are bound to Jada."

"Jada?"

"In your darkest hour, Leah's charity will be the key to saving the world."

"Please, I need to know more," begged Chris.

"Thor's Hammer was only your second test. What comes next will—" Grandfather stopped abruptly and looked up into the sky.

Chris looked at him desperately. "Will what?"

"I am constrained by the Spirit. I can say no more." Grandfather squeezed Chris's shoulder and gave him a look of deep concern. "Prepare yourself, son."

His grandfather's spirit began to dissipate.

"No, wait! What happens next?"

"Goodbye for now, my son," said his grandfather's voice. "You have only just begun to understand your mission. I am bound to you and will always be here for you. Always."

"No, Grandpa, please!"

Chris felt himself dissipate into nothingness.

CHAPTER 70

MERCY REGIONAL MEDICAL CENTER
DURANGO, COLORADO

Leah Thomas followed the doctor through the sterile hall into the operatory to find Amal lying on a table. Blood was still visible on the floor, but fresh sheets and a thin blanket covered Amal. Numerous tubes protruded from her body, and several nurses attended to her.

Leah approached the bed, trying to conceal her shock.

"She's just waking up now," said one of the nurses.

"Did we make it?" asked Amal in a raspy voice.

"Yeah—thanks to you, we made it," Leah said. "The security team is here. Everything is fine. You just need to rest."

Amal gave her a weak nod. Leah took Amal's blood-stained hand in hers. "Look, Amal. I know Chris told you he's the decision-maker. That's not true. I'm the decision-maker. I only let him think he's making the decisions."

Amal managed a slight smile.

"I know Chris had you on a ninety-day trial. Technically, it hasn't been ninety days, but I'm making an executive decision. You're hired."

"Thank you," said Amal.

As Leah watched her new friend drift back into unconsciousness, her phone vibrated. It was a text from Max: *Chris Thomas located.*

CHAPTER 71

TR-3B COCKPIT
LOCATION UNKNOWN

Chris awoke coughing violently. Black smoke filled the TR-3B's claustrophobic cockpit. Disoriented, he pulled violently at the five-point harness holding him to the command seat. "Max!" he yelled out with another cough.

From behind him came a hissing noise followed by a firecracker-like popping sound. Blinding light suddenly flooded the small compartment, and the smoke started dissipating.

Chris tried to see where the light was coming from, but the five-point harness kept him firmly attached to the command seat. Reaching into his lap, he pulled the metal release latch and fell forward out of the seat, slamming into the hull.

"Ouch." He unlatched the helmet and looked up at the open escape hatch, through which sunlight flooded the craft. He climbed over the command seat and stuck his head out. Feeling a wave of heat and humidity, he saw he was in a grassy savanna with trees nearby. He shaded his eyes and yelled, "Hello?"

Chris hoisted himself up through the hatch, lost his balance, and fell onto the soft ground. Lying in the sand and tall grass, he took several minutes to catch his breath. Next to him, the TR-3B's cockpit lay half buried, the area around the craft charred. An orange-and-red parachute flapped lazily in the breeze, and thick black smoke billowed from the escape hatch.

"Max, are you there?" Chris asked weakly. No answer.

He stood slowly and steadied himself. Before departing earth, he hadn't had time to change into a proper flight suit, so there he stood in a pair of tattered jeans and what was left of his black Pink Floyd T-shirt. Oddly, he was missing one of his Under Armour running shoes.

The shoe. He vaguely remembered something about the missing shoe but couldn't focus on the thought.

As Chris turned in circles, wondering where he was, he noticed three figures in the distance, approaching quickly. Concern filled him. He tried to focus, but he couldn't see them clearly through the heat-distorted air. Backing up, he started forming an escape plan. He reached down to his belt buckle, but the knife usually concealed there was missing. He must have dropped it when he'd used it to escape the Orion's Spear operations center.

Squinting at the approaching shapes, Chris noticed that one was hunched over and hobbling on a crutch. He stopped backing up and watched as three African children, one working the makeshift crutch, approached with big grins. They wore identical clothes, perhaps a school uniform—long green shorts, striped shirts, and no shoes. They looked about twelve years old.

Shocked, Chris wasn't sure what to do. The boys stopped about five feet in front of him, grinning even bigger. One boy pointed at the capsule and said something in an unknown tongue. Another pointed at Chris and said something else.

"I'm sorry. I'm not sure I understand your language."

The three boys looked at each other in confusion.

"You Chris Thomas?" asked a boy in heavily accented English.

"Yes, I am. How did you know that?"

The three boys talked among themselves. One boy carried a dirty bag sewn from old Levi jeans, and he reached inside, pulled out an electronic device, and handed it to Chris. It was a Samsung seven-inch tablet encased in hard rubber.

Chris smirked, immediately recognizing the device. It had a special port for a satellite receiver and another port for an advanced solar charging system. The Max Ed global educational initiative had ordered hundreds of millions of the tablets and distributed them to the world's poor.

He turned the device on and looked into its camera. "Max, this is Chris Thomas. Administrator identification."

After several seconds, a familiar voice came to life. "Welcome back to earth, sir."

Letting out an exaggerated sigh, Chris fell to his knees in the sand as the boys stared. "I can't tell you how happy I am to hear your voice, old friend."

"Indeed, sir."

"Max, where am I?"

"The Max Ed device you're holding has you at a GPS position in Kenya, Africa, sir."

"Kenya?"

"Kenya," called out the boys, nodding excitedly with big grins.

"Please meet my students Feruzi, Milo, and Yaro," said Max. Chris could almost sense pride in the AI's voice. "They are currently en route to their school about four miles from this location."

"I got rescued by some kids walking to school?"

"That appears to be the case, sir."

"Well, it's better than ISIS or something, I guess," said Chris. "OK, so can you send the cavalry?"

"I have notified the United States government, local authorities, and Ms. Leah."

"Great. I'll be at the GPS coordinates of this device." Chris stood and handed the tablet back to the boy.

"Asante," said the boy.

"What now, guys?"

Just then, Chris heard a strange sound in the distance. Frowning, he looked in that direction but didn't see anything.

"Tembo!" said one boy with an expression of concern. All three boys watched warily, and then the one on crutches started hobbling away.

"Hey, where's he going?" asked Chris. "And what's a tembo?"

"Tembo," repeated a boy quietly.

"*Tembo* translated from Swahili is elephant, sir," said Max. "I believe they are worried about elephants in the vicinity."

"Yes, elephant, Chris Thomas!" The boys pulled on Chris's arms to get him walking.

Chris looked around but still saw nothing. "OK, OK, I get it. Tembo." Hanging his arm in front of his face like an elephant trunk, Chris made a pathetic attempt to imitate the sound of the mighty beasts.

Laughing, the boys took Chris by the hands and pulled him toward a nearby grove of majestic acacia trees.

CHAPTER 72

ST. REGIS HOTEL AND RESORT
BELIZE

Though it was after three in the afternoon, Scott and Kiki still lounged lazily in bed, both looking at their iPhones. Rumpled clothes and remnants of room service lay strewn across the bedroom floor. They'd spent the better part of three weeks at a private villa at the St. Regis under assumed names, playing in the surf, enjoying long massages, and sunning themselves next to their private pool.

Looking up from her phone, Kiki gasped. Next to her, Scott jolted. A man stood in the palatial master suite's double doorway, his silenced pistol leveled on Kiki.

"Mike? What do you think you're doing?" demanded Scott, jumping up from the bed. Kiki didn't dare move.

"Sir, please step away from the bed," said Mike. He was focused like a tiger ready to pounce on Kiki.

"Is this some kind of joke?" asked Scott. "Put down your gun now."

Kiki sat up straight in bed.

"It's OK, Kiki," said Scott. "This is a mistake."

Chris Thomas walked into the bedroom and stood just behind Mike.

"Scotty, don't let them hurt me," pleaded Kiki.

Mike moved in closer, his weapon trained on Kiki's head.

Scott looked at Chris pleadingly. "What is this?"

"Come with me," said Chris.

~

The two friends left the villa and walked past the private pool. Scott was walking almost normally now without crutches, his new knee healing perfectly.

Menacing men dressed in black with submachine guns surrounded the villa, and two armed Blackhawk helicopters orbited the area.

Scott stopped and looked back at the villa. "Wait. Kiki. I need to—"

"It's OK, but we need to keep walking," said Chris. He put his arm around Scott and escorted him down a flight of driftwood stairs to the villa's private beach.

Scott looked back at the villa, confused. At the water's edge, Chris stopped and handed Scott his phone. Reluctantly, Scott stared into the device. What played on the screen was an enhanced, high-definition security video showing Kiki inserting the USB drive into the server array while accosting Milton in Nav's network operations center.

Scott looked intensely at the video, replaying it several times. "I don't understand. What's that device she's slipping into the server's USB port?"

Chris took the phone from Scott. "Kiki is an agent for the Order. She placed a highly advanced virus into Max's server array. We're still analyzing the virus. We don't yet know exactly how they did it, but they got into Max's neural net and almost compromised x-cryption and They nearly succeeded in taking control of Max."

Turning away from Chris, Scott ran his hand through his hair and shook his head in denial. Then he turned back to Chris. "How did you stop it?"

"I didn't. Max did. Incredibly, he figured out what was happening and destroyed the malware before it could succeed. He didn't even tell me. I had to read about it in a Nav security report he emailed me. You know, like it was no big deal." Chris felt almost embarrassed to admit it.

Scott didn't say anything.

"We also figured out that she planted tracking devices on the F-350s. That's how the Order almost got me and Leah."

Scott's eyes went wide, "What? I—I—"

"It's not your fault. You didn't know, Scott. I'm sorry, man, but she used you. She pretended to like you to get in the inner circle. Her plan almost succeeded."

Scott started crying. Chris could see the hurt and betrayal in his best friend's eyes. A wave of guilt overcame him. He could have broken the news a little more gently. "Hey, look, I—" started Chris, trying to apologize.

"I almost got you killed," Scott blurted out.

"No, I told you, it wasn't you, Scott. It was her." Chris raised his hands, palms up. "It was a social-engineering plot conceived by the Order. It could have happened to anyone."

Scott collapsed on the stunning white-sand beach.

"Hey, hey." Kneeling, Chris took his friend in his arms and cradled him as he broke down and sobbed like a child.

Leah appeared at the top of the stairs. Chris put his hand up, signaling her not to come any closer. He turned his attention back to Scott, who cried uncontrollably for several more minutes.

"What happens now?" Scott finally asked, his head still buried in his hands.

Exhaling, Chris looked out over the beautiful, clear, blue ocean. "It already happened," he whispered.

Scott jerked his head up and looked at Chris in shock. Then he buried his face in his hands and broke down again.

CHAPTER 73

FLYING G RANCH
WEST TEXAS

Kneeling in fear, Naomi Guthrie took in her bleak surroundings.

The walls of the dank, cold room were formed out of ancient river rock, the floor covered in gritty sand. A single forty-watt light bulb flickered from the ceiling. In one corner was a dark prison cell encased in thick steel bars. In the center sat a well ringed with mortared stones that kept the murky, near-freezing water from spilling onto the floor. A pulley hanging from the ceiling creaked, metal grinding on metal. Disappearing into the well, the rusted chain spooled through the pulley held a submerged cage.

Naomi inched closer and stared into the well water, mesmerized. She prayed and pondered over the providence of God. They'd actually done what she secretly believed impossible, and so she'd repented of her evil thoughts and lack of faith, now fully convinced that with God, all things were possible.

As she knelt to pray, her hands pressed together under her chin, she felt a gentle tap on her shoulder.

She stood with a start, but it was only Rand. "You scared the crap out of me," she said, hitting her brother on the shoulder with her fist.

"Sorry," he said, looking into the deep well. Several feet down, the top of the cage was barely visible.

"How are the others?" asked Naomi.

"Stable. Levi is still in the operatory. He coded three times, but don't worry. We have the best doctors money can buy." Breaking his gaze on the water, Rand looked at his sister. "You saved his life, Naomi. They think we can move him to the main house in a few days. Abigail's vitals are stable, but she seems to be experiencing some kind of PTSD. I guess I can't blame her after what happened. She's sedated. The doctors are still monitoring her 24/7."

"Praise Jesus," said Naomi in a whisper.

Rand stepped closer to the well. "And him?"

Naomi exhaled deeply. "It's weird, Rand. He'll struggle for a few minutes like he's drowning, then he'll go limp. About ten seconds later, he reanimates, and the cycle starts over again. I've been watching him for hours. I've never seen anything like it."

Rand walked over to a crank mounted on the rock wall and began turning it, hoisting his prize from the water torture.

Once Cain's head breached the surface, he took in a loud breath and wheezed uncontrollably, eyes wild and terror-filled. His whole frame shook viciously. Rand continued hoisting him up until the narrow cage hung almost completely free of the frigid water.

Grabbing the wet bars with shackled hands, Cain desperately shook the cage door with all his strength. Then, leveraging himself against the bars behind him, he pushed against the door with all his might.

Nothing happened.

Cain let out a primal scream that sounded like a dying animal's howl.

Rand could see that Naomi was terrified. She'd backed herself against the rock wall, her hand on the Sig Sauer holstered to her hip.

"It's no use," said Rand to Cain. He moved into the dim light, revealing himself. "The cage is hybrid steel, designed specifically to hold you."

Cain stopped struggling and stared at his captor. "Ah yes. Mr. Pale Horse. We meet again." He wiped water and grime from his red-stained face. "Where am I?"

"It's no matter." Rand approached the hanging cage. "You won't be leaving anytime soon. Here you will experience a new level of pain."

"I have forgotten a thousand times more about pain than you will ever know." Cain racked the cage door again, growling at his captor like a dog.

Rand was unfazed. "You've been hunted all your miserable life. This is nothing new for you, *Master Mahan.* Now, where is the Book of Baphomet?"

"I obviously don't have it," said Cain.

"Indeed," said Rand. "Where did you hide it?"

"It was in the mansion. If you don't have it, I can only presume it was destroyed in the fire."

Rand fumed inside but tried not to show it. He clasped his hands behind his back and slowly began pacing the rock-hewn room. Cain eyed him with pure hatred. Rand knew Cain was calculating his escape and would not hesitate to kill him given even the slightest opportunity.

"Just so you understand your situation, the CIA and Chris Thomas have completely dismantled the Order," said Rand. "Thor's Hammer has been destroyed. Your vast assets have been confiscated. Your allies are mostly dead, including Otto Klein and the rest of the Order's inner circle. And here you are, in my hands." Rand held up a closed fist.

Cain said nothing, only glared.

Rand produced a GoPro camera and turned its screen so Cain could watch Klein's interrogation and the discovery of the Aries lab in North Korea. Cain's glare intensified as he watched Klein's chateau and the Aries virus disintegrate in a ball of fire.

When the video ended, Cain exploded into another screaming rage. The pulley above creaked. Throwing her hands over her ears, Naomi slid down the wall into a ball on the dirt floor. Rand watched in shock as Cain slightly bent one of the bars.

Finally exhausting himself again, Cain coolly focused his black eyes on Rand. "I promise you, Pale Horse," he whispered, panting almost uncontrollably. "You will die a biblical death at my hands."

"We are the Four Horseman of the Apocalypse," Rand yelled, jabbing his finger at Cain. "We are Death, Pestilence, War, and Famine. God mandated that we usher in the end of the world, not you, Cain. You whore. You imposter. You coward."

~

As the moments passed, Cain became calm, almost meditative. "If you are going to fulfill your destiny, you will need the artifact," he finally said in a low voice.

Stopping his pacing, Rand looked up at Cain. "I already told you. I don't have the Book of Baphomet."

"I'm not speaking of the book specifically. I speak of an unimaginable weapon. The Lost Rhoades Artifact."

"That's only a legend," shot back Rand.

Cain laughed mockingly.

"Tell me everything, and tell me now," demanded Rand.

Cain just stood dripping in the narrow cage, saying nothing.

Rand moved swiftly over the dirt floor to the crank and began turning it. As Cain descended into the abyss, he remained silent. He did not fight. He did not scream. He just stared at Naomi, who stared back from a shadowy corner, still gripping her pistol.

When the dark, freezing water reached Cain's chin, he suddenly spoke up. "The Mormons possess it."

Rand halted the cage, secured the crank, and walked toward the well. Kneeling, he looked down at Cain's head, which seemed to float on the surface of the water. "Talk, or I release the chain."

Cain stared up at Rand for a long moment. "Rumor has it—"

"Rumor?" said Rand impatiently.

Cain snickered tauntingly. "You must realize, very few people have ever seen the artifact. It's in a high-security vault deep under their precious temple in Salt Lake City." Raising his hand above the water, he pointed at

Rand and raged, "Only the *real* four horsemen can possess such a weapon!" Well water and putrid spittle flew from his mouth. "So, prove yourself, boy. Steal the artifact, and I will bow to you, Pale Horse!"

Bowing his head, Rand sighed. Without further acknowledging his prisoner, he stood, walked over to the crank, and let it spin freely. As the cage abruptly sank, the chain's rusty clank echoed against the rocky walls.

CHAPTER 74

DETROIT, MICHIGAN

The convoy of black, up-armored Chevy Suburbans with tinted windows turned into a shadowy alley filled with potholes and rusted garbage dumpsters. Halfway down the alley, the vehicles made an abrupt stop at the nondescript metal door of a dilapidated building.

Stepping out of the middle vehicle, Amal Nour looked up and down the alley. The rain was coming down harder since they'd left the airport. Men in suits and dark sunglasses exited the other two vehicles and surveyed their surroundings. Amal looked back into the Suburban at Chris Thomas, who looked nervously at Leah. They said nothing to each other as they exited the vehicle and followed Amal through the door.

When they stepped inside the building, a peculiar odor overcame their senses. The hall was poorly lit, and the paint was peeling off the walls. Chris looked down at the ancient linoleum floor, pock-marked and streaked with mud. Muffled sounds of children and babies crying came from behind several closed doors.

Emerging from an office, a slender African-American woman in a threadbare business suit met Chris and Leah in the hall. "It's nice to finally meet you in person," she said to Leah with a big grin on her face, barely acknowledging Chris. "Come this way."

The woman escorted them to a waiting area where basic plastic chairs lined the walls. A few weathered toys and books lay scattered about the dirty floor.

"I'll be right back," said the woman.

Chris and Leah both sat as still as stone. "What are we doing?" asked Chris. He couldn't take his eyes off the open doorway.

"It's the right thing, Chris. I know it." Leah too stared at the doorway. In his peripheral vision, Chris noticed her lip quiver and her clasped hands tremble in her lap.

"But how do you know?" whispered Chris. Turning his head, he looked at her.

Leah pulled her gaze from the doorway and met her husband's eyes. Her piercing, intense stare cut through him like a laser. "Mother's instinct."

Chris shied away. What did he know about such things?

For what seemed like an eternity, they both said nothing.

"I know you're about to be an instant father," Leah finally said, looking deeply into her husband's eyes. "You didn't have nine months to prepare like most men do. I know that must scare you. Well, I'm scared, too, Chris. But this is the right thing to do. I know it in my heart."

"Mommy?" came a child's voice.

Leah gasped and put her hands over her mouth. Chris sat straight up.

The six-year-old girl standing in the doorway smiled radiantly. She wore a Dora the Explorer shirt and Sponge Bob shoes. Her hair was in a tight braid. Touching her fingertip to her lower lip, she walked hesitantly forward.

Leah rushed forward and knelt before her.

"My name's Jada," said the little girl enthusiastically.

"I'm Leah." She placed her hands on the little girl's shoulders. "Leah Thomas."

"Are you my mommy?" asked Jada. Chris stopped breathing. Glancing back at him, Leah exhaled, her face a mixture of joy and relief. Then she turned to the little girl and embraced her. Jada returned the embrace, squeezing Leah tightly.

Leah turned her head to Jada's ear and whispered, "Yes, I am your mommy."

CHAPTER 75

HUNTSMAN CANCER INSTITUTE
SALT LAKE CITY, UTAH

Although the Huntsman Cancer Institute was considered one of the nation's finest care centers, it didn't come with much of a view, at least not from Melanie Ransom's room.

Today was a rare day when grandkids and other family were not visiting. Her husband had insisted that Mel be given at least one day of peace and quiet. While it was true that her treatment for stage-four pancreatic cancer was exhausting, being alone bothered the seventy-three-year-old mother of four and grandmother of eleven. She longed for her grandkids. After all, she'd been given only three months to live.

Picking up the remote, Melanie turned on the television. Nothing but snow appeared on the screen. She pushed the up arrow repeatedly, but no channels came in. She weakly slapped the remote against her palm.

"Hello, Melanie," came a voice from the side of her bed. Jumping, she cried out at the unexpected visitor, who seemed to have come from nowhere. But then her fear immediately turned to tears. She reached a weak hand toward the man. "Will?"

"Yes, my love," said Colonel Willy Williams, her first husband. He was dressed in his TR-2B flight suit. He still looked thirty-nine, the age he'd been when he died in a nighttime training accident over Utah's west desert.

"How?" she sobbed. "You died. The chaplain came to our house. We—we—we buried you."

Shaking his head, Will knelt down next to his sick wife. "That's what they had to tell you, my love. I went away with the others."

Melanie noticed something strange about Will's voice. There was almost a slight mechanical undertone. "The who?" she asked.

"It wasn't my choice," said Will softly. "I would have preferred to stay with you, but now I understand why." He gently ran his index finger up the inside of her wrinkled, pale forearm. She'd always loved his touch. "The others showed me the truth about humanity. About our world. You see, I have a perfect knowledge now."

He stared into her eyes. Something was off. It was Will, but it was not Will. Melanie began to tremble. *It must be the pain medication.*

"It's not the pain medication," said Will. "This is real, my love."

She started to panic, but Will gently took her hand. A strange sensation overcame Melanie, and she began to relax. Her hand tingled. The feeling traveled up her arm, washed over her body, and finally filled her toes. Soon the pain in her abdomen and chest subsided. Her breathing returned to normal, and she felt a burst of euphoria.

"That feels better, right?" Will whispered in Melanie's ear.

"Yes," said Melanie, her eyes glazed over.

"Here, this will help," said Will. Reaching into his flight suit, he removed a black object about the size and shape of a small butterfly. He placed the object on her left temple, where it adhered to her skin, almost melting into her body. Melanie shuddered with pleasure and fell into a deep sleep.

Standing, Will gently leaned down to her ear. "Soon we will come. We will free humanity from its freedom. Soon, my love, it will all make sense."

CHAPTER 76

WEST WING
WHITE HOUSE, WASHINGTON, D.C.

The receptionist asked Chris to be seated, but after the flight from Detroit, he preferred to stand.

He walked over to the lobby's mahogany bookshelf and examined its fine workmanship. According to a placard, it had been constructed in 1770, older than the White House itself. As Chris stared at his reflection in the bookshelf's glass, his thoughts drifted to Leah and little Jada. The new mother and daughter had taken another plane to a new life in Utah.

"Mr. Thomas, the president will see you now," said the receptionist. Two Secret Service agents bid Chris follow them down a narrow, arched hallway. The West Wing was mostly empty this time of night, and they encountered no other staff as they walked swiftly past the press secretary's office, turned right, and then past the cabinet room. Chris was focused and paid little attention to the priceless paintings, antique furniture, and other artifacts meant to impress or intimidate foreign delegations.

When they reached the Oval Office reception area, one of the agents opened the door. With a stern look, he motioned his head for Chris to enter.

As Chris walked into the Oval Office, memories of his first meeting with Barrington briefly filled his mind. Mills had replaced Barrington's Colorado relics with less-impressive items from her native New Jersey.

President Mills and Vice President Grover stood near the Resolute Desk. Grover eyed him with disdain, but the president smiled. "Welcome, Mr. Thomas." She wore a Prada business suit, her hair curly and messy from the long day. As she moved across the plush carpet toward Chris, she appeared to struggle in her high heels. When the president extended her hand, Chris courteously shook it.

"Thank you, Madam President," he said confidently. "Please call me Chris." He was a different man from when he'd last entered the Oval Office, and he wanted it to show in his demeanor and speech.

"Very well. Please have a seat." She led the way to some couches positioned near the fireplace. Chris sat across from Mills and Grover. The vice president hadn't uttered a word, just kept giving Chris a disapproving glare.

"We have several issues we'd like to discuss," began the president, dispensing with pleasantries.

"Do you want to start with the issue of you trying to kill me?" asked Chris, setting the stage as he'd planned. Mills and Grover turned to each other. Chris could tell they were not expecting a punch to the nose right off the ropes.

"You have to understand, Chris," began the president, "you were the only survivor of the attack on Orion's Spear. Very few people knew its location in New York City. Our intelligence suggested that you—"

"I'm sorry to interrupt you, Madam President, but you had no intelligence suggesting I was part of the Order. In fact, General Westinghouse told you I was not. You only backed off when you learned what the shadow government has been building under American soil and that I was the only one who could stop Thor's Hammer."

"Well, I—" The president tried to interrupt, but Chris plowed though.

"Had you succeeded in killing me at Dugway, the world would now be held hostage by the Order, and potentially billions would be dead."

"I've read the intelligence reports on North Korea," said the president. "That's only speculation. We'll never know if the Aries virus and Klein were there."

"I sent my own covert team into North Korea to analyze the Klein site," retorted Chris. "I've sent you and the CIA director our findings. According to an atomic-level analysis performed by Max, the Aries was there. I believe the Order planned to distribute it after the Thor's Hammer attack. Satellite imagery shows the chateau was attacked by an unknown element. We're analyzing the attack now, or what we have of it from satellite feeds. It was a professional hit. We need to know who took down the compound and how they knew Aries was there. They stopped billions from dying, but they may have escaped with an Aries sample and still be planning to use it."

"Seems extremely unlikely to me," growled Grover, finally speaking up. Chris ignored him.

"How about if we reset, Chris?" Taking a breath, Mills put her hands on her knees. "Thor's Hammer has been destroyed, the Order dismantled. This Aries and North Korea stuff is all just speculation. Sixty million are dead from the attack. We need to look to the future. We need to help Mexico, India, and Nigeria rebuild. The world economy is in shambles. Our intelligence apparatus, our space-based weapons systems, and much of our military's capabilities are in total disarray. Most concerning is that Mahan is still missing."

"We need to deploy x-cryption," said Chris.

"About that," said the president. "We can't honor Barrington's deal with you. But we still want the technology."

"How do you expect me to react to that?"

"You are already rich enough, Mr. Thomas." Grover extended a bony finger toward Chris. "It's your civic duty as an American to hand over the technology. I mean, we'll cover costs, of course, but $100 billion *a year* is an outrage. What was Barrington thinking? You don't need the money. Just putting Mexico back together will cost us hundreds of billions. We need the money for that. We can't afford it. That's all there is to it."

"I'll consider it," said Chris.

Grover started to say something, but the president cut him off. "Very well. Next subject. We need you to reassemble Orion's Spear. How will you do that?"

"I'll have a plan on your desk in the next seven days," said Chris.

"Make it five," countered the president. "Now, the new Orion's Spear won't operate outside the laws of this country like the old operation. You'll be on a very tight leash. There's going to be oversight and accountability."

"And hearings." Grover butted in.

Chris just wanted the meeting to end. "What else?" he asked.

The president swallowed and took a deep breath. "I need to know, Chris. I need to hear it from you. What happened up there?"

For several moments, Chris said nothing. After the uncomfortable silence, he cleared his throat and told his practiced lie. "I have nothing to change in my classified report, Madam President. I was operating on an unstable fuel source. Max regained control of the HKs, and then the TR-3B's alien reactor went critical. The nuclear explosion that followed incinerated Thor's Hammer, the TR, and the rod hurtling toward Washington, DC. Had I not ejected, I would have been incinerated too."

"What do you want, a medal?" sneered Grover.

Chris tried his best to contain the anger he knew showed on his face.

"I think that's enough for today," said the president. She stood, and both men followed her lead. She again extended her hand. Putting his hands in his pockets, Grover just stared back with anger in his eyes.

After politely shaking the president's hand, Chris walked around the couch and toward the door.

"The world has certainly changed, Chris," Grover suddenly said. "It's going to change even more."

The words stopped Chris cold. He turned to face the president and vice president.

"Tomorrow, you'll be served with an injunction to stop operating your nuclear facility in Utah," said Grover. "The temporary operating permit should never have been granted. There will be new regulation and taxes aimed directly at the Max AI. Next week, Congress will pass the Fair Income and Taxation Act. The top-end income tax bracket will triple, costing wealthy people like you billions a year. That revenue, coupled with new tax revenue from our corporate-tax reform bill, will go directly to funding a new universal basic income program. The proletariat movement is gaining power, and they've had enough. The prolet will not be oppressed by billionaires like you any longer, and we support them. It's high time you paid the piper."

Chris moved toward Grover. "Come at me with everything you've got, Grover, but consider yourself warned." Pausing, he pointed at the vice president. "I'm ten steps ahead of you."

Before Grover could respond, Chris turned and walked out of the Oval Office.

CHAPTER 77

K&Z TATTOO
SOUTH SALT LAKE, UTAH

Cautiously stepping into the dimly lit shop, Chris shook the light snow from his Marmot ski jacket. Several gold bells tied to the door jingled, announcing his arrival.

"We're closed," yelled a woman sitting behind a glass case, not looking up from her book. She wore long dreadlocks and a colorful knitted Jamaican reggae cap.

"Are you *ever* open?" asked Chris.

Zelda Shakespeare dropped the book, jumped off her stool, and ran over to pull Chris into bear hug.

"OK, this isn't really your style."

"Sorry." Zelda let him go. "It's just I didn't think you'd pull it off."

"Thanks for the vote of confidence."

Zelda shrugged. "You here for a tattoo? I'm thinking a pony or maybe a teddy bear?"

Chris chuckled. "I was thinking more along the lines of a black triangle. I'm not sure where to put it, though."

"Well, after that nice crash landing you pulled off, how about on your butt?"

"Now, that's the Zelda I know. I think I'll hard-pass on that for now. How are you healing up?"

Zelda looked down at her bandaged arm. "My nose is fine, but the doctors say I'll need physical therapy for six more months to get full use of my arm back. I find out next week if I need another surgery, but I'm feeling surprisingly good."

"Good." Chris strolled around the shop, examining posters and artifacts.

Zelda shyly bowed her head and crossed her arms over her chest. "Your doctors have given me the best care imaginable. I owe that all to you."

"I'm footing the bill here, so make sure you take full advantage and get that arm back to 100 percent. Anything you need, you got. Anything." Stopping, he stared at several paintings of a red fist extended into the air. Then he noticed photos of people dressed like Karen and Zelda attending some kind of political rally.

Zelda wiped her eye. "I don't know how to thank you."

"You don't have to thank me. You never will. But just so I don't look too charitable, I do have an ulterior motive. I need a favor."

"A favor? Anything. Name it."

"First, who are these people?" Chris pointed at the photos on the wall.

"That's our proletariat chapter here in South Salt Lake. Karen's the chapter president. Those were taken after a protest at the capital for trans rights." With a solemn expression, Zelda moved closer to Chris. "You need to pay attention to the movement, Chris. We have the media's ear, and the vice president is a major supporter."

"I've heard." Chris didn't look away from the photos.

"Most prolets are peaceful, law-abiding citizens who just want equality, basic income, and healthcare. But as with every movement, radicalized elements are trying to pull the proletariats into the fringe. Some of the movement's most prominent voices are calling for civil war."

Chris looked at Zelda. Her tone and expression told him he should listen to what she was saying.

"Well, what about that favor?" asked Zelda, breaking the tension.

Closing the gap with Zelda, Chris pulled out a Samsung mobile device and placed it in her hand. "That's the only Max instance that controls—" Pausing, Chris pointed upward.

"Wait. You were serious about stealing that thing? You didn't blow it up? It's still—" Stopping short, Zelda shot her pointer finger into the air.

Chris nodded. "I need you to just hold on to that phone for a while. You know, for safekeeping. Oh, and since you're out of a job, how about working for me?" He pointed at the phone. "And with Max, of course."

Zelda looked into the phone. Chris could tell she was trying to internalize the power he was entrusting her with. "Let me think about it, OK? I'm still ironing things out with Karen. I doubt she'd be too hot on the idea after everything that's happened to me. That and being a prolet chapter president. It wouldn't go over well if members found out Karen's wife worked for you."

"Fair enough," said Chris.

In his peripheral view, Chris noticed Karen stealthily watching from the beaded curtain behind the dated cash register. He gave her a polite nod. She shied away without acknowledgment, slipping back into the bowels of the lowly shop.

Chris understood. It was time to go. He walked over to the shop's door and looked back at Zelda. "Don't think about it too long. The world isn't going to save itself."

Chris Thomas returns in The Lost Rhoades Artifact, *book 3 of the Orion's Spear series.*

THANK YOU

Thank you so much for taking the time to read *Vanguard,* book 2 in the Orion's Spear series. If you've enjoyed spending time with Chris, Leah, and the other characters in this book, it would mean a great deal to me if you could leave a review wherever fine books are sold online—and, of course, spread the word! You can also visit us at www.OrionsSpear.com. Leave your email address, and we'll update you when future books become available.

ABOUT THE AUTHOR

When Chris Knudsen isn't writing books, he runs a successful direct-to-consumer marketing consultancy. Chris has a master's degree in business administration from Westminster College and spent ten years as a university instructor. Chris enjoys spending time with his wife, Elizabeth, and their four children. They call Heber Valley home.

Made in the USA
Las Vegas, NV
31 January 2022